Northern Wolf

Northern Wolf Series

Book One

Daniel Greene

Cover Design by Tim Barber
Formatting by Polgarus Studio

ISBN: 978-0-9976096-9-1

For Craig, you sparked an eternal
passion for history that may never burn out.

CHAPTER 1

October 15th, 1862
Grand Rapids, Michigan

Johannes Wolf raised his dented pewter stein to the bartender. "Christoph, another." He let the stein settle back down on the heavy wooden bar, stained by hundreds of spilt beers over the decades. Wet rings left by his mug entertained him. He traced one with his finger round and round in his drunken state.

A gray-and-gold goateed bartender snatched the stein from Wolf's hand.

Wolf slurred his words, taken aback. "No need for anger, friend."

Christoph stared down at him, black bowtie sticking out over his white apron. "No need for drunkards who don't pay, friend."

The clamor of the local patrons around them rose in volume and Wolf spread his arms wide. "Surely, you can have some charity for a man down on his luck?" He raised thick eyebrows up in concession and adjusted his boot with a creak onto the beam that worked as a footrest.

"How long does one get to live on charity before they go and get themselves a job?"

Wolf shook his head. "Can't farm. Can't machine. Can't log."

Christoph banged the stein back on the bar. Amber-gold liquid sloshed inside only a touch over half full. "Can't brew his own beer."

Wolf raised his eyebrows and grasped the stein with both hands, whispering under his breath. "Can't pour beer neither."

The barkeep turned around, wiping a cup with a yellowing towel in one hand. He leaned toward Wolf, glaring at him with pale blue eyes. "You just be thankful that Bernard and I were close when we first came over or I'd have thrown you out a long time ago." He licked his lips, anticipating some sort of rebuttal.

Wolf wavered in drunken agreement. "My father's a good man, and I would pay if I could." He patted his metal brace engulfing his thigh and knee all the way down to his calf. It provided him with stability when he walked, otherwise his knee would bend and twist awkwardly and he would have no choice but to fall to the ground.

"He's an even better furniture maker." Wolf raised his beer in the air. "Not all of us have his skill. Prost." He lifted the stein to his lips, letting the golden lager bubble smoothly over his tongue. The carbonated liquid had a crisp, light, malty flavor finished with an aftertaste like a piece of crusty bread. It was warmer than he would have liked, but then again he was a charity case.

Christoph scrutinized him beneath flaxen eyebrows, rubbing mugs down. "Why don't you join the army or something? You've got a thick neck. Remind me of a lame ox. It'll give you pay. I hear thirteen dollars a month." He picked up another pewter stein. "Purpose. Hell, they sure need the bodies."

Slurping a gulp of beer, Wolf raised his eyebrows. "You know what you do to a lame ox?"

"What's that?"

His words went straight into his beer. "Put a bullet in it."

Alexander, another drunken compatriot, laughed. "You could eat it. I eaten ox plenty of times."

Wolf held his drink in the air. "You could eat me." He took another sip. "I would have joined at the beginning of this war, but they wouldn't take me. On account of the old leg."

Christoph shrugged. "Muster coming to town here. A whole new round of boys and old men for Little Mac to lead to the slaughter. He lost over 12,000 at Antietam." The bartender tossed down a newspaper.

Another young man stepped to the bar. He had curly blond hair and was over average height. His cheeks were soft and he wore a tailored brown coat and a fresh, cheery, energetic look to him. A disposition that irritated Wolf to no end in his current hazy state.

"Could I see that, Christoph?"

Christoph nodded and smiled at the young man. "Sure thing, Franz. Nice to see you, lad." He went to snatch the paper, but Wolf pounced on it first.

"Johannes. Let him see the paper. Not like you can read anyway."

"I can read." He could read, but in his drunkenness the tiny words were blurred together.

Hovering the yellowing Grand Rapids Daily Eagle close to his face, he was able to focus just enough to make out some of the words. Michigan was on the list of required states to provide troops for the ongoing civil war. A war that was supposed to have ended over a year ago, yet Union and Confederate armies still mangled each other day in and day out. He flipped to the back page; the news was still writing about a battle from the month before. Union General George B. McClellan had been too cautious, allowing the fickle General Robert E. Lee to escape the inconclusive battle at Antietam. Despite superior numeric advantages by McClellan, he had failed to end the war. Lee's escape stretched the uncivil conflict even further.

Wolf forced a high-pitched whistle through his lips. "He lost 12,000 in a single day and they call it a strategic victory."

Christoph shook his head in woeful disappointment. "We came here trying to forget that. We came here for a fresh start. It's like we brought the madness with us."

The older man prattled on like his father telling tales about the old country. "They're assembling a whole regiment?"

"Aye. Over a thousand men."

He grabbed the paper from Wolf and handed it to Franz.

Franz smiled and tipped the paper at Wolf in appreciation. "Thanks, Christoph."

"Wow, another muster," Franz said with a grin. "I'm old enough now too!"

Christoph shook his head as he scooped up another mug. "They just mustered the 7th Michigan out." He scratched his goatee. "Couldn't have been more than a couple weeks ago. Won't be any man left between the ages of eighteen and sixty before this war is over."

"I might have to give it a try." Franz snapped the paper with authority. "Soldiering has always been in our blood."

Wolf snorted. Soldiering was the last thing Franz needed to be doing. The man's affirmative words made Wolf want to strangle him. He'd known quite a few men his age who had gone off to serve and he'd been left behind with a bum leg, unfit for duty, jobless, and bitter. No glory. No honor. Nothing. Wolf turned to brawling to pass the time. One had to when they were a foreign cripple in a new land, despite the fact he'd lived there for years. Always ready to prove himself. Quick to take on a dare. There was no other way. Otherwise, he'd be another homeless invalid on the street with nothing to his name, not even a shred of respect.

"Franz, you couldn't fight a fly buzzing by your ear."

The young man narrowed his eyes and smirked. "I can fight fine." He nodded his head in affirmation. "I reckon I'd make a good soldier, just like father."

"Really?" Wolf's eyes slitted in Franz's direction. He couldn't ever remember scrapping with young Franz. Not that it mattered. He'd fought bigger, faster, stronger men. "Stand up. Let's see what you got." He started to roll a sleeve.

"I'm not fighting you, Mr. Wolf. I came here for a stein, not a fight."

Wolf grunted disbelief deep in his throat. "You softy."

Boisterous laughter caught his ear. Glancing over his shoulder in a stupor, a group of three men stood around a bar table across the room. They were all roughly the same height, well over six feet tall, with thick builds of men who worked hard for a living. Men that if you didn't have a horse, you could easily hook them to a plow as a replacement. Light-brown beards encircled round faces.

"Happy lot, aren't they?" Wolf said over his shoulder.

"Can't understand a word they say, but can't complain too much because they actually *pay*."

Wolf turned back to the barkeep. "Which boat they come off on?"

"Don't know. Money's real enough, isn't that the important part?"

Shaking his head, he muttered. "Taking what few jobs we have."

Christoph set the mug he cleaned harder then he needed to behind the bar. "What job?"

Wolf ground his teeth in his jaw, but it was his leg that hurt worse. The constant ache that saddled him with pain at all times.

One of the foreign men came over. "Yes?" he held a stein up. His meaty arm knocked Wolf, spilling the lager onto the floor with a splatter.

"Well, shit," Wolf called out. He shook out his hand in the direction of the floor and glared angrily at the man. "You going to buy me another?"

The heavily built man gave him a broad smile. "Yes?"

Wolf wiped excess liquid from his soiled jacket and shirt. "Where you from?" He took a few steps closer. His metal-encased leg creaked as he walked, his boot seemingly stomping the wood-planked floor with every step.

The man scrutinized him from above with apparent amusement. He smile grew broader. "Yes."

"You come in from New York or something? That's quite the accent you have."

The well-fed man blinked blue eyes not dissimilar from Wolf's own. "Yes."

Christoph filled his stein and gave it back to the man. The man set a coin on the bar and gestured his beer in thanks. "Jen Key."

The man lumbered back to his table.

"What the hell is *Jen Key*?"

Christoph shrugged his shoulders. "Don't care as long as he pays and in coin too."

The anger boiled in Wolf's gut and he rubbed his numbing face. *This bastard spilled my beer, said he'd pay and didn't.*

"You could go fight him," Franz said with a white smile. He lifted his full, foamy drink to his lips and took a sip. "Prost."

Wolf couldn't even get a job and these people were coming in by the day to take his, and spill his beer. "Why not?" He held up his hands as if he had nothing to lose.

Widening his eyes, Franz protested. "Johannes, I was joking."

Wolf ignored his puny protest. He shouted at the three men. "Hey!"

"No need for anything crazy, Johannes. Here." The bartender took his empty stein and poured more golden liquid inside.

Twisting his neck to the side in anger, Wolf said. "No, Christoph, the nerve of these heathens. Ain't right. If you spill a man's beer, you should buy him another."

Franz held up a small brown stamp. "I got you Johannes. No need."

Wolf leaned closer to the young man and breathed. "It's the principle of the matter."

He already felt pretty loose. The beer had seen to that, but he stretched his shoulders anyway. Despite Wolf's injury, his upper body was thicker, it had been joked that he had a laborer's body. Heavy in chest and shoulders that would have made him an exceptional farmer or miner. Neither of which he could do. He was tall, but not nearly as tall as these men. His hair had the same wave as his father's except his was the color of fresh honey where his father's had grayed like abandoned honeycomb.

He sounded like a tin man as he walked over to them. Marching up to the table, he eyed the men. "You spilled my beer." For the first time, as he looked each man in his eyes, he realized these men had to be brothers. Same light brown beards, builds, bulbous noses, and rounded jaw lines.

Two of them said something Wolf couldn't understand, gesturing at him. The one from the bar nodded. "Yes."

Wolf shook his head in disgust. "Speak English. God, where you from?" He'd been forced to learn at a young age when his parents immigrated to the United States from the German Swabia region. Wolf's father had ranted and raved about the necessity of speaking English, so much so, he forbade their native tongue and only spoke it on special occasions.

The grinning brute took a frothy sip of his beer. "Yes."

"How about you get me liter?" He pointed down at the man's quickly disappearing brew. "Lager." Jabbing a finger back at the man, he said. "You. Buy me."

The man grinned, turning back to his brothers. Gibberish spewed from his mouth and they laughed uproariously.

Wolf could feel the anger rising in his gut, the kind that allows a man to get past the fear of getting beaten to a pulp and steps him into action. Wrath fueled by alcohol. Tilting his head, he placed a rough hand on the man's thick chest. "I said, buy me a liter." He finished with a little shove.

The imposing man continued to smile and nod. "Yes."

Wolf swung as hard as he could with his mug into the side of his head. The foreign man's eyes elongated as the metal dented and he crumpled into a pile on the floor. Pushing the table, Wolf forced it into the other men. The brother on the right laid a ham-sized fist into Wolf's cheek, sending him stumbling backwards like a tumbleweed.

Fighting three men at once was a bad move and getting hit was a high probability. After all, he'd decided it was worth fighting three bigger men at once. Sometimes he enjoyed being hit, the intense thrill of the fight. His dim, drunkenly encouraged wits provided him with the rest he needed to fight. Not that he needed much to brawl. That's what happened when men didn't have much to lose and Wolf was one of those men. He was like the remaining tattered standard of a once-proud flag, now ripped and torn by the world at hand until only strips of fabric fluttered in the wind.

Other patrons of Christoph's fine establishment, Hans, Frank, and Franz, were trying to corral the men, grabbing at them, driving them toward the door, which only made the situation worse as the three foreign men thought they were being attacked.

With a crack, Wolf's back struck the bar. He used it to steady himself for a moment. Shaking his head, he tried to straighten his vision. The thick man shoved an intervening Franz to the ground and charged Wolf. Growling, he swung hard again over the top at a downward angle for the center of Wolf's face.

Wolf did the only thing he could do, duck. Pressing his chin to his chest, the blow glanced off the top of his head. Wolf was quick if he didn't have to run much. He hooked an arm into the man's kidney and then followed through with a jab to his gut. His opponent made a noise like an old dog trying to bark, wrapping heavy arms around Wolf's body.

His father had always jabbered on about how they'd descended from great warriors. Wolf wouldn't know if he was making wind or telling the truth, but he was strong and could scrap with the best.

The man lifted him and drove into the wall with immense strength. Wolf couldn't withstand his power with only a single healthy leg. Wolf centered himself and head butted the man in the nose. *Crack!* The man held on but blinked a half dozen times. Wolf took the break in events to torque his upper body and rolled the man sideways through the door. They toppled over one another and spun into the cold, wet mud of the outside.

The men struggled for control. Wolf managed to get on top. Squeezing the man's neck, he punched down into his face, the meat of his hand slapping his eye. The man twisted his head away trying to get free and Wolf raised a hand behind his ear for another punch.

"Johannes!" came a shout.

He squinted in confusion and a moment later a heavy stick connected with the side of his head. The blow lifted him off the other man and he landed on his back. Church bells tolled in his mind and his body was slow to respond. Trying to blink his eyes back into focus, he brought a battered hand up to the side of his head. The blood was swelling to the spot where the wood had met his skull. "Hell!"

Cries of men fighting surrounded him. He forced himself onto his elbows. Blue-clad constables skirmished the brawlers. They swung wildly with sticks into the rabble-rousers. The constable, that had thumped Wolf, beat his opponent even more mercilessly.

The man shouted gibberish at the constable. "Zartzymac!"

Cool mud caked to Wolf's hands as he pushed himself upright. He limped for the fighting men. "That's my sack of barley." The constable turned over his shoulder.

Using his strong leg, Wolf sprung into an all-out swing into the constable. He mostly missed, but struck the man in the jaw. The man's eyes closed as the blow knocked him into the mud.

He offered a hand to his former opponent. A first-rate scrap was all well and good, but getting caught was unacceptable. "Here."

The man studied him for a moment, unsure if he could trust a man who was raining fists upon him only moments prior.

"Let me help you."

The man grabbed his hand with a clap.

Leaning his weight onto his healthy leg, Wolf hoisted him to his feet.

The round-faced man wiped his nose. "Jen Key."

Wolf shrugged, tapping his own chest. "Jen, I'm Wolf."

The man smiled and, in broken English, he grunted. "Thank you."

Shrill whistles bleated the air like dying sheep and more constables were arriving. The crack of a hard stick along Wolf's back made him cringe and a gunshot filled the air. The men stopped fighting and gawked at a constable in a puffy cap and blue jacket, a round belly pushing out from underneath.

The constable held a small pepperbox pistol in the air. "This ends now!" He pointed the multiple-barrel firearm at the brawlers. "I don't mind puttin' a bullet in any of you stinking bodachs. Coming out here wakin' snakes. Peter, Joseph and Mary," he said in an Irish accent.

A constable tackled Wolf into the mud and, after a brief struggle, he clapped irons on Wolf's wrists. He was hauled standing with the rest of the fighters.

Franz and a few of the well-intentioned patrons of the bar were released with a sharp tongue lashing. Christoph was speaking to the constables and by the looks of his gestures, Wolf was going to be on the losing end of fault. He rolled his eyes at the bartender and brewer.

"Thanks. Thought we were friends."

The barkeep shook his head in loathing.

"I did it," he yelled at the constable.

"Ruined a good time for all," Christoph said. He gestured his fist angrily at Wolf. "I'll be telling your father."

Wolf gestured with his head. "They spilled my beer." He glanced over at the other men. "One of 'em."

Constable McCready sauntered past them, bushy sideburns and mustache twitching as he walked. He wasn't a tall man, but he had a rotund potbelly and wiry, strong arms.

Wolf was not friendly with the leading constable of Grand Rapids. They'd been aware of each other's existence for some time. The McCready family had been in the law enforcement business since they'd arrived in the western Michigan area, along with their twin McCormick cousins.

McCready jabbed his whipping stick into Wolf's belly, forcing a sputtering cough. "Nice to see you too."

"Get them out of my sight," he said and spit.

The brawlers were shoved into a line and slogged down the middle of the street.

McCready marched down the lane, chin held in the air. Smoke from oil lanterns lit the men's way through the dreary, soggy roads. Wolf knew the trek well to the jail. Around the corner and down to the right, off Campau Street where it intersected with Pike. One of the brothers slipped and fell in the mud, drawing the men to a halt.

"Get up, you Nancy," a constable shouted. He was one of the McCormick twins, Patrick or Timothy, but Wolf couldn't tell which one. The constable clubbed the man's shoulder with a thwack. "Get up."

The man rose to his knees and they continued their trudge to an elaborate Italianate building. The molding was black and curved above the windows. The brick was clean and white. It was more two buildings than one, separated by a tower with plain double doors. The rear of the building had small, equally spaced windows with metal bars covering them.

His eyes scanned for a way to escape. It wasn't his first time in the Kent County Jail. Constable McCready opened the tower door, letting his prisoners pass one at a time. "Welcome back, Mr. Wolf." He gave him a friendly shove inside the building. "Got your old cell ready for you."

CHAPTER 2

October 16th, 1862
Grand Rapids, Michigan

The entire rear of Constable McCready's house was lined with jail cells separated by iron bars. They reminded Wolf of circus cages better fit for exotic animals than people. The constable lived in the front of the towering home with his wife who cooked all the meals for the prisoners. The food wasn't too bad, mostly cabbage and potato soup, but he'd had far worse.

Wolf leaned against the wall near the back of his cell. A threadbare, flea-covered blanket and some hay were tossed on the floor. He knew it was more likely to soak up the piss and vomit from a drunk than to keep him comfortable. His relief bucket had filled over the course of the night and it stunk like a tavern outhouse.

The other three men were in the cage next to him. They sat on the ground and whispered in a foreign tongue to one another. Wolf rubbed his sore nose where one of the three, he couldn't tell them apart now, had hit him.

"All you had to do was buy me a stein," he said loudly. He glanced over at the men. They stared back, mistrust in their eyes. The one closest to him used a bar to pull himself off the ground and gripped the vertical bars.

"Mocno uderzyłeś." He held up a red-bruising fist in Wolf's direction.

Wolf stood, avoiding an unknown dark stain on the floor. The metal of his brace rubbed as he hobbled forward. "You need to learn English if you're going to survive here. Not your country."

The fleshy-cheeked man smiled. "You hit hard."

"You might have broke my nose." He smushed the cartilage with a finger with a tender grimace.

"Know English. Slow."

He patted his chest speaking like he would to an infant. "I'm Johannes Wolf."

The man's smile widened, revealing teeth. "I, Bogdan Poltorak." He pointed back at the other men. "He, Bartosz, and he, Bozimir."

"That's a mouthful." Wolf shook his head and stared the man in the eyes. "I'll never keep you straight."

Bogdan's grin stretched and he tapped his chest. "Polska."

Polish. "Swabia. I mean, I don't really remember it, but that's where I was born."

Bogdan blinked back his words and said, "Germański."

The door banged open at the end of the cells, revealing the constable. His curly brown hair was matted down and missed his puffy hat. A gold badge was buttoned on his breast. He led a single man in a dark blue jacket and sky blue pants with yellow stripes lining the sides. He wore a curved saber at his hip and a pistol hung off his belt in a shiny, black holster.

The men stopped in front of Wolf's cell. McCready eyed him with mistrust.

"This them?" the soldier said. His mustache was so thick Wolf thought that he might have been harboring a squirrel's tail on his upper lip. His shoulders were adorned with three downward-pointing chevrons with a diamond situated above.

"Drunkards and ruffians, the lot of 'em. They started a brawl at Kusterer's Brewery. They can't be trusted to watch your crop grow, First Sergeant O'Reilly. This lot ain't worth a nickel stamp."

O'Reilly's mustache twitched and he scratched at it with a finger. "Let me get a look at you."

Glowering, Wolf took a step closer. "You trying to sell us, McCready? Thought that wasn't legal no more on account of the President."

"Shut your damn mouth." McCready's cheeks grew ruddier with every word.

O'Reilly ignored the constable's outburst. "Looks fit enough. Let's see your teeth."

Wolf bared them.

"Looks healthy, strong shoulders." O'Reilly pointed at his knee. "What's wrong with your leg?"

"Accident, don't bend right."

The first sergeant surveyed his paper. "Shame, son. Can't use you, then." He gestured at the brothers. "What about these hulking brutes?"

They continued to the other cell. "What's their story?"

"Big Polish brigands. Strong and stupid, by the looks of 'em. Started with just a single family, but now they be trickling in twos and threes."

"I remember when that was us."

"They ain't like us."

The first sergeant studied his paper again. "We can handle strong and stupid. They just need to follow orders and fight."

"Oh, they can fight." McCready rotated his jaw in a circle. "Broke Constable Hart's arm and Patrick's ribs. No better than dogs, these ones."

O'Reilly smirked. "I can train a dog to do many tricks." He flipped a piece of paper, eyeing it. "All right, boys. Put your mark here." He tapped a black pencil on the paper.

Bogdan stared back at his brothers. They spoke Polish in hushed tones. "You let us go?"

McCready laughed and wiped his brow. "Told you they're stupid."

"But, by God, we need them." O'Reilly pointed the pencil at a line at the bottom. "Right here, lad. Scouting, spying, and protecting the flank. The cavalry way. Uncle O'Reilly will set you straight. Show you how."

Gripping the bars, Wolf pressed his face near the brothers. "No, don't sign."

All the men turned in his direction. McCready loosened the whipping stick looped on his belt. "You got a mouth on you, dontcha. You good-for-nothing, sauerkraut-eaten' piece o' dirt. Send you back, I will." He slipped his stick free and banged it on the bar. "Get back, you."

The cavalryman nodded, his mustache fluttering. "Now boy, mind your own damn business. These men want to be free, they'll join. Military done right by me. Gave me discipline and straightened me out. Regular pay too. It can do the same for these men." He smiled beneath his mustache at the other men with a slight affirming nod.

McCready swung his stick at Wolf again, and he took a step back for fear of breaking a finger. "Nothing can help you, stupid ox."

"I want to join. I'll sign."

O'Reilly's mouth tightened. "Boy, I'd take you. By God, we need more men if we're to win this war, but what can you do? You're hampered by your circumstance."

"I wouldn't take that one anyway. More trouble than he's worth," said McCready.

Wolf peered at his dried-mud-covered clothes and boots and collected himself. "Please. I can fight. If I sign, so will they."

O'Reilly shook his head. "Sorry, son, that's not your decision. But there'll be no war for you." He put the pencil through the bars. Bogdan took the pencil in his hand and O'Reilly drummed the line with his finger impatiently. "Right here, laddie."

"Bogdan, no," Wolf said.

Bogdan gazed back at him deciphering his meaning and hesitated.

"No," he repeated.

O'Reilly's mustache quivered, his voice rising in anger. "Boy, I can't help you. Now let these men speak for themselves."

McCready chimed in. "One more word out of you and I'll come in there and give you another thrashin'."

Wolf couldn't stop; this was his only chance to make something of himself. McCready was right. Kusterer was right. He wasn't worth much, but surely if he could enlist he could be something. "First Sergeant, you're cavalry?"

"We weren't always called the cavalry, but I been atop a horse for sixteen years."

"I can ride. I know how to do it well. I don't need a good leg for that."

O'Reilly rolled his mustache into his nose and glanced over at the constable.

McCready shrugged his shoulders. "He's a problem, always been, but he's got more fight than a bull in mating season."

Eyeing his paper, O'Reilly sighed. "Four in one day is a job well done. We been scraping the bottom of the barrel here. Ain't no one been turning out. Even for bounties."

McCready grimaced holding a hand over his heart. "You know me. Would have volunteered when the war began, but with the spells, my heart wouldn't last."

"Oh, I know, John."

A bit of doubt laced the first sergeant's voice, as if he'd heard it all before.

"If all the boy wants to do is fight, after this debacle of a war, then who am I to deny him the right to die? We'll find him something to do." He pointed a finger at Wolf. "You get these healthy brutes to sign up and you can enlist."

Wolf gave Bogdan a slight nod. "War. Freedom."

The Polish man's throat moved as he swallowed. He understood. He knew about this war between the United States and the Confederate States, he didn't understand the deep schism splitting the nation and maybe he didn't need to know why men were willing to kill each other, but he knew what war was. He turned and whispered something to his brothers. He took the pencil, eyeing Wolf with his dark blue eyes and, nodding his head, he signed.

"Good lad. Next," O'Reilly said. He flipped to a new page and Bartoscz and Bozimir did the same. "A hot meal, a horse, and a gun."

Bozimir handed him the pencil through the iron bars, and Wolf took the writing utensil in his hands. His father would understand. It would get his crippled dependent son out from under his roof.

O'Reilly glared through the bars. "Make your mark."

Wolf scribbled fierce across the line, pushing the lead deep into the paper. *Johannes Wolf. To serve as a soldier in the Army of the United States of America for the period of three years.*

McCready lifted a key on a gold chain from his pocket. "These drunkards are your problem now." He unlocked the iron gates and pushed them open. The hinges screeched with complaint.

Wolf limped from the confines of his cage.

Grinning beneath his mustache, O'Reilly looked the young men up and down. "All right, you liver-lipped strumpets, your ass is mine now. Let's move."

CHAPTER 3

October 17th, 1862
Grand Rapids, Michigan

"Son, don't fool yourself," his father said. He eyed Wolf over his spectacles, his glasses drifting to the edge of his nose. He pulled pork away from the bone with a fork, chewing with the haste of a man not knowing when he'd eat next. He licked juices from his finger. "And your mother didn't sleep a wink last night, thinking her son finally got knifed in the streets."

Well-crafted cedar furniture lined the room, dining room table, chairs, a dresser along with a glossy mirror on the wall. It held comfort, but was modest.

Wolf scooped a bite of potatoes and long strands of yellow, droopy sauerkraut into his mouth. "We muster in the square tomorrow morning."

"They don't want a maimed boy in their ranks."

"They do," he said hurriedly. He picked up a pork bone and tore into the pinkish white meat. His mother's was the best. Tender, juicy, filled with flavor. Between mouthfuls he said, "I signed the papers. It's official."

Bernard smoothed his mustache and set down his fork. "I was saddened when you hurt your leg. I knew a world would be taken from you, but you would live. I could pass on whatever I made here to you. Make sure you wouldn't want for anything." His brow furrowed. "But I was glad about your injury when this war started because I knew it would keep you from it. You're my only son." He clenched his jaw in emotion.

Wolf's sisters sat silently chewing their food. Both were younger than he and shared his broad shoulders, but thankfully resembled more their mother than their father. Josephine cocked her head. "Don't go, Johannes." Tears filled her delicate eyes. "You'll die."

Snorting at his sister's feelings, he grinned. "Don't be silly. I'll have glory and honor. Medals and ribbons."

"Don't be a fool. War never brought a man that."

Wolf shook his head. "What would you know about that?"

His father rubbed his mustache, irritated. "I know enough about war. Plenty of men have died already and civil wars are never over quick. They're always more brutal than against outsiders."

His family had fled the German States during the revolutions of '48 of which his father had been on the losing end of. They'd made a new life in America and a prosperous one like many of the other families that had fled. When the middle-class elements of the revolution split with the working class over priorities, the upper classes crushed the rebels. Many on the losing side had come to America as successful craftsmen, doctors, teachers, and other professionals.

"Father, this is my chance to make something of myself. There's nothing for me here." His words look like they'd struck his poor gray-haired father.

"Your family is here."

Wolf set down his fork. "I know, but there's nothing for me to do here and the cavalry has given me an opportunity." He leaned back in his chair. "How many times have you spoke out against the outrage of slavery? How many times have you said that to hold another man in bondage is a sin?" Resting his arms back on the table, he hovered over his plate. "I can make this right. That is this fight."

Bernard cleared his throat. "No, that is *their* fight. This is something the people here must fix." He wiped his mouth with a cloth, checkered black-and-white napkin. "But you're right. I have been outspoken, but that was before men started to kill one another over it. You know nothing of war and revolution."

"I know, I know. War is hell."

"Johannes, it is." His father's eyes held a tinge of fear laced with worry. "When you see men killed for the first time, it will be only the beginning of a nightmare. A nightmare that doesn't end even when the war does. We came to this place because they did what our country could not and created a constitution giving men freedom and representation."

"Then why won't you let me defend those things?"

Studying his plate in silence, Bernard collected himself. "You're my only son. I cannot feed you to the flames. I'm going to talk to this First Sergeant O'Reilly."

"No, father. You can't. I do not need your permission to do this. I am of more than age."

"A civil war is one of brother against brother and family against family. It is the ugliest of conflicts where even when one side wins, it still loses. We know this. We've been in it."

"We fight to keep this country together."

"This madness follows us." He shook his head in dismay. "Johannes, you are not a whole man."

His father's words stung like barbs stuck into his flesh. *If he doesn't think me a man, who will?* "I am a man. I'm nineteen. You weren't much older when you fought."

His quip fell on deaf ears. "You act like a boy, fighting in the streets. You're no man."

"Your shop took my leg! That's the reason I have to do this! I finally have another chance and you would steal that from me too?"

His father's eyes slanted in agony. "That was an accident. No one could have known that would've happened."

"But it did. I won't let you take this from me. It's all I have."

Bernard searched his plate for respite. He opened his mouth and closed it again. Peering at his son, his steel-blue eyes weighed his rebellious progeny. "I didn't want this for you, but you've taken your fate into your own hands as a man would and therefore, I cannot treat you like a boy."

Wolf's jaw dropped open a hair. He'd never heard his father speak in such a manner. "I…"

"Wait, I have something for you." He stood and walked to the old cedar dresser. Digging through a drawer, he removed a piece of raven-colored cloth. He held it in both hands as if it were the most revered of all saintly relics. On the end of the sash was an emblazoned golden wolf.

"I want you to have this, son." Bernard extended the cloth to him. "I wore this in the '48 rebellions and your grandfather wore it before him and his before him. The sash has been replaced many times, but this here." He pointed at the wolf. "This here goes back hundreds of years. This is a part of me, just like you are a part of me. This is also a part of you. Don't let anything happen to it." He held it out. "Take it."

Wolf's hands quivered as he held the black sash. The edge was starting to fray on one of the ends and the other was stained. "Thank you, father. I don't have any words."

"You don't need them." They embraced for a moment. Both his sisters were crying now. His father released him and tilted back and wiped his eye. "Now, no crying for men."

Bobbing his head in agreement, Wolf let out a short laugh.

"You listen to your sergeants and say your prayers."

"Yes, father."

"God will take care of your soul, and your sergeant will take care of your ass. They both know what they're doing. They've been around a long time."

Emotions welled inside him, but he corralled them. "Yes, Father."

"Don't volunteer for anything."

"Why?"

"Just don't."

Wolf nodded.

"If men are running, there's reason." His father's eyes blinked and grew distant. "Keep your head down when the balls fly, men tend to aim high."

"I will, father." He had no idea why men shoot high, but the warning was enough to heed.

"And you come back to us when this is over."

CHAPTER 4

October 18th, 1862
Grand Rapids, Michigan

It rained hard in the dim morning light, sounding off wood-shingled roofs and men's hats alike. The normally muddy, cart-ridden roads were pure mush. Over one hundred men stood around Wolf in a disorganized crowd. They wore all manner of clothes. Most dirty and plain, a few indicating signs of modest wealth. Majority were poor and young. Some had collected a bounty on behalf of a wealthier patron. A few had blankets, but no men had ponchos or adequate cover for the cold rain pummeling them from above.

The men muttered quietly to one another as they waited. The townspeople had drifted back inside their homes to dodge the foul weather. A few women stood beneath a building overhang watching their husbands or brothers or sons attend muster, handkerchiefs held to eyes.

Wolf wondered if the Polish brothers had bothered to show back up or if they'd skip town and avoid their obligations. He adjusted his weight to his back leg and felt his brace. Water covered the metal and it would need to be wiped down later or risk having the contraption rust.

A bugler sounded a quick, short tune, drawing everyone's eyes forward with excitement. An officer stepped his black horse closer to the volunteers. He wore a black hat that drooped with rain shadowing a darkly bearded face. His blue uniform was a darker shade from being wet and he draped a shell-style jacket over his shoulders. White gloves held the reins of his horse. He raised a careful hand and the bugler stopped.

"I'm Captain Peltier." He nodded solemnly. "You must be my boys then. I will be your company commander." Wolf caught a hint of an accent. *French perhaps?* "This is First Lieutenant Wells." The tightly cropped bearded captain gestured to a tall, slender, smooth-cheeked man next to him.

He wore a dark indigo-blue wool kepi, a cap of French origin that slanted toward the forehead like an angry duck, and the front had a square, flat, black brim. Lifting his chin, the lieutenant peered down his aristocratic nose at the men. His uniform was flawless even in the rain and his kepi was kept perfectly placed upon his head.

The captain continued with an almost saddened demeanor. "Raise your hands and repeat after me."

Wet, white hands were lifted into the air, arm cocked perpendicular with the ground.

"I, Andreas Peltier, do solemnly swear that I will support the constitution of the United States." The men fumbled along repeating the accented oath of allegiance at the behest of their captain.

"I, Johannes Wolf, do solemnly swear to bear true allegiance to the United States of America, and to serve them honestly and faithfully, against all their enemies or opposers whatsoever," he repeated after the captain, swearing an oath, the first oath he'd ever taken. He'd repeated things in church that bored him as much as he didn't understand them, but this made his skin prickle and his belly flutter.

"And to observe and obey the orders of the President of the United States of America, and the orders of the officers appointed over me."

The men lowered their hands one by one. Their oath had been sworn, words had been spoken and promised and they would live and die by them for their nation, but Wolf knew that it would be the enemy that would die, not these men. Not his neighbors. Excitement filled his belly despite his drenched exterior.

"We are to travel by rail to Washington, D.C. where you will be trained and outfitted appropriately. We are to link up with five other companies and together you will become the 13th Michigan Volunteer Cavalry. We will be small for a regiment, but hopefully we will acquire more recruits before the spring."

Captain Peltier waved at his squat first sergeant. "No use in getting you all sick while we stand around. First Sergeant O'Reilly, move them to the rail depot."

Wolf immediately recognized him as the man who'd enlisted them only a day prior. "Would you look at this lot?" the short mustached man shouted, his accent all Irish.

"All right, ya no-luck Johnnies, rows of ten. Let's make your townsfolk as proud as we can in this squirt." He took a man and shoved him in line. After mass confusion, squishing mud, the soaked men found their places.

The shower decided to flare up and water began to pool on top of the swampy streets, having fully saturated through the mud. Wolf tugged on his metal and leather brace. The water was dragging down the contraption so it would sag lower than it was effective, pulling his trousers.

Wolf found himself in a ragged line.

"Company," O'Reilly shouted. "Forward march." He trudged alongside the men while Captain Peltier walked his horse beside his recruits.

Between the droplets striking the buildings, and the out-of-sync squish of boots in mud, the men could hardly hear a thing, especially the marching cadence. The first sergeant may as well have been a hundred yards away. "Left, right, left, right. Jesus almighty, relieve me of these horrible sinners. If you were marching to heaven, you'd never make it to see St. Peter at the pearly gates. Gonna have to get the hay out back in camp. Teach you ingrates left from right."

Wolf hobbled in the middle hoping to be ignored by his officers and sergeants. They marched down the center of the lane toward the rail depot.

"Dear God, men, did no one teach you left from right?"

A man opened his door with a butcher's apron on and watched them pass from the shelter of his home. Others viewed the soaked recruits from windows and porches as the men marched through the pooling streets, but there was no fanfare in the rain. No flags waved. No kisses were blown from pretty young girls. There were no flowers for the men to be placed in hats and pockets. The new enlistees weren't in sharp uniforms, and were no spectacular sight to behold.

Wolf's leg gave out beneath him and he slipped in the mud. The man next to him caught him by his elbow. "Come, Johannes." He said *Johannes* like his father would, in perfect German form. The tall, broad-shouldered man straightened him out along with the man behind him. The man's face was familiar. "Wilhelm? Wilhelm Berles?"

The taller man was in his fifties, nodded his head with a quick grin beneath his curled mustache and rigid jawline. "Keep moving. No time to talk."

Gritting his teeth, Wolf smiled inwardly. Wilhelm had been a family friend of the Wolf's and he knew his father well. "Is Franz with you?"

"Yes, now focus on staying in line. We don't want any unnecessary attention. Low profiles are the best profiles in the army."

Focusing on the first sergeant's cadence, Wolf pressed on harder, keeping step with the men around him despite his handicap.

They marched through the center of the "Grab Corners," the hub of Grand Rapids. The white-painted, wood-boarded houses and brick shops passed by. Striped awnings over storefronts and barber's poles lined a wood-planked boardwalk. There was an auction house and clothing store, along with a four-story brick building with multiple signs peppering the front. The lowest one read "Millinery and Straw Goods."

He'd spent many an evening in the bars and poker rooms found in the basements of those very buildings. The difference between day and night in the Grab was stark. The later into the night it ticked, the seedier the clientele became.

Today, everything was quiet. The town showed no signs of life save for a couple of candles in the windows. Only chilled, wet rain wished the men farewell.

The rail depot was nothing more than a single-room shed on the side of the tracks. A four-car single stack locomotive sat waiting for them with the markings of M.C.R.R. The men hurried inside the cars eager to escape the rainy barrage. The last company of the 13th Michigan boarded the train that was more fit for cattle than men, for the three-day journey to Washington, D.C.

Wolf ran a hand through his wet hair and shook it outside the car.

"Johannes," came a feminine voice. He spied a young lady running through the rain, holding her dress high with one hand. Her baby-blue dress was splattered with mud and grime from the streets, her brown coat soaked with water.

"Josephine!" His heart jumped. He'd already said goodbye once and he would struggle to do it again. She ran up the ramp and wrapped her arms around him.

He gave a sad laugh into her hair. "You can't come with. This is a man's business."

"I'll miss you, Johannes."

"I'll miss you too."

She separated herself from him. Her blue eyes were not dissimilar to his own, but filled with salty tears. "I have something for you." She reached under her coat and pulled out a garment.

"Every unit needs its own flag," she said softly. "I worked on it all night. I had whatever Mama had, but it turned out all right."

Wolf unfurled the patchwork flag. It was a short flag, no more than two feet by two feet. The top was red and the lower part was black. A golden emblazoned wolf head was sewn on the bottom.

"It was Papa's wolf and I didn't have time for anything else."

"It's perfect," he whispered, admiring her stitch work.

She laugh-cried and hugged him again. "Be safe."

"I will come back."

"I know. Write me."

He tried to breathe in air to stifle his emotions. "I will." He was beginning to realize the personal sacrifice that came with leaving his family.

"All aboard," shouted the locomotive conductor.

She released him and ran back down the ramp to the cover of the depot. A sad smile whispered over her lips and she wiped the corner of her eyes. "I'll pray for you!"

"I'll need 'em!" He grinned, holding up the flag. "Thank you!"

First Sergeant O'Reilly stepped to the end of the plank. Water dripped off the black leather peak of his dark blue cap with gold crossed sabers and a 13 resting above the cavalry swords. "All aboard." He gave Wolf a smirk. "Wave goodbye to 'em, boy. Cause we're your family now."

Wolf scanned the town from the doorway of the train. The Grand River bubbled and flowed, inching up on the islands that sat in the middle, swollen from the downpour. Logs floated down the river to be milled and sent away. The duel steeples of St. Mark's Episcopal Church rose in the distance with the limestone church of St. Andrew's.

"She's a beaut, ain't she?" Wilhelm said from nearby. He pointed at St. Andrew's. "That limestone came from the bottom of the Grand River."

"I didn't know that."

"Don't suppose you would. It was built when you were a small lad."

Wilhelm put a fatherly hand on his shoulder. "What have you there?"

"A battle flag."

Wilhelm took the flag in his hand. "This is well done." He gave Wolf an approving nod. "I assume you didn't do this?"

Laughing, he said, "No, Josephine did." He pointed at the train depot.

Wilhelm gave her a wave. "She's got a big heart."

"She does."

"Let me talk to the first sergeant and get this up to company standard. It will be a fine reminder of home."

"But the world awaits us."

"And you'll long for home. Everyone does in some way."

The doors slid closed. Wilhelm waved Wolf over to the floor. "Sit with me and my boy. We have a long journey."

Franz gave him a cheerful grin. "Told ya I'd fight."

The wall was rough and splintered and Wolf leaned against it. "Yeah, yeah."

"We're going to the capital. I've always wanted to see it," Franz said.

"We're going to war. Best remember why you're there," Wilhelm said.

"Adventure," Wolf said.

Wilhelm shook his head. "You boys have much to learn."

The two young men raised their eyebrows at one another. *What did Wilhelm know anyway?*

The locomotive engine roared to a start and then lurched to a roll. Three long shrill whistles pierced the air and the last company of the 13th Michigan Cavalry left their home behind.

CHAPTER 5

October 21st, 1862
Washington, D.C.

The journey by railroad took almost three days before they'd reached the capital of the United States of America, Washington, D.C. They switched rails twelve times through the travels, each and every rail different than the last. The worn out recruits forced to wait in the brisk fall weather for their next train.

When they arrived at the train depot near Washington, they stepped out into an expansive rail yard in a whirlwind of chaos. Tired men in plain clothes exited trains along with the men from Grand Rapids. Hundreds and thousands of new recruits in the process of arriving for their enlistment. Soldiers in uniform, intermixed with the others, as well as laborers unloading supplies for the war effort. Few women graced the train yard with their presence.

Wolf hobbled down the inclined ramp, both his legs tight and in need of a stretch. He was happy to be free of the stinking cattle car, as most men were ripe and in sorry need of a bath.

Franz stepped near him and shaded his eyes. "Would you look at that, father." He pointed a finger toward Washington. A white building with a massive unfinished dome stood in the small city. It was as if they stared through a mist into the past where the mighty Athenians constructed a temple for the gods.

Wilhelm nodded. "That's the Capitol Building. Where our government holds congress and we're represented by an elected official."

"It's glorious!" Franz exclaimed, happiness enveloping his bare cheeks.

A broad-shouldered man with three point-down chevrons under three arcs stood waiting at the bottom of the ramp. First Sergeant O'Reilly stood on his right. They both stared at a sheet of paper. "Well, we don't bloody well pay you to gawk at the gosh darn Capitol, now do we? Make haste," the sergeant major called at them.

"Come on, lads," Wilhelm gave them a gentle push down the incline. "These men shouldn't be kept waiting.

When Wolf reached the bottom, the thick sergeant major looked through him, his voice sounding like a sawmill. He spit a throaty black glob on the ground before he spoke. "That was haste?" He spit again, a growl forming. "Bloody civilians. Name and company?"

"Johannes Wolf, Company F."

The bull-necked sergeant major marked something on the paper. His eyes darted down to Wolf's leg. "Mister O'Reilly, you're gonna have your work cut out for you."

Eyes reached the shorter first sergeant. The stout man squinted his eyes at Wolf. "That we will, Sergeant Major. That we will."

The sergeant major shook his head in apparent disgust for Wolf. "Move over with the others and try not to get lost between here and there, volunteer."

Wolf stepped into the small mob of men from Grand Rapids. Men unloaded horses from freight cars and long boxes from another car. Teamsters drove wagons through groups hollering to get out of the way. A company of infantry marched in rank and file, causing a jam of people. It smelled like horse and shit, and Wolf could care less because everything was new.

Washington had grown much larger than it apparently had been. Hasty barracks and tents had been added along muddy streets. The streets were busy, horses and carriages clopped, and it appeared that most manner of men were moving on some business related to war.

A short, dark-haired man joined Wolf in his observations. He had a toothpick in his mouth and he ran it along the crevices between his teeth. He scratched at his head picking at lice.

"You hungry?"

Wolf's stomach growled in response. The men ate what they had brought with them, but hadn't been given any rations. Apples, crackers, bread, and dried beef had helped them along their way because when they stopped, it was only to change trains not to rest or eat.

"Very."

The young man winked at Wolf. "Hold on for a minute."

"I'll stay put."

The dark-haired young man disappeared. Wolf stood on his tiptoes trying to get a view of where he went through the crowds.

Wilhelm and Franz joined him.

Wilhelm watched the men around them. "Looks like Lincoln turned our capital into a military camp, and not a very organized one at that."

"Watch yourself's!" A man shouted as he led a team of horses hauling stacked crates, all labeled U.S. Army on them.

Stepping to the side, the man hollered and whipped the air for the other men to make way.

"I suppose we should be grateful Maryland didn't go secessionist, otherwise he'd be surrounded."

"What's a secessionist?" the dark-haired man asked, appearing at Wolf's side without making a sound. He handed him a thick loaf of golden bread. Rich and savory smells tickled Wolf's nose and he held the bread close breathing in its essence.

Wilhelm glanced over his nose at the boy. "A person who secedes from something."

The young man shoved some bread in his mouth and chewed loudly. "Don't we want to succeed?"

A short grin settled on Wilhelm's lips. "No not succeed. Secede. Like to separate. Like what we did from England a long time ago."

"Where did you find this?" Wolf asked the young man, marveling at such delicious food.

The young man ripped a chunk off his piece. "I seceded this from the quartermaster's private box."

Tearing a hunk off, Wolf shoveled it in his mouth. It tasted as divine as he ever thought bread could taste, melting into pure ecstasy. Handing it off to Wilhelm, he tore his share and passed it to Franz. Wolf chewed quickly, trying to dispose of the evidence.

Franz held his bread eye level. "This was stolen?"

Wilhelm cuffed the boy on the back of the head. "This ain't home. You eat what you can get. I command it."

Lifting his brows, Franz complied with his father's request, munching the bread slowly.

The two sergeants were atop mounts now walking them near the recruits.

The sergeant major yelled down at them. "By the grace of God, your entire company has made it here without anyone falling off. Which means you're too stupid to run away. Get in a line. Do it." He finished his sentence with a phlegmy spit.

The men scrambled to obey. They stuck out chests for the senior noncommissioned officer. Ignoring them, the sergeant major walked his horse through the bustling crowd. Confused, the men stood in the cold for almost ten minutes.

"Hey, O'Reilly, what are we doing here?" shouted a man.

The first sergeant shook his head. "Waiting."

"Why?"

"It's the army. That's what we do. Wait. Until it's not time to wait. Then we hurry."

More time fleeted and the men waited, watching their own breaths mist in the air. Other companies of recruits marched past, blue-uniformed federal soldiers leading the civilian-clad men in browns, blacks, blues, and grays.

The sergeant major returned with a short, fat officer atop a healthy brown mare. He peered down at the ground as if he despised it and by proxy the company of men before him. He wore a dark blue uniform, he had a round face and it was hard to see his eyes beneath his wide-brimmed hat. The officer walked his horse forward, hooves slapping the hard mud, until he was within a few feet of the new recruits. Captain Peltier and Lieutenant Wells trailed behind. Peltier's horse shied away from the other two who sat very close together.

A voice came from beneath the hat like an irritated preacher. "You men have all willingly enlisted in the Army of the Potomac and taken your oath of allegiance. President Lincoln sends his regards." A grin crossed his lips, but only he found his joke funny. His horse's hooves stamped, shifting beneath his weight.

The officer's face turned sour. "However, by the looks of this sorry lot, I'm not sure how grateful we should be." He paused for a moment. "I am Colonel Moore, your regimental commander. You are the last men we could scrounge up for this command. Most of the other men of your humble town have already enlisted or can afford to pay their way out, which leaves me the scraps." He said something to the other officers beside him. "By the looks of these mangy fellows, I should have pushed for a better appointment."

"We ain't going to get nothing but scraps with his lard arse leading us," the thief said.

Wolf stifled a grin.

The youthful thief ran fingers through greasy hair and it stayed in place. He was a noticeable six inches shorter than Wolf. "Name's Roberts."

"Johannes Wolf."

The man kept his eyes forward. "Better not let anyone else hear that."

"Why's that?" he asked nervously.

"Isn't Johannes John in German?"

"I suppose it is. Are you German?" The young man didn't look German. He had a swarthier look to him.

Rubbing his upper lip, Roberts smirked. "Not even a lick." He jabbed a finger in his chest. "Me, I'm English, at least my ma was. Not really sure what me pa was." His eyes rolled upward as he thought and he shrugged his shoulders. "But back to you, Johannes. Don't you know who we're going to fight?"

"The rebels, Southerners, Confederates, or at least *secessionists* from the Union of the United States of America."

"Ha. All them big words. What are you, some sort of scholar?" He snorted.

"You dummy, we're going to fight Johnny Reb. I wouldn't tell no one your name just in case they get the wrong idea, *Johannes*."

"Okay, Roberts. I won't say nothin'."

"Good on you. Let me tell you something. I ain't here by chance. Three meals a day. Regular pay. Uniform. Beats living on the streets stealing to eat." He said with an affirmative nod. "Picked me up a bounty too. For some rich lumber baron's boy. Soon I'll have all the money I could ever want."

"Yet you stole earlier."

Roberts laughed. "Old habits die hard."

The colonel's harangue drew their attention. "I expect my men to be in tip-top shape. Ready for anything and sharp. I hold order and discipline in the highest regard. You will be punished if you break conduct." He turned his horse around and walked back across the row of recruits. "We have so much work to do to get you men parade ready." He pointed at the towering sergeant major, his senior noncommissioned officer of the regiment, a rank above his quartermaster sergeant. "Sar Major, good luck." The colonel gave a subtle, unamused gesture with two fingers.

A youthful man with a blue cap and yellow layering his front held a bugle in one hand like it was his weapon. He put his instrument to his lips and let out a high-pitched tune.

The sergeant major stepped his horse forward. He unraveled a blue flag trimmed with gold tasseling from its pole. He untangled the flag and let the edges spread like a bird's wings. A mighty eagle flew at its center bearing a striped shield over its chest. In scrolled lettering along the bottom, it read, "Thirteenth Michigan Cavalry." He released the edge and it drooped lamely to the side.

Sergeant major's voice was harsh and deep. "These are your regimental battle colors. Every single one of you sons of whores better be dead before this falls into the hands of your enemy. I don't care if you're holding your guts in with one hand and your other arm is blown off. You will remove your hand from your guts, let them fall to the ground, and take up this flag. Is that understood?"

The men around him were silent, a few men looked away from the senior noncommissioned officer in disgust at his words.

"Yes, sir," he said. There were mutterings of the same thing.

"Apparently, they sent me the deaf, dumb, and stupid." The sergeant major rode his horse within inches of the front row of men causing a few to step back. "Well, which is it?" He pointed at a man with his reins. A scrawny farmer with sandy-blond hair from Hastings.

"None, sir," he yelped.

"Now, I couldn't hear you, you cherry."

The young man's face reddened. Being called a woman of loose morals wasn't a common thing for a rural farmer, and one may even take it as a large enough insult to start a confrontation.

The sergeant major spoke slower. "So that makes you either deaf, dumb, or stupid. And you answered me then, so you ain't deaf. Hell, I would have loved a deaf boy over a stupid one. So which are you? Dumb or stupid?"

"I'm not stupid," said the young man.

The noncommissioned officer leaned off his horse getting close to the recruit's face. "I guess that makes you dumb then." He turned away. His horse's hooves thumping hardened mud with little give. He eyed the dreary, fluff-clouded skies in torment. "Now, I pray to God every night that he will send me soldiers that are capable of defeating those dirty rotten scoundrels to the south and he sends me this lot. I reckon I deserve this, but a soldier or two would have been an ounce of a blessing." He turned his horse abruptly toward the men, mouthing words to himself.

Hacking tobacco onto the ground, he continued. "I know many of you aren't actually from here, but you're going to fight under her flag and fight you will or I'll kill ya me'self." He raised the flag higher into the air. "This is what unifies you. This is what binds you to the man next to you. If you fight for anything, you fight for these colors. Anything less is shameful." Black spit flew from his mouth. "These are your colors. Will you defend them with your life?"

"Sir, yes sir!" the recruits shouted. The fervor of the warrior brotherhood rose inside Wolf's gut.

A glint of pride crossed the sergeant major's face, but then it faded and drooped in exasperation with the limp flag. "Do any of you have wives?"

The men nodded and murmured yes. Almost half were married.

The sergeant major's mouth sneered into a frown. "Sisters?"

"Aye," Wolf said loudly.

Echoes of affirmation rose up from the recruits.

The sergeant major shook his head at them. "You should have sent me them instead."

Moore gestured for his man to calm. "That's enough. We still have a good deal of training to do before we enlist their wives and sisters. Captain Peltier." He waved his officer as if he were shooing him. "You may lead your company back to Meridian Hill."

"Sir!" Wolf called out.

The sergeant major's eyes bulged and O'Reilly appeared to be in the final stages of shitting a brick in his pants. Squinting his eyes, Moore made as if he were so high above them he couldn't make Wolf out.

"Sir, permission to speak."

A throaty laugh came from Moore. "What is it that cannot wait?"

"Sir, we have a company standard."

Lifting his hands in the air, he held up the newly cut guidon for the company.

An interested smile carved onto the colonel's fleshy lips. "So the ladies from that frontier village sent their men away with a gift. I'd say I was impressed, but I've been there. First Sergeant."

O'Reilly stepped his horse close to the front rank and Wolf passed through the men. He handed the flag to the grizzled first sergeant. Angered, he ripped it out of his hands. "We will talk about this later."

The first sergeant walked it over to the colonel. Moore held it in front of him like he was reading a paper. He gave a truncated laugh. "What do we have here? Black and red? Stitching could use some work." He turned to Wells and Peltier. "Remind me not to get my clothes tailored in Grand Rapids."

Wells gave a hearty laugh for much too long and Peltier grimaced a bit beneath his black beard.

Moore shoved a white-gloved finger at the emblazoned wolf head. "What's this a little gold doggy? Woof. Woof."

"It's a wolf, sir," he threw out.

Moore ignored his newest private. "What do you think, Lieutenant?" He raised his eyebrows. "Do you want this ragged dog to represent you on the field of battle?"

Wells did a fine, haughty laugh. "I'd prefer the stars and stripes, sir or the regimental colors over this patchwork quilt."

"And you, Captain?"

Peltier's horse shifted beneath him. His superior wanted him to play along and mock the lower ranking soldiers. "I believe whatever symbol makes the men fight harder is a good one. Let the men keep their standard."

Moore's mirth died down. "I suppose you're right. All right, sergeant, get the standard airborne. Captain, let's move these men to camp, now." He glared over at Wolf who retreated back to his position.

Peltier twisted his horse in front of them. "Company, advance."

"Hay-foot, Straw-foot, Hay-foot, Straw-foot," O'Reilly yelled and the men began their march into Washington.

CHAPTER 6

October 21st, 1862
Washington, D.C.

The company joined the other five companies of the 13th Michigan Cavalry camped near Meridian Hill, northwest of the federal district. As they were the last unit to join the regiment, all the other troopers had already been outfitted with uniforms, weapons, and mounts, making F Company feel wholly inadequate.

The other men pointed and stared at the newest members of their unit. A man stepped out from a cluster of soldiers. "The old yellow dog company. The last to arrive and first to run away!" A roar of laughter followed the newcomers with their homemade standard.

Fire rose in his belly without the help of alcohol, but he knew he was going to get a thrashing from First Sergeant O'Reilly for speaking out of rank, so he doused the flames with whatever personal control he could muster.

"They're asking for a fight," Wolf said as they continued to march to the men around him. "When we get done here. We'll have words."

"Don't listen to them, boy," Wilhelm said. "A man with a strong voice often has a weak walk. Army discipline ain't no night in the jail. They'll flog ya, put you on a wheel, or make you ride the wooden horse."

"Wooden horse?"

"A wooden horse that you straddle with no saddle or stirrups. Gets you in the arse."

Wolf shook his head in impatient acceptance. He didn't want to be flogged or forced to ride the wooden horse like he was in a Puritan village, but he wanted those men to shut their mouths. And he'd see to it if need be, despite Wilhelm's warning.

They drew to a halt. After splitting the men into two roughly even platoons, Peltier left them with the regiment's quartermaster sergeant. He was pale, skinny and sweaty, often leaving his desk to find the latrines, delegating the issuance of supplies to his subordinates.

"Stay away from him, boys," Wilhelm said.

"Why's that, Pa? He seems nice enough," Franz said.

"He's sick. Illness kills more men than the battlefield. You'd do well to remember that."

Wolf and Franz rolled their eyes at their cautious patron. They were young and didn't worry about catching a chill, as Wolf's mother used to call it.

They waited their turn until each man was issued a dark blue cavalry jacket. It had a series of twelve brass buttons down the front and was edged with their service branch color. Yellow embroidering trimmed around the collar and the cuffs of the wrist. Plain sleeves designated them as privates.

The reinforced trousers were sky blue with a single matching stripe down the center of the pant leg. They all received forage caps, a floppy version of the pre-war shako that Wolf thought resembled deflated accordions when resting atop men's heads.

Wolf admired his belt buckle attached to smooth black leather. It was made of brass and an American bald eagle perched, wings widespread, surrounded by a wreath. The Latin phrase *E Pluribus Unum* stretched along a banner above the eagle's head.

"What's *E Pluribus Unum* mean?" Wolf wondered aloud.

A gray-bearded man with a skeletal face perked up at the question. He had an almost grandfatherly look to him and the thought crossed Wolf's mind that he may be lost.

The man close-lipped smiled. "Out of many, One. It's an old motto from the Revolution."

Wolf pondered this for a moment. "You think the rebels have the same motto on their belts? I mean, we came from the same origin."

"Suppose they could, couldn't they? Don't think too much about that. They are not righteous in their purpose. God is for the liberators, not the despots. Pray, young man, that he blesses us."

"We'll be liberators." It gave him confidence knowing they had the righteousness of God at their backs. He'd never thought that God would take a stake in the fight, but this ancient man was convinced that God was with them, so Wolf accepted his wisdom.

"Yes, we will." The grandfatherly man smiled. "I was a Quaker before now. Our faith prohibits war or violence."

"I think you're in the wrong place then," Wolf said with a laugh. He wondered how the man would get back to Michigan. "Does the captain know about this?"

The elder man's voice turned grave like he was standing at a pulpit. "No, I go where God leads. It may be the devil's work that I'm to do, but it's God's will. We will free the slaves from their bondage. I am Zachariah Shugart." They shook hands and were soon bombarded with laughter.

The Polish brothers held up their pants and laughed with one another. "What are they laughing about?" Wolf asked Bartoscz. He spoke the best English out of the three.

Mirth masked his face. "They are thankful that the Union army knew they were coming."

"Why's that?"

"They made them the reinforced pants to keep in their long members." Their brash humor sat well with Wolf, but was stamped out by the approaching Lieutenant Wells.

Postured erectly with his dimpled chin jutting from his face, he reminded Wolf of a stallion's member. Alongside him was a man of average height. He didn't wear the dark blue uniform but a black jacket and overcoat with a short ebony top hat. A half-grown beard had sprouted on his cheeks as if he'd just decided one day to stop shaving.

Clasping his hands behind his back, Wells said. "Men, I would like you to meet Sergeant Cobb. He is a veteran from the 1st Michigan Cavalry. He's seen a lot so heed what he says and do as he says. He'll be a part of 1st Platoon so you will answer to him."

Wolf held up his black leather, knee-high riding boots with a smirk at Roberts. "These for women?"

"Be thankful you got the knee highs," Cobb said.

"Why is that, sir?

"None of us got 'em in the beginning. We had to buy 'em from the crook sutler." Cobb carried on down the line of men eyeing the sutler's tent from afar with malice.

"Where's your uniform?" Van Horn said. He had slipped on a cavalry jacket that was too small for him, cuffs stopping above his wrists.

Cobb grinned. "You'll learn soon enough, boy."

Van Horn was no boy and the tall Dutchman frowned. "I ain't a boy."

"You are until you seen the elephant." Cobb referred to gaining experience in battle, war, death, and destruction, all experiences that came at a psychological, emotional, and physical cost. Where through the smoky mist men tried to rip each other to shreds with cannon, muskets, swords, and their bare hands when the opportunity arose. The elephant was being witness to man's true beastly nature.

Lieutenant Wells spoke down to them. "Yes, Mr. Cobb has been through many battles and he will now instruct you on the importance of discipline. Something of which you men are sorely lacking after the stunt the gimp played today with the company standard."

Heat rose in Wolf's cheeks. If they were in a tavern, he'd be throwing punches at the tall man regardless of his dangerous long reach. But he knew enough to quiet his tongue. Wells could see his discomfort and stepped closer. "Is there something you'd like to say, *private*?" His eyes darted down to Wolf's lips and he waited a moment for Wolf to dig himself in a hole that he could never escape. A hole which the officer could bury him in. Vengeful eyes continued to dare Wolf and he could feel his jaw clenching. Wolf averted his eyes.

Wells nastily smiled from above. "Sergeant, make sure they are thoroughly disciplined. They must learn their place. No room for miscreants and vagabonds in this army."

Rubbing his chin, Cobb nodded. "Of course, sir. It will be done."

Taking his time, Wells turned away. "Very well. Carry on. I expect very tired men on latrine duty later." He strolled away whistling "The Battle Hymn of the Republic."

Cobb studied his unit. "I don't know what you've done, but you made him mad. If he's mad, I'm mad, and you should be thankful you aren't in the wilderness with a Mosby ranger breathing down your soft pink necks with a Arkansas pig-sticker at your throat. Instead you're in the capital city of this nation surrounded by a ring of forts." He took a breath. "So I'm going to work the ungratefulness out of ya." Almost nonchalantly he added, "To the log."

With plenty of complaints, the platoon marched over to logs for building. About two feet thick, they were over thirty feet tall. Cobb shouted. "Get that log up, boys!"

The men bent over trying to get a grip. Cobb chuckled, slapping his knee. "If you don't work together, you're going to get chewed to pieces out there."

Wilhelm's voice rose out of the clamor of grumbles and grunts. "Everybody get a hand under it. Then on three we hoist." Wolf knew he'd been a soldier before immigrating to the United States.

"Ready, set, heave." The men groaned as they lifted the log into the air. They rested it across each other's shoulders.

"March," Cobb ordered with a sigh.

The men marched.

***

After they had learned to parade with a log, the men tromped, minus the burden, to the stables directed by First Sergeant O'Reilly. The stables were a whirlwind of flies and gnats and the stench of horse dung hung heavy in the air like a summer rain. As they stood in the open, outside the stable, they could overhear O'Reilly arguing with the stable master.

"A Company got bays, B Company got browns, C Company grays, D Company blacks, and we get the *leftovers*. Ain't right."

The stable master had muscular forearms and sleeves rolled to his elbows and appeared less than amused by the first sergeant's inquisition.

"It's what we got left. Listen, O'Reilly, it ain't nothing against you. You showed up last, you get last pick."

"Oh, McMasters, you're a no-good son of a goat."

McMasters licked his lips and stared down at the short first sergeant. "You get what ya get."

The first sergeant's veins bulged in his neck, but he spun on his men instead. "All right, men, come and grab your horses."

Rapidly, O'Reilly went about setting man with horse, saving the larger horses for the larger men, but it was clear that these mounts were of lower quality than the others in the stable. F Company's mounts were older, skinnier, with swayed backs, and weak dispositions.

"Okay, Private Wolf. You're with this one here."

The horse was a brown gelding with a white patch over his nose.

"His name is Billy," O'Reilly said, slapping the horse's backside.

"Billy," Wolf repeated.

The first sergeant carried on matchmaking.

"Billy." He patted the horse's flank. Its skin twitched, bouncing flies away, and his tail swung, brushing them away despite their persistence. "You know, Billy, my father taught me how to ride and care for you so you will be in good hands. I'll take care of you and you'll take care of me, and we'll take care of each other." The horse turned his long equine head toward Wolf and stared at him with an open eye. He kicked a hoof into the stable mud. "You're going to let us run."

Wolf eyeballed his leg brace with disdain. This horse would make him a fighting man, an army man, something he could never dream of until now. He continued stroking the horse's flank. "We're going to run."

CHAPTER 7

December 14th, 1862
Washington, D.C.

Sunlight cracked the horizon and the shrill notes of the bugler cut the chill December air with the rousing sound of reveille. The men had to learn over thirty-seven different bugle calls. Each meant a differing order in battle. But this was the one call that always pulled them away from the bosom of sleep.

Wolf pushed himself onto his elbows and wiped his eyes. A cream canvas tent rippled overhead outlined by carved wooden poles. Each trooper was issued a half shelter, and when teamed up with another trooper they could create a whole shelter. The shelter was held together with buttons and had grommets for stakes to hold the tent down with wooden pegs.

He flexed his maimed leg. He reached blindly to his right and his fingers locked around his metal brace. Night was the only time he removed the supportive encasement, letting his skin breathe. He draped it over his foot and pulled it up his sky-blue pant leg.

"Up and at 'em, my precious cherries," shouted First Sergeant O'Reilly from outside.

The camp was almost two miles from Washington on a relatively flat land that was prone to flooding despite the elevation of the position. More than half the days they awoke wet from the saturated earth. It was cool there, but nothing like Michigan. He imagined they'd have snow on the ground by now.

His tent mate clipped on his belt and scooped his saber and stuck his blue cap on his head. "Chipper old Leprechaun this morning, ain't he?"

"Wonder why he's so happy?" Wolf tightened the leather strap that ran along the top of his brace and belted it into place. He tested it out. It resisted his movement with a groan of metal on metal.

"Latrine duty, I'm sure." The black-haired private rubbed his young mustache. He was only seventeen and the Sergeant had looked the other way when signing him to fulfill the rich patron's bounty. The regiment was already understaffed after the 6th and 7th Michigan Cavalries had nabbed most of the higher quality recruits. They had basically dredged the gutters of Grand Rapids to piece together the last of six depleted companies.

The men had been plagued by the menial soldierly tasks required of a new recruit, building breastworks, cleaning weapons, digging latrines, and attempting to teach the men to ride. It was apparent that almost none of the new recruits had any equestrian experience, something that put them at a distinct disadvantage to their Southern opponents.

Squeak. The brace complained as he stepped into the brisk air of the outside. Trees had been cleared for firewood leaving general desolation around them. The large white tent of the sutler rested about 100 yards away. George Peterson was a crook with an easy smile and a quick shake. He loved to relieve the men of any and all valuables for items not provided by the military. Extra food, drink, clothes, and even a few nice looking pistols that Wolf could never afford. Peterson claimed that the two women always with him were his nieces, but it was rumored that they were actually prostitutes. Knowing of the man, Wolf supposed the girls could be both.

Roberts joined him. "As soon as we get paid, I'm gonna see what all the fuss is about with Peterson's Mary. Nice red hair on that one."

Wolf eyed the tent. He'd noticed her too. She was a cute girl with flaming red hair and long legs that reminded Wolf of a deer.

The cavalry company formed rank in front of squat O'Reilly. "Straighten that blouse, trooper," he said, tugging at a man's dark blue fatigue tunic. The trooper smoothed his tunic that fit like a suit jacket under his overcoat that acted as a poncho and a way to keep rain off and cold out.

"Just cause you got your overcoats on don't mean you can look like bloody hell underneath." The men wore their double-breasted overcoats to keep warm in the winter months. Every piece of issued clothing was made from wool, which Wolf appreciated.

"Form ranks." The company grouped into a column, four men across. "Advance, march." The troopers made proper form over to an open field. "Company halt." The dismounted cavalrymen stopped in ranks. "Right, face." The troopers twisted on their right heel and faced the company first sergeant. "Break out into split platoons for saber drills."

Each company broke into two platoons of forty men. 1st Platoon was composed of thirty-six troopers, two sergeants and four corporals, depending on illness. In turn each platoon broke down into two half-strength units. It wasn't a formal designation, but when it came to scouting, training, and other maneuvers made below a platoon level, the men worked in smaller units led by a single sergeant, two corporals, and roughly fifteen troopers.

Wolf scrambled to get in line with half of 1st Platoon.

The troopers filled a single line with a corporal on either end. There were the three Polish brothers, almost indistinguishable with their hulking frames and round faces. Wolf and Roberts, Wilhelm and Franz, Van Horn, and three men just eighteen. Lent was a mousy young man with brown hair, Henry Hunt was an orphan with red hair, and Jerry Gratz was a young Austrian immigrant, tall with blond hair and coffee-colored eyes. On the far end was the other corporal, Zachariah Shugart. His fatherly look and apparent wisdom had earned him corporal stripes almost immediately.

Sergeant Cobb was proving himself to be a highly unmotivated instructor. His training was always short, but mostly he delegated training to his subordinates out of pure boredom.

"Troopers, draw."

Wolf gripped the handle of his sword, the model 1860 light cavalry saber, a little over two pounds outside its sheath, steel blade and brass hand guard, the handle wrapped in leather. It was curved for slashing or piercing and from tip to hilt forty-one inches long.

With his other hand he held the sheath at his left hip. The blades scraped metal on metal as they were released from their homes. Wolf brought the curved sword to his right shoulder and let it rest there.

Cobb strolled in front of them. "These are the same actions as when you are atop of a horse. Corporal Berles, you may lead them in drill."

Wilhelm stepped out of rank and went to the front of the men. He'd been immediately promoted to corporal because of his previous background in a German Uhlan, a light cavalry unit popular in Europe. It quickly became apparent that while Sergeant Cobb had experience in this war, Corporal Berles had years of cavalry drill under his belt as well as combat experience. He conducted most of the troopers' drill and training, leaving Sergeant Cobb to other pursuits around camp.

"Troopers, present arms." His voice boomed with easy command, but more of an angry father than an antagonistic sergeant.

Wolf twisted his saber so the hand guard was in the center of his chest and the blade was flat and sideways in front of his face. Berles marched down the line. His thin mustache was waxed in a rounded fashion. He abruptly stopped in front of Bartoscz.

"Now, Bart. You have to keep this part oiled or it will rust. Do you understand?"

"Yes, sir."

Berles nodded. He carried on down the line, his back straight like a rod. "Good. Move to guard."

The men split their stance, the right roughly two feet from the left. "Now molinet left. Now molinet right. Good. Now molinet rear." Giving the other men a wide berth, the troopers rotated their shoulders and wrists in full circles. It was a warm up of what was to come, loosening up the joints before getting into the movements meant to kill the enemy.

"Move to point." Wolf raised his sword hand level with his shoulder and jabbed the saber forward, outstretching his arm. He systematically brought his arm back and lowered the saber to his side.

"Remember men, sticking them with the pointy end is always the most effective killing blow. Slashing is well and nice on a force, but nothing kills a man better than a point through the heart."

"Point left." They followed the same motion but this time lunged the blade to the left side of their body.

"On a horse, we must be careful to avoid harming them. They are your lifeblood. You live and die with your mount."

"Point rear," Berles shouted.

Wolf turned and swung the sword over his right shoulder. With his right arm half extended, he thrust it behind him, blade horizontal, edge upwards.

"Good, Johannes," Berles said as he walked by.

"Franz, edge up. It's hard to parry with the edge down. Your enemy's blade will run along the curve like slippery ice and slice into your arm. Unacceptable."

The troopers worked the forms all morning, different cuts, parries, and thrusts for both mounted and infantry opponents with adequate breaks from Berles. Cobb seemed generally indifferent to if Berles drilled them to death or not at all.

They broke for lunch and Wolf sat with his comrades around a large campfire near the center of four of their tents.

Franz smiled as he cooked a rash of bacon in a small skillet over the fire. His curly blond hair stuck out from the sides of his cap. Wolf leaned in, nibbling on a hard cracker that tasted more like flour than anything else, trying to get more of the heat.

Corporal Berles took a seat with a yellowing newspaper in one hand. He took out his wooden pipe and packed it with rich tobacco and stuck it in his mouth. With an ember from the fire, he lit the pipe and opened his paper, puffing his cheeks to get it going.

"Bacon?" Franz asked.

Wilhelm waved him off. "Give it to one of the brothers. Dan did the best today." The men had taken to calling the Polish brothers by diminutives of their original names. Bogdan was Dan, Bartoscz was Bart and Bozimir was Berry.

Bogdan smiled. "Yes."

Franz placed a limp piece of greasy bacon on his plate.

Bart held up his plate. "Yes?"

Franz glared at him. "Okay." He placed a piece on Bart's plate.

"Yes?" Berry said.

Franz sighed and placed his last piece of bacon on Berry's plate. "I'll see if I can get some more from the quartermaster." He left the fire, shoulders slumped.

Wilhelm masked a grin as he watched his son leave. "He'll learn." He held the paper out. "Christ," he cursed. "We've been crushed."

"What happened?" Wolf asked. Any news of the war while they sat in camp was welcomed. Rumors wormed through the ranks at all times, but solid if only semi-reliable accounts from the paper were worth gold to the men.

"Burnside demolished our army at Fredericksburg." He eyed Wolf. "Over 12,000 casualties."

"Where's Fredericksburg?" Roberts asked. He munched an apple he almost couldn't hold with one hand. He was a fine tent mate to have and Wolf never was hungry when he was around.

"About forty miles south of here."

Van Horn's face was stoic. "They could be here in a few days."

"They could," Wilhelm said. He looked back at the paper. "A stunning defeat. Federal troops butchered on the river. Richmond erupts in jubilation. Two generals were killed. More men wasted on fruitless battles."

"Lincoln isn't fit to lead us," Van Horn said.

"Shut your mouth, fool. You're in his army and you fight for his Union," Wilhelm ordered.

The Dutchman wouldn't budge. "All we've done is lost. How can we expect to win this?"

"No conflict worth fighting is complete without sacrifice."

"Wilhelm, we don't even have guns. What are we going to do, charge them with sabers?"

"Have faith, brothers," Corporal Shugart said. His long beard was mostly gray and he had a slight bend in his back. "Our cause is just. God will give us the strength to win this struggle and smite the evil, slaving Southerners. We stood up to them at the Kentucky Raid of '47 and we'll do it again."

"I don't think God is listening, old man," Sergeant Cobb said from behind them. His black hat was off-kilter like he'd been drinking.

"Sir," the unit murmured.

Cobb gave them a nasty smile. "They'll get us our equipment soon. They're going to need more men for the meat grinder." He pointed at them. "And here we are, fresh little piggies for the grinding." He circled their fire like a shark. "You think this is new? Ha. This is how we got here. First and Second Bull Run, Antietam, now Fredericksburg. We've been through it before. Lee'll invade now and who will stand up to him? Little Mac? Ha! Burnside's proven all he can do is get our boys slaughtered. Hooker? You read what he'll do to us, futile frontal assaults all day long until we're all piles of red mush, our souls singing the Battle Hymn straight up to St. Pete. The Dutchman was right, Lincoln can't lead us cause he can't find a general who can."

"God will guide us," Shugart said softly.

Cobb snorted. "You all would have done good and stayed home fucking your wives until Lee sacks Washington."

Wilhelm stood abruptly, smoke billowing from his pipe. "That's enough, Sergeant. Can't you see these boys are taking in what you're saying? They're looking to you for strength. Don't cut us down before we get to the field."

The troopers looked away, the insubordination by Corporal Berles on their behalf striking contrast to their sergeant.

Cobb held up a hand. "I ain't gonna pull rank on a man twice my age, one that should know better, but I'm saying the truth."

"Leave your truth out of this. Someone will take charge."

Laughing, Cobb gave Wilhelm a mirthless grin. "You're one stupid German. You can lead them through filling in the sink, Corporal. I'll be in my tent."

The sink was a common term for the camp latrine. After the long pit was filled with the excrements of the men, they would fill the stinking trench and dig another nearby. Bushes and branches were stacked around the long ditch to provide some privacy, but it was mostly open and the ripe sewage had a fierce smell to it.

Cobb walked away, grabbing a camp girl by her waist. Red-haired Mary looked back at them and Cobb pulled her away.

Wilhelm stood for a moment, watching the Sergeant disappear. "Classless wretch," he said under his breath. "You heard him. Grab your shovels."

CHAPTER 8

May 7th, 1863
Washington, D.C.

Wolf crouched near his mount's neck. He rode with his saber along his side, carefully avoiding his horse. The drill was speed attacking. He pulled back just a bit on Billy's reins right before he reached the first straw man. Yellow straw bristled from gray sleeves and a watermelon head stood defiantly on the field. He cocked his arm at his elbow and pierced the melon with a thrust. Twirling his wrist as he weaved the horse to the right, he cut downward and to his left. The cut shaved an inch off the side of the melon.

He weaved the horse to the other side of the next enemy and slashed to his right whipping his arm. He spurred his horse for the last practice dummy. This was a wooden horse with a scarecrow on top that looked rather ridiculous. Billy moved into a full gallop and raced past the wooden horse. Wolf twisted in his saddle for a rear cut. His sword swooshed overhead. The straw rebel living to fight another day.

Wilhelm and Cobb observed on horses near the end of the makeshift course.

"Well done, Johannes. Finest in the platoon. All but the last opponent."

Wolf moved his sword to carry saber letting his little finger wrap around the outside of the hilt resting on his thigh and smiled. "Thank you, sir."

"Back in line, Private," Cobb said with a disinterested yawn. "Killing straw men is one thing, but real men fight back." Ignoring the truth of his sergeant,

Wolf steered his horse with his knees and rode back to his comrades. His leg ached in the saddle, but he felt alive. When he was atop his mount, he could sprint like the wind. The animal gave him a new leg, and he loved his gelding for it, taking the utmost care of grooming and feeding him on a more than regular basis. Even if the aged gelding was outside regulation.

His platoon finished the drill. Bart and Roberts were capable riders and saber-fighters, Dan dropped his saber during his run and Shugart almost fell from his horse. Most of the troopers were new to horses with only a couple men outside of the veterans having much experience. They moved into platoon tactics and then into company formation and, joining with three other companies, participated in squadron maneuvers. They were painfully slow and First Sergeant O'Reilly let them know, but they were getting better even if they were as green as a pea.

New life had been breathed into the 13th because they'd finally been issued carbines and pistols, all except F Company who'd been snubbed in the order.

Command of the army had fallen under "Fighting Joe" Hooker and despite their losses was conducting an offensive campaign against Lee and threatened Richmond and therefore the end of the war was near. Their unit hadn't been sent into the field yet, but maybe they wouldn't even have to fight. A disappointing prospect because he'd wanted a chance to prove himself, but had grown comfortable to the soldier's camp life of training, marching, gambling, and drinking when O'Reilly turned a blind eye.

The men took their horses back to stable. Wolf removed his McClellan saddle from Billy's back. It was a standard issued saddle developed by Little Mac before the war started. Its design, as he claimed it, was a modification of the Hungarian design in Prussian service, but it most closely resembled the Spanish tree saddle. Wilhelm was most certain it wasn't a Prussian design. Those saddles were much heavier and could be used with lances like a medieval knight jousting.

Wolf draped the saddle on the railing his horse was tied to. With a stiff-haired brush, he started to groom Billy.

"Wolf," came a voice. He looked behind him. Only the meaty flank of a mare was visible. "Psst." Roberts waved a bottle at him from underneath.

"Tonight, we have some fun."

Smiling, Wolf wiped the sweat from his brow. "Better get out from under there or he'll piss on ya." Washington was devastatingly humid compared to West Michigan even in early spring and now the woolen uniforms seemed scratchy, hot, and unbearable. He was beginning to see why some of the veteran soldiers wore civilian garb. Every chance they got the troopers were stripping off jackets and gear to stay cool, but with no tree cover their tents provided the only shade.

"Where'd you get that?"

"Ha. Well, just say I found it."

"You didn't pay? Even better."

Dan's rotund head popped above his horse. "Bottle, yes?"

Putting a finger to his lips, Wolf said softly. "Yes."

A wide smile cut Dan's face and he turned to his other side and yelled something in Polish to his brothers. They all smiled over their horses at Wolf and Roberts, nodding their heads like a Jack-in-the-box.

"Wolf, those guys are brutes." Roberts stretched his arms to the sky. "They're gonna drink the whole damn thing."

"I signed on with them. They're good guys and I owe 'em."

"I know."

Wolf bent low and looked underneath Roberts's horse. "You'll just have to steal another."

"I risk getting flogged every time I 'forage' us something to drink."

"And it's worth every drop."

"Coming from the guy who doesn't have to risk anything to drink it."

Wolf chuckled and went back to rubbing down his horse. "Atta boy."

"Excuse me," a private shouted from across the way. His forage cap was pushed up on his forehead, the hat still managing to slope downward as if it were putting all its weight into pushing the flat brim onto his face. He was with two other soldiers.

Wolf stopped brushing down his mount. "Yeah?"

The man picked lice from his yellow beard. He had more graybacks, a term for lice, than the Confederate army. "Was wondering if you could wipe down me mount too. She's over there. God bless."

Curiously, Wolf glanced at Roberts, looking for confirmation that the men were serious. The private sneered in response.

"Do it yourself."

One of his allies laughed with a deep voice. "You could wipe down me cock."

Wolf focused on caring for Billy. Words of Wilhelm filtered through his mind. *Stay out of trouble. Getting in a fight is worse in the army. Nothing to prove. Nothing to prove.* He knew when a man was digging for a brawl and this private had came over with singular purpose of instigating one.

"Well that's funny. I thought you two were laborers. Isn't that what that flag means? Yellow dog company." He licked his lips and grinned brown-stained teeth.

"We're F Company of the 13th Michigan."

"F Company are the laborers, right?"

"Bugger off man," Roberts said, from over his horse. He hardly reached the horse's back. "We got sabers just like the rest of y'all."

The man edged closer to the small thief. "Big words for a little puke who hasn't seen a goddamn lick of nothing."

"What you seen?" Roberts said.

Wolf continued grooming Billy, trying to control himself. *Nothing to prove.*

The trooper fixed his jacket. "Haven't yet, but I can tell a company of cowards when I see's one and that yellow dog there sums it all together. I wouldn't let you's hold my horse for a fight."

"That's enough." Wolf set his brush back in his bag folding the flap over carefully.

The man smirked at him. "And what would a crippled Dutch like yourself do about it?"

"We can fight."

Their antagonizer looked at both his friends. "You'll run the first bullet that comes your way."

"Nah. We'll fight. I just have this gut feeling 'bout it."

The man stepped within a few inches of Wolf. His rancid rotten egg breath assaulted his nostrils. He kept his eyes cool and unimpressed.

"Wolf, let's get back to camp."

His eyes never broke contact. After a few moments of the standoff, he averted his eyes back to Roberts. "You're right. Let's head back."

The man's evil smile grew larger waving a sad child-like farewell. "Run away, yellow dogs."

A quick spin and Wolf's fist snapped like a flash into the man's nose. *Crack!* His head jerked back, his feet following beneath him. He bent over, holding his face. His tall friend now took his opportunity to windmill his fist into Wolf's jaw. The blow sent him stumbling backward. Using Billy to stabilize himself, he bounded back into the scuffle. His gelding neighed in discontent and stomped his hooves.

The man swung wildly over the top and Wolf shifted his head far to the side. The man missed, his problem was that he was going for a knockout punch leaving himself exposed. Throwing a hook into his ribs, Wolf rapidly followed with another hook and uppercut into the soldier's chin. He fell into the mud on his back with a splash.

Wolf spun seeking the third assailant, but was too late as Roberts crawled under his horse and jumped on the back of the third. Violent arms wrapped Wolf's neck, but Wolf's arm was trapped between them. Clasping his hands, he locked them together around the other man. His strong arms squeezed his assailant and it became a wrestling match of who could overpower the other.

Adjusting his hips a moment before, he threw them both into the horse-tread muddy enclosure. They rolled through the muck destroying their uniforms.

Yells from the edge of camp startled the young troopers and he knew they'd been caught. *They're gonna send us to the Wooden Horse, right up your arse.* The two men released each other. They stood stinking in horse piss and shit.

The commotion drew the men away from their conflict. The other man spit. Wolf gave him a glance and moved closer to the road leaning on the fence. Through a dust cloud, white-topped wagons came into view pulled by teams of horses.

The other men joined him looking like they'd jumped into a pile of manure. They reached the side of the road and Roberts stood alongside him. "New recruits?"

"Nah, recruits come by train, not wagon," the ringleader said, he spit again. "Got shit in my mouth."

Wolf smirked, but held his tongue, not wanting to start another round.

"Only wounded come in like that," said another. The words quieted all of them.

As the wagon's got closer, sorry faces stared back, heads bandaged, arms in slings, tattered bloody uniforms. Then the next wagon rolled by. The sounds of outright sobbing trickled out. More defeated men sat inside, crippled, maimed and broken from war. The wagons crushed any mirth the men still had and replaced it with the reality of war. The long line of white-canvased wagons extended down the thoroughfare and disappeared out of sight.

A man sat on the back of the next wagon and Wolf called out to him. "What happened?"

The man had a black mustache and goatee. He coughed. "Hooker happened. We more than doubled them and they chewed us up and spit us out like an owl pellet."

"How'd you get done in?" shouted the ringleader.

"Stuart led Jackson's men right into our flank. Never thought they'd come from that direction. Shattered us. Hampton danced circles around us. It was like they couldn't be killed. Those Red Shirts." The man's face twisted. "The Devil's Banshees."

The wagon train of wounded and dying passed by like battered blue ghosts to the hundred different hospitals that had sprung up around Washington once the war started. The groans of the afflicted haunted Wolf for nights to come, lingering in the shadows near twilight. Hooker had been thoroughly beaten at Chancellorsville, and Lincoln and Congress were in a scramble to find someone who had the gall to fight with a belly of courage and an ounce of foresight.

"Come on, boys. Let's not waste our fight on these dogs. Someone's got to win this war." He waved his fellow privates to follow him. "I'll see you laborers again when I need my horse groomed."

"We'll be waiting," Wolf hollered back.

Wilhelm leaned over the split-fence railing, apparently privy to the entire encounter. "You boys think it's fun to brawl it out over a gosh darn flag?"

Wolf wiped mud and dirt from his uniform flinging it on the ground. "They questioned our honor."

"Then let 'em. They'll learn we're a force to be reckoned with. Show it on the field. Fighting each other is only going to get us killed out there where it counts."

Roberts looked like he'd tried to bathe in a mud puddle. It dripped off his face and hands.

"Gotta get cleaned up before the Sergeant sees us," Roberts said.

"I'll say. They might try to send us to work with the other coloreds by the looks of you." They gave half-hearted laughs and hurried back into the camp, avoiding the other troopers, but they both knew the other masked his true feelings about the wounded that had just rolled through.

Near their bivouac, Sergeant Cobb lounged with his feet up in front of his tent. He perked up a bit as they crossed his path. "What happened to you, men?"

Roberts turned his eyes to the side, leaving Wolf to lie to their sergeant. He coughed into his hand. "Uh, we fell. You know horses." And as an afterthought. "Sir."

Cobb twisted his face and nose away from the men. "You boys stink. Get that cleaned up, now."

"Yes, sir," the young men said, saluting and moving toward the river.

***

The next morning, First Sergeant O'Reilly called reveille and the men of F Company made formation in front of their tents.

"Looks like they're finally serious about getting us in the fight." Privates set down elongated boxes on top of one another. "Get 'em open lads."

The privates took fat crowbars to the wooden boxes, prying the wood around the edges until they were open.

O'Reilly bent down and lifted a firearm. A genuine smile stretched on his mustached face. "Finally, some firepower, boys. What we have here is a Sharps carbine. Bout eight pounds, .52 caliber, and 39 inches long with a 22-inch barrel. Stock is hard walnut. You could use it to crush a skull if need be." He flipped the carbine around, showing them. "This instrument of death will work under almost any condition. I've seen it fired after a cavalryman dragged it behind his horse for two miles in the mud." He gestured over at another box. "Get that one open too."

A Sharps carbine with strap and Colt Army .44 caliber pistol were given to every man in the company that hadn't already been issued one. They weren't given any ammunition or percussion caps, but they were instructed on proper maintenance and loading procedures and given no time for firearms practice.

Standing nearby with arms across his chest, Cobb smirked. "Ha, they just gave you what was left. I heard that a few of the other Michigan regiments received new Spencer rifles. Seven shots per load out. Copper cartridges. Now, that's what you want. Sharps are a fine firearm, but nothing like the Spencer."

"I don't even care." Wolf's excitement was not to be deterred, his sergeant could naysay all he wanted, but they had guns, they were men. The fact that he had not one but two firearms made him feel like he could take on the entire Confederate army, and at the current rate of Union debacles he might have to.

Men on horseback galloped in their direction as the men held their weapons to the sky in joy, for they were true soldiers.

Wolf brought his carbine close then placed the weapon to his shoulder, taking fictional aim at an attacking rebel.

"Pew."

Now, there were no doubts in their minds. They were troopers, not mere groomsmen of horses.

CHAPTER 9

June 26th, 1863
Washington, D.C.

"You open the handle like this." First Sergeant O'Reilly worked the Sharps carbine by flipping out the trigger guard that lowered the breech mechanism for the firearm.

"Take out your carbine cartridge. Place the cartridge into the breech and slip the guard closed. Now you want to make sure to slice the end of the cartridge linen, leaving some powder for your cap to ignite." His thumb set the hammer halfway back. "You put the hammer half-cocked. Put a percussion cap on there. Cock the hammer the rest of the way, and then fire." He quickly placed the short carbine, excellent for horseback, to his shoulder and discharged the weapon. In a second, he had the gun breech open and was slipping another cartridge inside. He snapped the mechanism closed, rapidly moving his fingers as he set his cap and fired another.

"And that's how it's done." He showed them the carbine. "You need to be able to do this as fast as seven times a minute."

The men of F Company murmured among themselves. They hadn't even been allowed to fire the weapons, only practice loading, and cleaning the weapons repeatedly. The regiment's morale had dipped even lower when the 5th, 6th, and 7th Michigan Regiments were led into the field by Brigadier General Copeland and the 13th Michigan had been left behind to protect the capital. It didn't help their reputation in the eyes of the other soldiers, who already felt that the 13th was lacking in martial spirit and that angst dripped down the companies, ending on F Company.

"If you can do that, you'll bypass any Johnny Reb muzzle-loader. These level the odds. Hopefully make up for your green ass in the field."

Captain Peltier came riding up, his horse panting fiercely followed by his lieutenants. The first sergeant rested the carbine on the ground.

"Company, stand at attention." The men put their carbines stock down on the earth. Backs were straight, chests out, hands at hips. The first sergeant saluted their commanding officer.

Peltier gave him a hurried salute back. "We are on the move in an hour. Lee's invading north. We are to ride hard to link up with the rest of the brigade."

"Yes, sir," O'Reilly shouted. The captain turned his horse around and rode off followed in tow by his junior officers.

"Should have left with them weeks ago," Roberts whispered.

"It's the army. Sometimes the head doesn't know what the foot's doing."

O'Reilly turned back on his men, a tinge of excitement in his voice. "Well, you heard the captain. We're headed to War. We break camp in an hour. Then we have some hard riding ahead. Dismissed."

Wolf rushed back to his tent with Roberts. The thrill of going to war danced among the men. Guard duty, camp life, training, and boredom were about to be left in the dust. They were about to get into the action. Stop Lee. Win the war.

They disassembled their domicile swiftly and tossed tent stakes into the fire. They folded half-shelters and bedrolls into one, Wolf's fingers enthusiastically squashing the two materials into a tight wrap.

"You hear that, Wolf? We're gonna fight!" Roberts said.

"I know. We're finally going to show Johnny Reb how it's done."

Roberts grinned beneath his darkening-in mustache. "No more latrine duty from Sergeant Cobb. We're big fish now."

Wolf gave a hearty laugh. The glory of war would soon be theirs, but the visions of those wounded men always crept into his mind every time he thought about glory. He shoved the maimed men away. "We're gonna end this war. One glorious charge and we'll send them running."

Roberts wiped a hand over his greasy hair and snatched his pack, draping it over his shoulder. "Race you to the horses."

"Screw you."

Roberts didn't wait for him and took off. They rejoined at the quartermaster sergeant's tent. The regiment had received a new quartermaster after the last one perished in a hospital from his illness. Their new one was the opposite, pink like a sausage and round like a kettle pot. Quartermaster Appleby was prepared and ready to distribute linen and paper cartridges for both the carbines and pistols.

The heavyset quartermaster grunted at them. "Got you as much as we could for this fight." The cartridges consisted of a pre-measured load of black powder and a ball, wrapped in a waxy, oily paper or linen that had been dried. It was infinitely easier than measuring and carrying all the individual components of firing a weapon. For their pistols, to load each chamber, one only had to slip the cartridge into the front of the chamber and seat the ball with the loading lever ram. Then a percussion cap was placed onto the raised aperture, called a nipple, at the back end of the chamber.

"These are for your sardine box to keep your pepperbox operational." He handed them percussion caps for their firearms. "Won't keep you in the fight all day, but at least you won't be cannon fodder neither. We'll get you more once we get situated."

Wolf tucked the ammunition in one pouch on his belt and tucked the caps into another right next to his belt buckle. His Colt Army revolver was heavy and unwieldy, and firing from horseback seemed like an impossible feat unless you were within a dozen feet from what you were shooting.

The men collected their mounts from the stables. Wolf threw his horse blanket over Billy's back. The gelding could sense his excitement and tossed his head.

"I know, boy. We're going to war."

Billy tucked his head back down and eyed him from the side.

"We'll get there soon enough. Long ride, fella." After tossing his saddle blanket on Billy, he ensured that the hairs on Billy's back weren't matted or rubbing the opposite direction of how his hair grew. Wolf placed his saddle onto his horse and placed Billy's tail through the crupper, a piece of tack that kept the saddle in place on the horse's back. He tightened the cinch around its belly. He straightened his reins and made sure his effects, forage for the horse, and bedroll were all secure.

The bugle sounded out the call to mount up.

Roberts, lighter on his feet, was already atop his mare. "Come on, Wolf, we're going to miss the war!"

The company was in the middle of forming ranks. The Poltorak brothers were in formation, even old Shugart was mounted and steering his animal toward the others.

Mounting the horse wasn't an easy endeavor for a man with a lame leg, even with months of practice.

"All right, Billy, you ready?"

The horse didn't respond and Wolf gripped the mane with his left hand, and the reins and high pommel with the other, attempting to vault himself atop the animal. He easily placed his right foot through the stirrup. He let his carbine swing to his side along its strap.

Wilhelm left rank and was waving at him to hurry. Sergeant Cobb looked on in disinterested satisfaction. Wolf grimaced as he forced his boot in and finally felt one with the animal. He patted his mount's flank.

"Come on, Billy," he said loudly and the horse trotted into the column. He joined the men at the rear.

"We were worried you'd decided to stay here," Cobb mocked. His black hat tilted to the side. "If you're smart, you would have."

"Not in a million years. We're finally going to fight."

"Not the first boy with visions of glory and honor in his head. Most of them lay one foot under, pushed into a shallow grave with the rest of the like-minded *brave* fellows."

The company of cavalry formed into a column in ranks of four horsemen. Wilhelm, Wolf, Roberts, and Bart formed one rank. Each rank either had a corporal or sergeant in it to lead and support the more novice troops.

Wilhelm sat tall in his saddle, easily controlling his mount. "I was like you once, Wolf. War will take your innocence, but that doesn't mean it's not a fight worth fighting. Some causes are worth the risk."

The bugler let out another shrill bellow. The column moved at a slow walk until it joined with the other companies of the 13th Michigan Cavalry. The time in camp had sent every company's numbers drifting downward with no fresh recruits to take their place. Wolf had felt lucky he hadn't caught the "Virginia Two-step" that had laid up so many of the men, rendering them weak and unable to fight. If it got bad enough, they could die too.

The captain turned to O'Reilly. "All men accounted for, First Sergeant?"

The Irishman bobbed his head. "All eighty-four men. We're leaving twelve in the sick tent with various illness and four in the ground from disease."

"Very well, First Sergeant. You may proceed."

O'Reilly turned his horse down the flank of the column. "Greener than the hills of Donegal, but you're more ready than the last few regiments I been in. Let's get you blooded." The men hooted and hollered at the sound of that and the first sergeant returned to the head of the column.

And the men sat in the hot humid air waiting for their orders to depart. The sun beat down and the men kept patient rank. And soon sweat dripped from chins and cheeks.

"What are we waitin' for?" Roberts asked.

"No idea."

"You boys know the drill, we hurry and we wait."

Billy decided it was time for a snack; he tugged at his reins, stretching his neck for beaten down yellow grass. As the men waited, it battered the nervous energy associated with going to war.

After the men had lost count of time, the first sergeant's voice yelled loud from the front of the company. "Let's march." The horses' hooves clopped the earth. F Company followed in line behind the rest.

The column stretched almost a half mile along the dry dirt road. The supplies and camp followers took their place behind the 13th Michigan. The drone of an army going to war played out. Sabers rattled, horses neighed, men made small talk, and wagon wheels ground along.

They marched their horses out of Washington north, out of the federal district and into Maryland. The most direct route toward the rest of the brigade under Copeland, a small fraction of General Hooker's army on an interception route to catch Lee's invading army.

CHAPTER 10

June 28th, 1863
Southern Maryland

Brigadier General Wade Hampton III looked out over the swollen Potomac River. The river had grown with each of the rains and now stretched almost a mile across. It had taken his command hours to ford the river, but he had done so, knowing that he was out of sight from Northern eyes. He'd been shown the abandoned Rowser's Ford passage by a sympathetic Virginian.

His eyes peered south. The land was lush with summer growth, green and vibrant. Even now he was only about eight miles from the federal capital. With proper deception, a bold jab at the enemy capital could end the conflict despite the heavy fortifications surrounding the city. They would swoop in like demons in the night and they could end this war.

The man on the horse next to him waited patiently, but his mount was uneasy, tossing its head and stamping its hooves into the earth. Hampton couldn't tell if it was from the rocky passage across the flowing waters or it sensed his master's restlessness. The man had captain's bars on his shoulders and was one of Hampton's finest warriors, and also one of his harshest. A trait he hid under a charming exterior.

Captain Marshall Payne had a honey-rich drawl to his voice. "Sir, look at the plentifulness of this land."

Hampton easily steered his mare away from the river and the forested banks retreated to lush farmland. The horses walked as they brought up the rear of his command that was the vanguard of Stuart's cavalry and the eyes and ears of the Army of Northern Virginia. They were to meet with Lee and win their historic victory on Northern soil. It was something that they'd sought time and time again during this war. It would demoralize the Yankees further until they capitulated. Hampton looked back south. Same with capturing their exposed capital. He smiled as he imagined Lincoln fleeing the city dressed as a woman to evade detection.

His subordinate was correct. The farmlands of Maryland left nothing of want. Neither would his home state of South Carolina in peacetime, but this was not a time of peace.

The land was all shades of vibrant green and fertile brown. Grain and clover, pig and cattle, acres of pasture untouched by the war that ravaged a once great nation. A nation that had grown apart and exercised its right to stay that way.

"So much for the taking, General," Payne said.

Hampton couldn't tell if he was asking a question or making a statement, nor did he suppose to care. The captain wouldn't take any action without his explicit order, but he was subtly voicing his desire to do just that.

"Not yet, Captain. Send out scouts, but nothing else. This won't be like fighting in Virginia, don't expect friendly faces." His subordinate had a fine understanding of an irregular style warfare that bordered on total war. Payne could sniff out a farmer hiding an egg and he could put a church to the torch without batting an eye all in the name of saving the South. Lee's invasion was designed to bring the North to its knees and convince the foreigners of England and France to come to the South's aid. Break the damn blockade like in the Revolution, only this time it could be the Brits helping. The irony wasn't lost on him. He was sure his captain's tactics would still be necessary and vital to their survival.

The gray-, brown-, and tan-clad horsemen marched in their column. Horses made the only sounds, clip-clopping along. Hampton didn't mind a bit of silence. He didn't like to make small talk. He hated the perfume-laced conversations of elitist gossip. He was straight and forward and he was Stuart's hammer on the field. His men were all recruited, raised, and outfitted by himself in South Carolina. He'd been the richest planter in the state before the war and he intended to keep it that way by winning.

A man started to sing. The words were indistinguishable at first until the men around them picked up the tune. "Hurrah, hurrah, for Southern rights, hurrah!" *The Bonnie Blue Flag.* An unofficial anthem for the army. They had good reason to be happy. They were going to end the war and they hadn't met a foe yet they couldn't lick in a fight and ride circles around in the field.

The singing gave way to cheering further ahead the column. High-pitched whooping tickled their ears near the rear.

Payne eyed his superior officer. "Sir, should I investigate?"

Hampton almost felt bad keeping the busy Payne in check. "Sounds happy. There'd be gunshots or cannon if it required our attention." Hampton could feel Payne's piercing blue eyes on him, but the thick-shouldered general kept his bushy-bearded face forward. Payne should know better than to question him, even non-verbally.

Payne's hair fell almost to his shoulders in looping brown curls. A red blouse billowed from underneath his gray captain's jacket with yellow trimming. He had an umber goatee below piercing blue eyes.

His company all wore the same crimson blouses and were affectionately called the "Red Shirts" by the rest of the men. They were unusual in the fact that most of even the privates within their ranks came from wealthy families. They'd grown in reputation and his command hardly ever fell below full staffing. Other men sought out the Red Shirts and had to be accepted into their ranks, each man earning his red shirt with exceptional bravery on the battlefield. It wasn't a normal circumstance, but then again nothing about this scrappy army was.

Just ahead of them, the men brought up a cheer as a three-story white-sided building came into view. People hung out of windows waving at the passing troops. As they neared the structure, and his eyes could focus, it became apparent they were young women.

A leering smile curved on Payne's face. "Will you look at that? Even the women on Northern soil love us."

Hampton let a small smirk touch his lips, his cheek twitching under the unusual sentiment. "Stuart is going to have a field day with them."

"Yes sir, he is."

"We'll probably end up riding parade for them."

Young women hung from every window and Hampton was glad none of his men had forced their way in, not that he had expected them to, but he was pleased he wouldn't have to deal with the aftermath of cleaning up their mess.

Young women leaned out of the windows. Black, blonde, brown, red, and orange hair, and everything between, accompanied by tender, smooth faces that twinkled at the Southern horsemen as they passed. Other braver young women gathered outside the building.

Like their hair, every color of dress was fit perfectly to their bodies. They showed bare arms and their hair was a wonderment of curls and pins. Their lips were rosy and bosoms rounded. They were a sight for any man's eyes. Enough to draw horsemen from ranks and loud pledges of victory were promised in the women's honor.

"And I thought the South held all the finest women folk," Payne said.

A young black-haired woman stepped closer to Payne. Her words sounded like singing birds in the morning. "May I pin you, good sir?"

"Why, of course, my most fine woman." The captain gracefully bent down in the saddle and the woman fastened a lock of hair to his jacket. He inspected it. "By golly, I must be the luckiest man on earth to receive such a priceless gift."

The young woman's face turned redder than a beet. "My name is Hannah, if it pleases."

Payne grinned handsomely. "Oh, it pleases me. It pleases me to the end of time, my lady."

A blonde and brunette approached Hampton. They handed him a basket of baked cookies.

"My thanks to you." He grabbed the rim of his black slouch hat.

"Our pleasure." The young women curtsied.

Payne turned his horse around in a circle. "Your gentle souls are why we fight. Many blessed thanks for your kindness." He gave a bow deserved of an actor on stage from atop his mount.

Hampton nodded his head to the young ladies. He'd been married twice now and had a horde of children. It stung him to see the fairer sex because, if his younger brother Frank were here, he would have much to say to them. Things to make them smile. Things that would make Hampton laugh at his brother's playfulness.

Frank had always been the talker in the family, while Wade had been the silent doer. But none of that mattered now because Frank had been slain at the Battle of Brandy Station, leaving Wade with vibrant memories that would fade with age. It still didn't feel real, like Frank was only in another place. Still living and breathing and laughing. But he wasn't.

"Come, Captain."

Payne had his saber unsheathed and was giving the ladies a small demonstration of his fictitious sword work against the enemy to the oohs and ahs of the gentler folk.

"I bid you adieu, ladies." Payne sheathed his weapon and kicked his horse to catch Hampton, leaving swooning women breathless in his wake.

"Nothing like the love of a woman to help you win the war."

Hampton was silent. He hadn't seen his wife in months nor felt the touch of a camp follower like many of the other men on campaign were wont to do. Some only wanted to be held. Only wanting a woman's embrace to make them feel human again. Others went for man's primal needs. Merely a pleasant distraction in the game of war, one that made men feel less like monsters and more like men again. Like the sexual act could somehow counterbalance the violent ones.

Dust took to the air as a rider pounded down the line. A junior officer with freckles and strawberry blond hair peeking out from his cap, dressed in gray, pulled his horse to a halt near Hampton. An eager kid with potential, had the bar of a lieutenant on his shoulder. He thought his name was Charles? One of the Benningtons? No matter.

"Sir," he said hurriedly. A hand leapt for his forehead in a quick salute.

Hampton returned the salute with a gloved hand. "Speak."

"Sir, we've run into an enemy wagon train."

"And?"

"Captain Blackford has begun to chase." The aide smiled beneath a light mustache. "It must have been meant for Hooker, sir. Ham, sugar, ammunition, clothes, and—" The aide stopped as a broad smile split his cherry lips. "Whiskey, sir. Barrels and barrels of glorious whiskey."

Hampton nodded in satisfaction. "That is well done. Give Captain Blackford my thanks and I'd like to see a bottle of that whiskey when we make camp later, but see to it it's not any bust-head." The last thing he wanted was a hangover from cheap alcohol when he was in the saddle. "Can you see to that?"

"Of course, sir."

"You may continue on and notify Stuart."

The aide saluted and kicked his horse into a trot.

"This is going to be easy," Payne remarked. He waited a moment. "Easier than falling from a log in a pond."

"Nothing is easy, Captain."

"Then we should make it harder on them," Payne said. His voice had turned methodical like he'd become a machine.

Hampton gradually nodded his head. It was time to let his hound off his leash. He couldn't restrain his man from seeking out and destroying whatever he could find.

"You may take your company and commence your operations."

Payne visibly took in a breath. "We shall bring fear to the oppressors."

Hampton avoided eye contact with the man. He was a necessary evil for the war. "Only Yankees. I don't want to hear about sympathizers falling under your hand."

Placing a gentle hand over his heart, Payne said. "I will only take the fight to those who mean our great nation harm."

Waving him off, he said, "Then take your leave."

Payne saluted his superior and kicked his horse into a gallop to gather his Red Shirts. *It must be done. They must know the pain of invasion. By God, we do. A victory here will bring us one step closer to freedom.*

CHAPTER 11

June 29th, 1863
South of Westminster, Maryland

On the third day, the 13th Michigan's column walked into a federal camp south of Westminster, Maryland. Tired horses were urged through the pickets and along paths of the rowed tents of the other regiments. The Michigan Brigade troopers watched them arrive with equal parts disdain and disinterest. The cause mattered not, whether it was being the newest mustered unit, rivalry, or otherwise. The message was clear: you haven't proven yourself and you can't be trusted until you do.

Cobb kept his face forward as they walked. "You know, Wolf. Even if we do fight. The 13th will have to protect the supplies. No glory there."

Wilhelm clicked, but held his tongue.

"Yes, sir," Wolf responded.

"It's good you know our place." He gave him a baleful look. "You'll thank me when you live."

Wolf peered at Roberts, shrugging his shoulders. "I'm just happy to be on the move."

"What was that, private?" Cobb said louder.

"Just happy to be on the move, sir," Roberts said.

"Latrine duty when we get camped, private."

Roberts looked down at his horse. "Dammit."

Wolf studied the white tents and smoky haze cloaking the camp. "I'll help."

***

They claimed an area nearby a shallow creek the men used for water. The bottom was blanketed with pebbles with swarms of minnows darting every which way and frogs croaked cheerfully to announce the presence of dusk. A hum of excitement captured the encampment, shadowing over everything and everyone equally.

Roberts and Wolf dug away as the other men in the unit set up their tents and relaxed after their long journey, cooking food and drying sweaty clothes.

Sticking his shovel in the ground with his foot, Wolf wiped his forehead. The heat in Maryland hadn't relented, stifling the men while they worked.

Roberts handed him a canteen and Wolf took a long swig. The water was tepid at best, but it washed over his throat like a sweet elixir.

"A smaller latrine will do," Wolf said. It stretched over eight feet and was close enough to the creek that the men could wash after. "We won't be here long." He handed the canteen back. "Whatever gets us in a bedroll."

"Come on, we still have to set up our tent." Shovels to shoulders, the two young men marched back to the company's tents.

Wolf attached his tent canvas to Roberts's and stepped back to view their work. The satisfactory straight poles had been taken up by the other regiments leaving little adequate supporting wood that wasn't meant for kindling. Their tent sloped to the right.

"We won't be here long," Roberts said.

Wolf gave him side eye. "I'll sleep on the left."

"I'll race ya to the fire for first choice?"

"Not a chance."

They joined their fellow men around a campfire.

"Our two best diggers," Van Horn said. His humorless face almost cracked a smile.

"At your service," Wolf said with a bow.

"Saved you boys some ham and bacon," Franz said with a grin, handing them a plate.

"Many thanks."

The beating of hooves reverberated the earth, drawing the troopers' attention. A gang of riders rode into the center of F Company. The man leading them wore a black suit trimmed in gold. His wide collared navy shirt was folded over his jacket and a red necktie bustled from the collar.

"Would you look at his dandy?" Roberts said. He tossed a handful of berries in his mouth.

Franz bobbed his head, curls bouncing. "O'Reilly is going to tear him a new one."

Dan looked at Wolf. "Pretty man." He turned to his brothers, speaking in Polish, and they laughed.

The first sergeant marched toward the riders and, to the squad's surprise, he saluted the man. The man brought a white-gloved hand to his forehead in a quick return of the gesture. His long blond hair bounced beneath his broad-brimmed hat.

O'Reilly pointed toward the regimental headquarters. The dandy spurred his horse on and they galloped off toward the command. His followers galloped after him, flags now visible in the dark, whipping with the wind.

Wilhelm watched him go. "He's wearing a general's star on his sleeve."

"Can't be. He's only a few years older than me. If that!"

Cobb grinned as he eyed the general ride away. "He be the youngest general in the entire Union army. Never thought I'd see that."

"Who is this man?"

"You don't recognize him? That's George Armstrong Custer, and I bet he's here to lead a regiment or maybe the brigade. Can you imagine that?"

"He's mighty young to be leading so many men," Wilhelm said.

"And he ain't afraid of a fight, that one. He'd charge the Rebs just to prove a point."

Wilhelm twisted his mustache. "Brash, young, and brave. That's how men get killed. I'd take disciplined, prudent and experienced any day."

Cobb smiled which was more of a sneer than anything else. "But you'll get brash and brave, my good German soldier." He leaned closer to Wilhelm. "And more dead boys."

A gruff voice came from the side. O'Reilly eyed the sergeant with extreme malice. "Now, Sergeant Cobb, I know you weren't filling our young recruits ears with blasphemous talk of the devil."

"No, sir."

"A blessing to me ears 'cause I won't have any naysaying while I'm in charge here. Is that clear?"

Cobb dipped his chin. "Yes, sir."

"Let's keep your tent empty tonight. I don't want you discharging because you stuck in some loose cherry."

"Yes, First Sergeant."

O'Reilly left them and Cobb continued to stare at the ground. "Why are you standing around? Latrine duty for all you. Move."

"Sir, sink's been dug," Wolf said. A snicker escaped from one of the men.

Twisting his face, their sergeant pointed toward the creek. "Dig it again."

Wolf shared a look with Roberts.

"You heard him boys," Wilhelm said. "Grab your shovels." With a groan the unit got to its feet and shouldered their implements of labor.

CHAPTER 12

June 29th, 1863
South of Westminster, Maryland

George Armstrong Custer dismounted his black horse and handed the reins to his orderly, Joseph Fought. Nervous energy roiled in his belly like thunderstorms battling inside. Energy that had kept him awake for over a day. He'd made the largest jump in rank of any officer in American history, going from lieutenant, brevet captain, straight to brigade command as a brigadier general.

"You look the part, Autie," Joseph said over the horse. His orderly had scoured the camp the night before, finding an old Jewish man who'd given them the proper stars befit his new rank and sewn them into place by candlelight.

"Let's stick to General until we're in private, Private." His mustache quivered as he spoke.

The young orderly, only a few years younger than Custer, blushed with embarrassment. He felt a pang of guilt admonishing his loyal man, but generals didn't feel guilt about terms of respect and ranks, the army was built on it. Joseph had been with him since the beginning, but he needed to act the part and play the part if he was to be the general he was meant to be. And he was meant to be a general, of that he had no doubt. Although, he balked at the idea that he would be one so soon. Just the night past, the men ribbed him for having such ambitions. They'd laughed and teased him, the way soldiers do, only for him to find out they'd seen his appointment letter while he'd been out inspecting pickets in the twilight hours. An official memo addressed to Brigadier General George Armstrong Custer, U.S.A. Vols. He kept that securely in his jacket pocket.

Straightening his jacket, he stopped outside Brigadier General Copeland's command tent. Light shone from underneath the flaps. The general was awake, a good sign. Lee was on the march, Stuart was on the loose somewhere in Northern territory, and the Union needed leadership now more than ever.

"Sir, George Custer," he said from the other side of the tent.

"You may come in," came Copeland's voice.

Custer pushed open the tent flaps and entered the command tent.

Copeland sat in a campaign folding chair. He wore an airy white long-sleeve shirt, his jacket draped on his officer's camp cot. His formidable if tangled brown-and-gray beard hung to his chest, but his body was thin. He glanced at Custer with intelligent eyes. The skin beneath his eyes sagged with tiredness.

"Captain, I didn't expect you."

A sickly gaunt pale man stood in the corner of the tent. His hair receded to the back of his skull and a stringy beard hung off his jaw like he'd swam in the ocean and emerged with seaweed on his face. "Do you know Colonel Town of the 1st Michigan?"

Custer dipped his chin. "It's a pleasure, sir."

"And Colonel Moore," Copeland gestured to a hovering heavyset man with a brown beard and beady eyes. Custer's immediate instinct was to distrust him. He gave him a slight nod. "As well as Colonel Mann of the fresh 7th Michigan." Wild hair hung to his shoulders and off his face alike. He'd met Mann before.

An uneasy Mann smiled at Custer. "Good to see you, Autie."

Custer regarded him coolly. "Sir, I come from Meade and Pleasonton."

Copeland weighed his words and found them wanting. "Changing commanders now is like switching horses while crossing a river. Let me see it."

Thumbing the orders for a moment, his hand shook as he handed over the letter. "Sir, might we read it in private?"

Skepticism narrowed Copeland's eyes. "Nonsense, we don't have secrets from these men. They are prudent." Custer held his tongue in check knowing that the general was about to be hammered in front of his subordinates, and soon to be his men.

Taking the white envelope, Copeland carefully opened it. He removed the paper inside, unfolding it. His eyes quickly skimmed the information, years of being a judge put to use. He folded the letter as if it had reached out and slapped him.

His words came quick. "Captain, I recognize Pleasonton's signature and that of Meade, but surely a young man such as yourself is not ready for a command of this magnitude." He eyed Custer with confused anger. He now spied the single stars on Custer's shoulders. "You're a general? You can't be but twenty."

This kind of scrutiny he was accustomed too. *This is your destiny, not his.* "Twenty-three, sir."

Copeland laughed in disbelief. Moore smiled, trying to mimic Copeland's mood like a fat chameleon tasting the room. "This has got to be a joke?"

"Sir, I am afraid not. I'm to assume command of this brigade and you are to report to Washington for your new command."

"Do not proceed to tell me what I am to do," Copeland demanded. "You're only a pup. This is war for the big dogs, not pups."

Custer's mustache twitched. *Stay calm, Autie. These men are watching your every move to find a reason to not like you.* "That is not my order, sir, but General Pleasonton's."

Tossing the letter on the table, Copeland shook his head. "I've done everything they've asked and more. I've fought this ugly war and with a change of the winds they throw me out. Politics have too much sway in this army." He stared at the table. "We have a war to fight and I'm sent away like a bad dog." Pointing, he said, "The enemy's that way."

Receiving no reprieve from his orders, he let his hand fall. He glared at Custer, vengeance glittering in his eyes. "I'm going to protest this all the way to the top."

"That is your right, sir, but until then I must speak with my regimental commanders. You are more than welcome to stay. Your input is both respected and appreciated."

Copeland's body trembled. "You come in here with your gold-embroidered hussar jacket and navy shirts, non-regulation rebel boots, like a trumped-up dandy and you expect me to *stay* and assist you?" He took a deep breath, realizing he was unraveling in front of his men. He wasn't wrong in that this was a rapid and unexpected shake up in the cavalry corps of the Army of the Potomac, all of which was set in motion with Hooker's defeat at Chancellorsville and the demotion of Major General Stoneman. With the elevation of Custer's friend and political ally Pleasonton, he was determined to make his rise in status not a fluke. He had the guts to lead men. Some men only have it because of their youth, but he'd always been fearless, at least he never let his fears show. He kept his demeanor cool in the face of Copeland's flames.

"I expect you to follow your orders as dictated by our superiors."

Copeland turned to his orderly. "Saddle my horse. I'm riding to meet Meade now." He threw on his jacket with the determination of a slighted man. Pride tattered, but not yet broken, he snatched up his sword and left the tent.

The three other colonels watched Custer. He knew Mann and of Town, but didn't know Moore, who appeared to be a lackey of whoever was in charge. One could never escape the weak underlings and political appointees that somehow found themselves in charge of men far greater than themselves.

Moore hastily saluted. "General, sir." *Eager, but appears lacking in martial prowess. Would I let the man watch my back? No. I bet he can't even handle a weapon. His men will serve as last in my line.*

Custer glanced at the other men, greatly his senior, and until a day ago higher in rank as well. Town put a hand up to his forehead, followed by Mann. "General," they said.

Now, came the really uncomfortable part. He had great friends throughout his different postings. He loved the camaraderie and the brotherhood that came with. These men could easily be companions, but they weren't, the dynamics had changed. They were subordinates and he had to break them of any thoughts that they were deserving of the post he'd been assigned.

"I'll expect you to salute me whenever we meet. You are to attend reveille every morning."

He eyed Moore. He lacked weapons of any kind, as if they were below him. *By God, we are at war, man.* "We are within range of the enemy so expect him. Never be without pistol and saber. We are *here* for war. Is this clear?"

Moore nervously smoothed his uniform. "Of course, sir."

Colonel Town hacked into his hand. He removed a handkerchief from his jacket pocket and wiped crimson from the corner of his mouth.

"I trust that you are well enough to command, Colonel?"

Narrowing his eyes, he grimaced, his voice coming out weakly. "Of course, sir. It's the consumption. If a bullet doesn't get me, it will for certain." His inky eyes didn't lie. "I'd rather it be a bullet, sir."

Custer nodded his understanding. Don't deny this man an honorable death when his life was already cut so much shorter than it could be.

"Tomorrow we cross the Mason-Dixon Line. Back to our home turf. Buford is north and we're going to vanguard for Meade. We need to spread our units out and try to find Lee or Stuart. Either will do. Then we fight. Gentleman, are we ready for a scrap?"

"Yes, sir," Town said loudly, taking all the air from his lungs. The other two were silent.

Custer eyed the other two coldly. "I need everyone ready. Your men's spirit starts at the top. We must foster an unstoppable élan. Can I count on you?"

"Yes, sir," all three of his colonels said.

A small grin spread on Custer's face. "Then let's find a scrap."

CHAPTER 13

June 30th, 1863
South of Hanover, Pennsylvania

The sound of horse hooves and rattling sabers sang in the air, the dust kept down by an early morning rain. The clouds were clearing, revealing a light blue sky. Soon the sun would beat mercilessly through the leaves overhead, reaching for the men with sweltering fingers, but it hadn't yet.

They had crossed the Mason-Dixon Line in darkness, spearheading the newly appointed Meade's army into the north. Rumors ran abundant through the ranks that the people here were sympathetic to the invaders, souring the men's mood.

The 5th and 6th Michigan Cavalries had been sent out on scouting missions, leaving the 1st Michigan in the lead, trailed by the green 7th and 13th Michigan Regiments. Farnsworth's 1st Brigade followed them along with the 3rd Cavalry Division commander Hugh Judson Kilpatrick.

While the men and animals attempted to embrace the morning in relative peace, Cobb had decided to discuss in detail the capabilities of the average Confederate soldier. "They're rotten and scoundrels to the last man. Devious as the devil himself. Look one way, he's there, gone the next."

"What do they look like?" asked Roberts.

Cobb's mouth made a revolting sneer. "They're ugly. Uglier than this lot, and let me tell you that's ugly. Covered in dirt, they're more beast than man. They fight like it too. Animals." He glanced over at Wolf. "Don't you surrender to 'em, they'd soon as stick ya than take you prisoner."

"I'm not planning on surrendering."

"Seen twice the man of you surrender. Surrounded, friends dying all around you, it will cross your mind." His voice grew feminine. "Live, oh let me live, oh Jesus, but it's only the Rebs screaming at the top of their lungs that'll answer you. Most men will fold."

"Why the Rebs be screamin' all the time?" Roberts asked.

Cobb took a swig of water from his canteen and swirled it around before laughing loud. "You never heard of the 'Rebel Yell'?"

The men nearby mumbled their no's. Wolf patted Billy's flanks as if to calm him.

"Men piss themselves when they hear it. They all do it at once, mix between Injun and a howling dog. Then they charge, whooping like redskins. But I'm sure you men will stand tall in the face of it."

"They will," Wilhelm said. He handled his horse with ease as if he were born in the saddle. "And if they don't, that is a reflection of their noncommissioned officer."

As if Wilhelm had ruined all his fun, Cobb gave him a nasty look. "Why you here, old man? Don't you have a son that can die in your place?"

"I'm here because my son is here and no father should send their son to a war he wouldn't fight. I been with the 1st Baden Uhlans in my younger years and fought in the revolutions."

"So, if you know better, then why would the likes of you even want to fight in this godforsaken war? You weren't even born here."

"You're right. I wasn't. But I came here to live and I intend to do so in peace. If I have to fight to have peace, I'll do it."

"Fucking crazy Dutch."

Wilhelm wasn't amused. "This land gave us all a fresh start. Gave us hope. I'll do the same for it."

Shaking his head in disgust, Cobb spat, "Well, I been here long enough and don't see why we're killing each other. Nobody gives two flying donkeys about the Negroes." He pointed at Berles. "I bet you don't."

"This land bleeds because one enslaves the other. I fight to stem the flow."

"Slavery's immoral. That's why we're here," Shugart hollered back at them. "You can't say that men are free while some are enslaved."

Cobb glared at the old man's back. "What, you think you owe these coloreds something?"

Shugart stared over his shoulder. "I owe them as much as I owe any man."

"They ain't like you and me." Licking his lips, he shook his head.

"They are. The color doesn't matter. The actions of the man do."

Cobb searched the sky for answers. "Dear God, would you listen to this?" He met Shugart's gaze. "There ain't no Negro that's my equal. Why have you given me every bleeding Republican heart in the Union under my command?"

"With all due respect, Sergeant Cobb, I've met many a Negro that is far superior to you in character and disposition," said Shugart.

"I can't believe the words coming out of your old as shit mouth. You must be senile to say something like that. Or take it back."

"I am of sound body and mind, God willing it will stay that way."

Sergeant Cobb steered his horse from the column and rode it alongside his corporal. "You're sound of body and mind?"

"I am, sir."

"You just earned yourself picket duty tonight and tomorrow night. You can sleep in the saddle. Perhaps you will learn something about the *disposition* of men."

The troopers turned their heads away from the disciplinary action by the angry sergeant as a rider galloped down the column.

His mount panted with the effort, sweat and snot running from its mouth and nose. The rider met with Captain Peltier and First Sergeant O'Reilly trotted his horse along the company.

"Captain asked me for my favorite sergeant and Cobb's unit was the first name to crop up in me old noggin." The retributive tone was enough to know this wasn't a lucrative assignment.

"Of course, First Sergeant." Cobb nodded his acknowledgement, touching the rim of his hat.

O'Reilly ran an eye over the cavalrymen. "Prepare your men. We are coming up on Hanover. Your men will scout to the east."

"Yes, sir," Cobb said. The cynical sergeant turned to his unit. "All right, you heard the first sergeant. Let's go see what we can see."

CHAPTER 14

June 30th, 1863
York County, Pennsylvania

The trees blocked the morning sunshine, but the summer sun threatened them, baking them inside their scratchy woolen coats. Any remaining precipitation left on the ground had evaporated.

Wolf unbuttoned his top buttons, letting the jacket hang to the sides. His father's black sash draped around his neck, blocking the sunlight from burning his skin. There was no wind on the forest road and he wished he was back in Michigan where the summers were more temperate than the dripping Pennsylvania humidity.

They'd passed three Pennsylvania Dutch farms earlier, who were really of German descent. Wolf was surprised to see strong healthy men of fighting age so nonchalant that a war was raging around them. Wilhelm spoke to each one in German, which immediately made the men trust the troopers. One farmer's wife even offered them a basket of blueberries, which the men devoured without batting an eye, the juicy tart berries refreshing in the oppressive warmth.

Roberts scouted far out front of the half-platoon. He was small and adept enough at blending in that he was an easy pick. His form was only a dark blue, twisted shadow ahead. The rest of the unit walked their horses single file, heads dipped in avoidance of the rising temperature. Corporal Berles traveled behind about twenty yards, ensuring that the men weren't surprised from the rear.

Horses beat soft hooves into a narrow forest trail. It was more of a deer path than a trail made for men on horseback. They walked the animals, not wanting to give away their position for want of speed. Spindly branches and leaves slapped and tugged at the troopers with every tree they passed. The green undergrowth of vines, ferns, and grass tried to reclaim the path they tread.

"We'll ride out about five miles and circle a mile or so north and then proceed west back to Hanover," Cobb said.

"You think they're out here?" Private Lent said. He was a small man with the appearance of a scared mouse boy with his clean-shaven face and petite features. Sweaty, drab brown hair stuck to his forehead and every few seconds he glanced to his right beneath a forage cap that was a size too large for the young man.

The vibrant green leaves of the trees waved and rippled as a light breeze drifted through them like the trickle of a stream. Wolf enjoyed the soft pardon from the heat.

"They're out there. I heard Lee was going for Harrisburg, but it's not him I'm worried about. No, sir." He ducked beneath a tree branch.

Lent stuttered with nervousness. "W—W—Who you worried about, Cobb?"

"Nobody knows where The Knight of the Golden Spurs and his Invincibles are. That's a problem for big, bad Kill-Cavalry and the Boy General." His tone turned mocking. "What a duo we have leading us."

Hooves clip-clopped as Lent thought about the Knight and his warriors. "The Knight of the Golden Spurs? Invincibles?" His eyes darted faster to the right.

"He speaks of Jeb Stuart, boy," Private Van Horn said. He rode his horse in a stiff manner, not allowing himself to go with the animal. He would be sore everyday because of it, but he was a stubborn man refusing to learn better.

"Six thousand of the Confederacy's finest horsemen. They're the knights of the South. Creme de la creme. Unbeatable in the field." His voice changed into a mocking tone. "Been besting us for years, but don't you worry, that's all gonna change with the 13th Michigan. Sure will." Cobb laughed at his joke.

Curly hair bobbed beneath Franz's cap as he leaned over. "Well, what's that make us?"

"What's that make us?" The sergeant looked out into the trees, debating in his mind what kind of men they were. "You men aren't fit to muck their stables. Let alone fight them."

Lent gulped nervously. "I don't want to fight them."

"No, you wouldn't, nor any of his lieutenants. There's the giant Wade Hampton. Bigger than those Polish brothers that nobody can understand and mean as badger." He pointed at Bart and Dan. The heavily built brothers' broad backs stretched their cavalry jackets tight. Thick necks begging for space from collared shirts and cheeks rosy from the heat.

"Big men can get knocked out like anyone else," Wolf said.

Swaying in the saddle, Cobb said. "Aye, they can, but it's a lot harder. Old Hampton is the richest man in the South, so they say." He pursed his lips, thinking. "Then there's Marshall Payne and his Red Shirts."

"Who are the Red Shirts?" Wolf asked. He couldn't understand all this talk from Cobb. The Confederates sounded like ancient warrior heroes of legend. How could they fight them and win if they were so fierce, noble, and unconquerable? Their mythos astonished him.

Disgusted, Cobb shook his head. "The most brutal of all Stuart's units. Burn everything they can. They say those shirts started as white and they wash them in the blood of their defeated enemies, and, of course, they can't be killed."

"Hogwash, Sergeant. All men can be killed," Shugart said, his graying beard shuddering. "All men die, God sees to that."

Cobb pushed his top hat on his forehead and gave the old corporal a mocking glare. "All men do die. Some sooner than others." His eyes left the old abolitionist. "I'm telling the boys what they say. They deserve to know the enemy they face."

A chuckle came from Shugart. "That's right, some sooner than others. I go in peace when He takes me. But you're telling ghost stories, Sergeant." He turned to the rest of the unit. "He's duping you boys. Plenty of Rebs have died in this war. We must stand tall in our convictions, for we fight not only to defend the Republic but your fellow man. Tis noble to give one's life for such institutions."

"Bugger your convictions, old man. I ain't duping nobody. I seen the Red Shirts once. Slashed one with my saber too. Didn't even faze the man. I may as well have patted him on the back and gave him a cookie on the way by."

"They're monsters," Franz said.

"How did you escape?" Wolf asked. The younger men of the unit had veered their horses closer to the veteran Cobb. He was their connection to a distant enemy.

His shoulders rocking from side to side in conjunction with his horse, Cobb held them in suspense for seconds. "We retreated."

"Where are they now?" Lent squeaked.

"You're a smart one ain't ya? Very good question. You'll be a general by the end of this campaign with a head on your shoulders like that."

Lent looked around wondering if the sergeant was actually offering him a compliment, a dumb grin on his lips.

"If we knew where he was, we wouldn't need to ride out and scout, now would we?"

The words shattered Lent's pride and his eyes dropped to his horse in shame.

"Keep your eyes up, boy. We ain't paying you to ride with your head down."

Frowning, Lent lifted his eyes.

Cobb's voice softened. "Last we known of him, he was near Aldie, Virginia, but he's disappeared now. Vanished into the countryside like they do."

Roberts trotted back toward the unit and pulled his mount to a halt. "There's a homestead ahead," he breathed.

"And?" Cobb questioned.

"There's horses out front."

The sergeant narrowed his eyes. "How many?"

"Four."

"Anyone outside?"

"No." Roberts's horse turned in an uneasy circle.

"Hmm. Seems like a lot of horses for a visit. Maybe they seen something. Shugart. Take Lent, Gratz and the Polish brothers. Circle around the woods and come at the homestead from the other side. Don't be seen."

Wilhelm caught the rest of the unit. His eyes had the steel glint of action to them. "What's happened?"

"There's a homestead that warrants a lookin'." Cobb turned back to the group. "The rest of you, with me."

Shugart's men disappeared into the timber, the blue coats swallowed by the forest. They walked their horses to within eyesight of the farm and waited for Shugart to get into position.

The homestead consisted of a small single-room cabin with thatched roofing. A boxy window was the only decoration on the rough frontier building. A small plot of vegetables grew next to the structure and the clearing opened up to poorly kept fields of grain. A pink and gray-splotched pig rooted around in a tree-branch pen on the other side of the cabin and four horses were tethered near the door. The door opened, revealing a man.

"Follow my lead." Half the unit came into the clearing in the woods, riding in ranks of two.

A man in a leather buckskin coat and faded black trousers was packing something into his saddle. As the half unit fanned out into a semi-circle around the front of the cabin, he looked and pushed his brown wide-brimmed hat upward on his head.

Wilhelm's voice was softer than a summer breeze on the edge of a storm. "Get those guns loose in your leather."

Wolf's heart thundered in his chest. He let his hand drift to his hip and unbuttoned his holster flap containing his Colt revolver. He then rested his shooting hand on his gun belt near the handle. Billy could sense his sudden uneasiness and stamped a hoof.

The man eyed them calmly. "Well, I'll be, federal cavalry all the way up here. How can I be of humble assistance?" He gave a mock bow to the troopers.

Cobb edged his horse forward. "You live here?"

The man smiled, he was missing a front tooth and his beard was only partially grown. "Well, you see. I was just visiting my sister here. Her husband died in this here war so we was just checking in on her." He nodded as he spoke. "Paying our respects like."

"Then you wouldn't mind if we spoke to her?"

The man's smile broadened. "Not at all." He turned and yelled at the cabin. "Sandra. We got some nice soldiers that want to talk to you."

A few moments later, a woman came through the door. She wore a simple, light brown, homespun dress the top few buttons undone dangerously low. Her black hair hung partially in a bun. Her cheeks were rosy and her eyes red around the edges as if she'd been crying. She straightened the shoulders of her garment as she stepped outside.

The man eyed her with loving adore. "I was just telling these soldiers the terrible news about how your husband died in the war and we were paying a visit." The way he spoke made Wolf's skin prickle. He oozed too much charm on her and it was clear she did not feel the same way. Something was wrong here and he was sure the other men could sense it too.

With respect, Cobb removed his hat and wiped his brow. "Ma'am, is it true your husband's dead?"

She lowered her chin and averted her eyes.

"Ma'am, are you okay?" Cobb said, suddenly a white knight of virtue.

She nodded again, wringing her hands in front of her.

"I am sorry for your loss, but have you seen any rebels in these parts? Any men riding that don't belong?"

She shook her head silently no.

"She speak?" the sergeant asked the man.

"Quiet as a church mouse, this one."

"Something isn't right," Berles whispered next to Wolf.

"Can't say we've seen any dirty rotten scoundrels 'round here, Sergeant, but we will be sure to let you know if we do. Where y'all camped?"

"You can find us in Hanover."

"That's mighty swell," the man gave a genuine smile, the gap in his front teeth black.

Cobb placed his hat back atop his head. "Thank you, we'll be on our way."

Wilhelm urged his horse forward a few steps. "Ma'am, you wouldn't mind for some water. Would you? My canteen needs fillin'," he said loud. He swung his leg off and climbed down from his steed, taking steps in their direction.

"Corporal, we should be on our way," Cobb said.

Wilhelm waved him off. "After a bit of water."

She looked at the man next to her with wide eyes. Wilhelm got within feet of the two. "Surely you can spare some water for us?"

After a moment of silence, the man grinned. "Of course she can. Run along, Sandra. So distraught. This whole war is a shame." The woman bowed her head slightly and walked to a ground well nearby.

Everyone watched her walking away. Wolf's gut started to turn with tension like it did before a fight.

She rolled out the bucket with a splash and reeled it back up in sweeping motions.

Wilhelm twisted one side of his mustache. "Say, did you say you came with others? I count four horses here."

The man laughed, sounding like a mischievous raccoon. "I must've forgot. I'm here with my brothers."

"Sandra's brothers then no doubt."

"No doubt. Our brothers." The man licked his lips, still smiling.

"Say, that's a different accent. Where you from?" the man asked Wilhelm.

"I'm German."

The man nodded his head in little shakes. "I think I got some Dutch somewhere in my lineage. Never can tell nowadays. My pappy was a mean Irish bastard."

Sandra came back with a wooden bucket in one hand and she set it down next to the men, shying away.

"Don't mind me," Wilhelm said. He bent down and dipped his canteen in the bucket.

The man watched Wilhelm as he squatted near the bucket. His canteen gulped water inside. Van Horn edged his horse near the side of the homestead.

The air was beginning to stifle, making it feel like they were in a tropical oven. The soft whisks of horse tails treaded lightly along with a hoof stomp every few seconds as the horse's deflected the flies landing incessantly on them. The pig rolled and rooted around in its pen, snorting away.

Wilhelm took a look at Sandra. "How many brothers do you have?"

"Three," she said too fast.

"Three? But there's four horses."

"Well, you see—" the man started.

"No, my friend. Let Sandra speak." He stood tall and screwed the cap to his canteen back on, his voice coming firm with authority. "Go ahead."

The man put an arm around Sandra and she looked like she wanted to melt and flutter away into the wind. "My sweet, sweet sister is so timid and the sight of you strapping fellows with your shiny guns. You've scared her and, with all due respect, we must retire."

A grave smile flashed on Wilhelm's lips. "My condolences." He waited a moment before continuing. "But that Jefferson Davis is a real cunt, ain't he?"

The man's grin faded like a stick of butter in a skillet, his eyes growing in size. Wolf could tell he was rolling his tongue on the backs of his teeth. "Why?" He jammed his tongue down into his lower lip. "Why'd you go on and say that?"

"Because, he is, and that Lee is his Nancy boy."

The man blinked, his eyes darting to the other soldiers. Wolf's gut rumbled. The tension rising in the air.

Glass shattered in the cabin's single window. Gunfire boomed from inside. Wilhelm drew his pistol while the man grasped beneath his coat. The corporal popped a shot from his revolver into the man's belly and the man fell back inside the cabin.

Wolf's horse turned in a circle and he fumbled with his reins and the pistol on his hip. Cobb's carbine leapt to his shoulder and he discharged a shot toward the door while Wilhelm grabbed Sandra and shielded her with his body as he forced her away from the cabin. Three men burst from the doorway, all dressed in civilian attire.

Fire exploded from the ends of pistols as the men fired at the cavalrymen, leaving smoke in its place. Private Hunt tumbled from his saddle, his back smacking the earth with a thud.

Wolf's hand found the handle of his revolver and he instinctually had brought the weapon level with his eye. The Colt was light in his hand but the barrel drifted down as he used his single bead sight. The trigger was heavy and seconds turned into an eternity as he focused on firing his gun. Hunt's horse bolted, crashing through the timber. Franz was holding his firearm pointed at the sky, unable to fire. Roberts had ridden his horse away from the cabin and was drifting back toward it, his revolver in hand.

Bang. Wolf's pistol reported and his shot went way wide. Dirt exploded into a cloud in the air. His inaugural shot done, he found the next shots easier. He pulled the trigger again and again. Their enemies mounted horses, spinning them in circles, shooting at the scattering Northerners.

Roberts fired his pistol and went for a reload. The rebels bolted for the woods. Cobb's carbine kicked off and the rear rider fell. Within an instant, a small volley erupted from the trees and two more riders tumbled from their saddles. Their bodies rolled as he hit the underbrush, trampling it. The man with the belly wound clutched his horse and spurred the animal into action.

"Don't let them escape!" With the lever out, Cobb jammed a cartridge into the breech of his carbine.

Wolf goaded his horse. "Come on, Billy!" He sped in pursuit of the rider. His saber clanged against his leg as he pushed the gelding into a full gallop. The injured man turned and fired his pistol backward. The bullet whizzed by, missing the mark.

Grasping the horse's neck, he kept his head near Billy. Trees whipped them as if in punishment for passing through the forest with such carelessness.

Wolf's hand wavered and jostled as he took aim at the fleeing man. He pulled the trigger, his weapon expelling the bullet with fire, and had no idea where the shot went. The other man rode hard down a ravine and the horses naturally slowed their speed. The Confederate reached the bottom first and sped his horse for a shallow creek.

Seconds later, Wolf crossed the same ground. "Come on, Billy!" The wind rose to meet them as they raced and his hat flew off and his sash snapped. The man jumped his horse over a log and Wolf's confidence in the chase started to fade. *I've never jumped anything.*

"Billy!" His mount ignored the rider's protests and leapt over the impeding log.

Moments later, the rebel's horse lost its footing in the small creek, sending its rider headfirst into cool waters. The man rolled in the shallows, coming up for air with a froggy groan.

Wolf pulled Billy's reins to a halt and leveled his sidearm at the man.

"Ohhhh," he moaned, his eyes squinting in pain. "You Yanks killed me."

"Don't move." He thumbed the hammer and it cocked back.

The rebel clutched his stomach tightly with both his arms. He resembled a mangy dog sopping wet. "I yield. I yield." He held up a single hand his other pressing on his belly leaking blood into the water.

The rebel's horse screamed. It was shrill and high-pitched and made Wolf's hair stand on his arms. It tried to walk on its broken leg and then would collapse, eyes larger than pieces of coal.

"By God man, put her down already. Poor beast. Have mercy." He gestured with his hand. "I ain't going no where." He pointed with his hand again and placed it over his heart. "I swear it."

Wolf swung his leg over Billy and hobbled over to where the horse had collapsed a half dozen times.

Putting a hand in the air, he spoke softly to the dying creature. "Shh. Be calm." The beast stared at him with black, terrified eyes.

The rebel sat in the stream. "Go on, do the right thing."

As the animal calmed, he inched closer. Fear and pain dominated the beast and it made Wolf sick to watch. He placed a gentle hand on the creature, trying to ease its fear. The horse panted, chest heaving and lips quivering.

He eyed its leg, blood oozed from a white, creamy, bone-exposed fracture sticking from the horse's flesh.

"Do it, Billy Yank," the rebel shouted. "She don't deserve to suffer."

Wolf pointed his gun at the injured mount. The whole situation struck him as odd; he'd been about to kill a man, but killing a horse just seemed so disparate. Worse by comparison and revolting. It was innocent of the vices of man and its entire life was based around serving and man took them to war and they were slaughtered by men just like men. But he wondered if they ever had any idea why.

The trigger relinquished itself to Wolf's command and his gun banged alone in the forest. The sound of man's violence overcame the bubbling of the creek and the calls of the birds as one of its beasts returned prematurely back to the earth.

The horse laid its head down still. A leg twitched and he thought that it still breathed, but it was dead. Billy pulled on his reins, seeming to understand that Wolf had just killed one of his brethren.

"Okay, Johnny Reb. Let's go back." He turned around and stared the rebel square in the eyes. The man lunged for his gun with both hands and Wolf was driven backward in surprise into the shallow water. The man scampered on top, the pistol plopping into the cool stream, rapidly sinking to the bottom. The stream relieved him of all his heat, but with no way to enjoy the refreshment with the enemy soldier driving down upon him.

The rebel's hands clasped his neck and he squeezed. His fingers entrapped his throat, begging to murder him, each finger crushing the life from Wolf's body. The rocks and pebbles in the bottom of the creek ground into his back and the water threatened to take him before the man did. Struggling, Wolf pushed his head above the water. He chopped the man's hands, striking him in the face, and he could breathe again. Fresh, clean, Pennsylvania air filled his lungs and Wolf crawled to the edge of the creek. Hands searched the bottom for his revolver, frantically turning stones and pebbles alike. Over his shoulder, the rebel bore down on him again.

A thick Bowie knife appeared in the rebel's hand and he lunged it toward Wolf's chest. His hands slipped as he tore at the slick rebel's wrist, and he threw his body behind the knife hand, adding weight to his attack.

The rebel frowned, baring his browning teeth as he inched the knife closer and closer. "Shhh. Quiet now, boy. Just take it."

"No. No!" The blade gained ground every inch nearer to his chest until the tip touched his heavy woolen uniform. The point of the wicked steel pricked his skin, pushing into the upper layers of his flesh.

"Almost there, boy. It'll all be over. Shhh." His face was so close to Wolf that he could make out every feature. His choppy beard, the blackheads on the tip of his nose, his deep brown eyes, one eye that drooped slightly more than the other. He was amazed at the detail to which he was seeing these things all while trying to not die. It was like he was in a state of hyper focus, every tiny fraction of the knife in his chest bringing panicked torture.

CHAPTER 15

June 30th, 1863
York County, Pennsylvania

Thwack! The man's eyes rolled into the back of his head and his body grew heavily limp. Wolf rolled, tossing him into the creek. Wilhelm stood above them both, Sharps carbine in his hands.

"You all right?" He gave Wolf a hand and helped him to his feet. "Did you get cut?" Wilhelm reached for him and patted down his chest scrutinizing him for injury.

Everything was still a whirlwind of confusion after surviving his brush with death. He rubbed his neck and felt the place where the rebel had tried to end him. Crimson droplets graced his fingertips. "A bit."

The corporal yanked his wet jacket back. He pinched the wound with two fingers and slapped it. "Not enough to care about."

Wolf nodded dumbly, still in shock over the fight.

Shaking his shoulder, Wilhelm said, "Let's get this prisoner back to the cabin." They dragged the rebel's limp body back to the creek embankment and tied his hands together with rope. They tossed the man onto the back of Billy and they walked back to the homestead.

They hitched their reins where the rebels had theirs earlier. Now, a dozen horses stood outside. Shugart's men had revealed themselves waiting for Wilhelm's return.

Franz waved at them. "You caught him!"

"Johannes did," Wilhelm said with a little smirk.

"Well done," Franz said. "I can't believe it. We've won our first battle!"

Rolling his eyes, Cobb chided the man. "That was hardly a battle, boy. Not even a skirmish. I already told you boys, there ain't no glory in the cavalry."

Franz helped his father carry the prisoner by hand and foot into the cabin. The rest of the men followed them inside.

As expected, the interior of the cabin was humble. It was a single open room, with a fireplace, bed, table and three chairs. The floor was wood and adorned with a tattered blue rug that frayed errant thread along the edges.

Sandra sat in a chair with her hands holding her head. Cobb sat in the other chair with Shugart.

She looked as the men carried in their prisoner. "No." She pointed outside. "Get him out of here." She stood, her finger wavering at the door. "Now."

Cobb removed his hat. "Ma'am, no need to be frantic."

"He's a dog," she cried. "A wicked dog."

"I know." Shugart put a comforting hand on her shoulder and she flinched. He pulled his hand away as if he'd been struck.

"Don't touch me," she whispered.

"My apologies," Shugart said with a sad look in his eye. "I will pray for you."

"A lot of good that will do."

Shugart shut his mouth and bowed his head.

Directing them to a chair, Cobb ignored the woman's pleas. "Put him here." They set the prisoner on the chair and Cobb secured him with extra rope around his ankles to the chair legs.

Shugart studied the rebel's belly leaking reddish contents onto his pants. "A grave wound."

An uncaring look crossed Cobb. "What the hell do I care?" He leaned back in and slapped the rebel's face. "Wake up, now."

He waited a moment and smacked the rebel a bit harder the next time. A pink handprint emerged on the rebel's cheek. He glanced at Shugart. "Will you go take a look at Private Hunt? I don't think it's bad, but I don't want him mustering out before we can reach the surgeon."

The rebel's chin rose and he blinked, his eyes coming into focus. A loud moan escaped his lips. "God damn, my *belly*." He writhed in pain but the rope kept him in place. "No, no, no."

"Johnny Reb, now I want to get you back to a surgeon, but we need to talk."

"Why, Billy Yank? I don't have no stories to tell."

Cobb's grimy fingers squeezed the rebel's mouth as if he were estimating cattle age by studying their teeth. "Where's the rest of your unit? Who's your commanding officer?"

The rebel coughed and wheezed. "We're partisans. No unit. No commander. Sympathizers."

Letting him go in disgust, Cobb spoke. "Sure." He took his black hat off and set it on the table. "You overhear anything ma'am?"

Her face twisted in hatred. "They're part of Lee's command. Virginians."

Dark eyes lit under Cobb's brow. "Bobby Lee?"

"Fitzhugh," she said.

The rebel turned his head toward her. "Now, why you gone and do that? We was nice to ya."

She leaned forward and spit on his face. The glob ran down his cheek like it was trying to find the quickest way off.

"You gone and made our lady upset, and we take care of our ladies in the North. Right and proper. Ain't that right, boys?"

The men muttered their acknowledgement.

The rebel coughed. "No proper female folk in these parts anyway. Bunch of brutish abolitionists."

Sandra folded her arms over her chest. "I ain't no abolitionist and I ain't no lady."

"Old Lincoln is a damn dirty colored lover, but you're right. You ain't no lady."

She stepped closer and slapped him hard. *Smack!* His head rocketed to the side.

Recovering, the rebel rotated his jaw. "Hits like a bear."

"Franz, would you be kind enough to take the lady outside."

Franz stepped closer and offered her a gentle hand. "Ma'am."

"Get your hands away from me, you little cherub." With a glare at Cobb, she said, "This is my house."

"And soon as we get what we need, it will return back to your lovely hands."

Sandra's eyes narrowed to slits, but she stormed outside, followed by Franz tailing her like a whipped dog.

The sergeant leaned back in. "Where's the rest of your men?" He got even closer. "Now, boy."

Johnny Reb coughed and his face winced in pain as he rolled his head backward. "Oh, it hurts. Let me go back. Please." He moaned in agonizing discomfort.

"Not until you tell me where your men are."

"No, please. You already got me good. Let me go back and get fixed by me own kin."

Cobb shook his head in disgust, bending down next to the man's face. "Where's your command and how many?" He punched the rebel in the stomach. It was a quick jab and not even that hard, but with the bullet wound in his belly the man wailed something fierce.

The rebel breathed hard, his chest rapidly inhaling and exhaling, grunting with effort. "Oh, God." He repeated over and over.

"That was me being nice, Johnny Reb."

The rebel squeezed his eyes shut and muttered to himself. Cobb wound up again for another gut punch.

"Please. It's Stuart's entire command. Colonel Lee is me Colonel. Bless him. Please leave me be. No more punching."

Surprise flashed in Cobb's eyes. "Stuart's entire command?"

"How many men?" Wilhelm said.

The rebel's eyes were bloodshot and bulging round. "I don't know. Maybe five thousand cavalry."

"Five thousand. Dear God," Cobb said.

"Where are they?" Wilhelm said. "We'll get you to a doctor, but where is your army?"

"Southwest of here about six maybe seven miles."

"Six miles. We must've practically marched right by them," Wilhelm said.

The rebel's breathing came labored. "We were supposed to link up with General Lee, but haven't yet."

"Where's Lee?"

Johnny Reb turned his head away. "I don't know. We's be looking for him."

The sergeant's face hardened and he clenched his fist like he was about to punch him again.

Wilhelm raised a hand. "No, Cobb. This man is in enough pain. He can't tell us more."

"He's lyin'," Cobb said, winding his fist. "They all lie to save their scalps."

Wilhelm's voice became stern like a father. "No, he ain't. I can tell."

The sergeant blew air through his nose. "Fine." He unrolled his sleeves and shouldered his way back into his black jacket.

The rebel smiled faintly. "Now, my sweet Billy Yank. You gonna untie me and patch me up?"

"No," Cobb said, emotionless. He scooped his black top hat off the table. "Everyone outside."

Wolf trailed the other troopers into the sunlight and untied Billy. He looked back at the rebel, feeling a pang of guilt for his suffering. That man had tried to kill him and here he was getting all softhearted for him.

The man's head was down to his chest and he was crying. "God be merciful." It was truly pathetic to watch a man broken down in the pits of agony.

Wolf turned away. "What are we going to do with him?"

"None of your concern, Private," Cobb said, fixing his horse's reins.

With her arms folded across her chest, Sandra stood outside with Franz. Shugart had finished bandaging Hunt and they sat beneath a tree under its protective shade. The pig rooted around in the pen, chewing loudly and sniffing with its nose.

"Mount up." The men mounted their horses. Wolf slipped his bad foot into a stirrup and pulled himself atop Billy. The rebel's body trembled as he cried inside the cabin.

Cobb looked down at Sandra. "Now, I trust you will look after Johnny?"

Tears filled her eyes. She shook with contemptuous anger. "You want me to look after that piece of trash? After what he done?"

"Yes, ma'am. He's your responsibility."

She sighed and looked away.

"I trust you will take *care* of him."

Her eyes went cold and fierce. "I will."

"Good." He turned his horse around in a circle. "Who's the fastest rider?"

The men looked at one another, but it was Wilhelm's voice that came through. "Wolf is."

"You heard what that Reb said. I need you to go straight to the general and tell him. Stuart is close. Fitzhugh Lee is with him. At least a full brigade. Can you do that?"

"Yes, sir."

"Then why are you still here?"

Wolf prodded Billy with his heels. "Ja!"

CHAPTER 16

June 30th, 1863
Hanover, Pennsylvania

Wolf pushed Billy as hard as he dared through the forest. Twigs and branches tugged and swatted at him. Being careful to keep on a beaten trail, before long he found himself on a dirt, rural road spacious enough for two wagons to pass one another at the same time. He took the country road for over two miles, passing farms and green pastures alike until he could make out the homes and structures of a small town of what he thought should be Hanover.

Empty dirt roads greeted him, soulless save for a brown dog sniffing a tree and lifting a leg. Whitewashed houses with black shutters passed him by. The sounds of people clapping and cheering steered him toward the center of the town. The packed earth lane led him to the backs of people.

Three-story red brick businesses stood near the square along with clusters of townspeople. Houses lined the other side of the square, all the homes connected. Wolf slowed his horse to a walk.

The people wore fine coats and dresses, top hats and buns, vests and rolled-sleeves, braving the heat to clap and cheer the passing Union soldiers. One of the citizens noticed him and smiled. He was an older gentleman with white hair and matching drooping mustache like willow branches on either side of his face.

"God bless you, fair soldier. Water? Bread?" He nudged his wife with an elbow startling her. She gave him a surprised, grandmotherly smile, warm and sincere. She stepped closer and dug her hand into a basket, handing him a chunk of golden-brown crusty bread.

Wolf took the warm bread in his hand, sniffing it. The smell of baked goods tantalized his nostrils. Their warmheartedness took him aback. "Where is this? Hanover?"

The man quizzically frowned. "Why yes. Thank God you've come. Those vile Southerners have invaded and you've come to protect us from their horrible ways."

Wolf took the hard-crusted bread and stuffed it in his mouth. It was warm and sweet and fresh. Nothing like the hard tack, or the sawdusty flour biscuits they'd sometimes get or any shoddy goods the army dolled out on a regular basis. He shoved the rest in his pack.

Chewing gleefully, he mumbled a quick, "Thank you," to the old couple. "Ja," he called to Billy and kicked the horse through the crowd merging near the column of cavalry.

A plain wool bunting pennant flag of white with two blue, crossed sabers at the center passed by.

The men regarded him with curious looks like he was mad, or worse a deserter with a change of heart in the face of impending contact with the enemy. Or they thought he was out fraternizing with the local female population and neglecting his duties. One of the men took a flower from a pretty girl on the edge of the street, sticking it through his jacket's buttonhole.

"Whose command is this?"

A sergeant with a gray-and-black speckled beard turned his way. Even he had a half smile on his veteran face. *The joys of fighting on home turf.* "Who would have thought they'd come out for us like this?" He shook his head in astonishment. "We're Farnsworth's 1st Brigade. Who you looking for?"

"General Custer. I have an urgent message."

The sergeant pointed a finger north of the square. "Boy General. Should be 'bout two miles ahead."

"Rebs are coming," Wolf said.

The sergeant looked him up and down like he was crazy. "When are they not?"

"Ja!" Billy swiftly found his gallop. They passed row after row of blue Federal cavalry. Regimental flags billowed, snapping smartly in the wind. Guidons fluttered. The men laughed and enjoyed their homecoming parade. They were showered with gifts from the magnanimous townsfolk and basked in the benevolence of the people. Boys got kisses from the girls and fresh fruit and cookies.

They all blurred by and Wolf ignored the ache in his leg as he rode. He finally came to a standard he recognized. The 13th Michigan. He could hear the men holler after him as he passed by. Shouts of "Wolf" faintly breached his ears.

"Must see the general," he yelled as he passed.

He rode Billy to a knot of officers and a flag bearer. General Custer wore his signature black velvet coat over a spread-collared naval shirt with a red necktie curling out from beneath topped off with a wide-brimmed hat.

Colonel Moore and Lieutenant Wells sat on their horses nearby along with the general's orderly. On his other side, a slender colonel sat next to him who looked like he couldn't grow a beard until you saw the wavy whiskers running off his chin like hanging moss.

"General," Wolf breathed.

General Custer glanced at him with deep-blue eyes. The left part of his mouth threatened to turn into a smile. He had a borderline long nose with a slight downward slant at the tip, covering his golden mustache.

Colonel Moore had an irritated look on his face as if Wolf's presence embarrassed him. His beady eyes were debating which punishment to place upon his private's head every moment he lingered.

"Where are you coming from all in a hurry?" Custer said. The left part of his mouth smiled in amusement. "I pray you bring us good news and a salute."

Wolf composed himself, bringing a hand to his forehead in respect. "Sorry, sir."

"Don't you know you're not supposed to give a report by starting with the word sorry?"

"No, sir."

Custer blinked and stifled a chuckle.

"I believe he's one of mine, General." Colonel Moore said and with added malice. "You are part of the 13th are you not, Private?"

Wolf managed to nod. "Yes, sir. I am, F Company."

"He is part of my platoon," Wells added reluctantly. "We don't get to pick our men."

With a white glove, Custer waved the two men off. "Well, out with it then. I don't expect you rode that poor beast half to death just for the fun of it."

"Yes, sir." Wolf gulped in air. "We caught a rebel scouting party southwest of here about five miles." He pointed over his shoulder.

Custer's eyes lit up with the idea of rebels to fight. He licked his lips with anticipation. "You bested them, I take it?"

"We did, sir." The rebel's face driving his knife into Wolf's breast flashed before his eyes. "Three of them were killed and the other wounded."

The general's mustache fluttered. "A job well done."

Wolf nodded. "Thank you, sir." Most of the fighting had been done by the veteran soldiers, Corporal Wilhelm and Sergeant Cobb. A few of the men hadn't even fired a shot, let alone hit anyone.

"He told us that Stuart's entire cavalry division of five thousand men are close, only a few miles south from here."

Custer reached up and smoothed his mustache, his eyes growing distant. "They could strike at us any moment. Lee must be near." He waved an officer to join him. "Lieutenant."

A young officer steered his horse close to Custer. "Sir."

"I need you to get word to the 5th and 6th that we found Stuart. Get them back into Hanover. Same goes to Kilpatrick. Do you understand?"

"Yes, sir." The junior officer urged his mount into action and, with a clank of his saber, he was off.

Custer twisted his fair head to his regimental commanders. "I need you both to hightail back to Hanover. Moore I want you to swing your regiment south and west. We're going to see if we can get Stuart to commit. You're going to flank them."

The officers gave quick salutes.

"Sounds like our Golden Knight wants a scrap." Custer gave him a fierce grin and he turned toward Wolf. "How about it, Private? Let's go see if Stuart is as superb a commander as everyone says he is."

Wolf's gut churned with a fighter's butter, the confidence of the general was infectious. "I love a good brawl, sir."

"Private," Colonel Moore said. "Back to your unit." He pointed a glove at the column. "Lieutenant Wells, you will address our young private on the proper way to speak to a general."

Wells's chin lifted up a bit higher than normal. "He will be dealt with."

They all saluted General Custer as another aide from Farnsworth galloped on scene.

"We're engaged, sir!" He gestured back in the direction of Hanover.

Custer grinned. "Tell Elon to hold his ground, I will move to support."

Wolf followed his officers back down the column toward the rest of the 13th Michigan Cavalry. *A battle is coming.*

CHAPTER 17

June 30th, 1863
Hanover, Pennsylvania

Wolf and the two officers trotted back along the column to the 13th Michigan. Men were turning their horses around as the rippling sounds of muskets, rifles, and carbines rattled in the distance.

"Although you lack the proper respect for your superiors, I can put you to use, Private. Tell Captain Peltier we are engaged and that he is to take his company and hold our flank between Gettysburg and Littlestown Roads. The 7th is moving there now and we are to support them. Your company is to anchor the 13th. Is this clear?"

"Yes, sir."

"Ride ahead, while I gather the rest of the regiment. It will take time to get this command counter-marched."

Shouting, Wolf steered his horse in the new direction. "Ja." He passed over a mile of concerned cavalryman riding in a column of rows of fours. The new recruits let their sabers rattle at their hips while the veterans strapped the blades to their saddles.

He finally found Captain Peltier talking with Second Lieutenant Jay Little, a strapping young man from a prominent family in Grand Rapids. Concern stippled the captain's face.

"Sir, I come from the colonel. We are to wheel back southwest and support the 7th on the right flank. Farnsworth is engaged in Hanover."

"It sounds like a legit fight," Peltier said. His eyes shifted back down the road toward Hanover. "Let's move with haste, men, we have a flank to protect. Little, you may lead."

"Company, halt," shouted Second Lieutenant Little.

The horseman brought their horses to a stand still. "Company, left fours."

The front rank of F Company wheeled around and off the road. Men removed carbines from shoulders as they reversed direction, shoving the stock into their hips to keep the gun steadier as they rode, ready to dismount at a moment's notice.

"Well done, Lieutenant," the Captain said with a nod.

Rejoining his detached unit near the rear of the company, he settled into rank with the other scouts who had returned behind him. He took a spot next to Wilhelm.

Cobb eyed the second lieutenant with disdain, muttering to himself. "Everything is nice and pretty before a proper fight. That boy is fresher than a green turd and will get us killed."

"At least he's not a prick like the other one."

"I'll take a prick that doesn't get us killed over a nice officer who doesn't know his head from his arse."

Wilhelm gazed at the road ahead warily. "We crossed Hanover about ten minutes before the last of Farnsworth. Glad we didn't get caught in that mess." The booms of cannon captured the troopers' attention. "Sounds like a proper fight."

They followed the four horsemen in front of them as the bugler sounded, signaling an increase in speed to a trot. After some time, the outer buildings of the town, a couple barns and houses along with a water pump appeared. As they rode closer to the center of Hanover, they could make out the 18th Pennsylvania's flag, blue with gold trim, stallions propping up a shield with an eagle. Along with the 5th New York's, the blue with gold-trimmed flags waving from Farnsworth's brigade. The cavalrymen were dismounted, forming a line between the buildings. Every fourth man held horses for his comrades. It was the only way to ensure the animals didn't bolt during a battle.

Civilians scrambled with shotguns and smooth-bore muskets, helping the soldiers build makeshift barriers that they could take cover behind. Boxes, carts and wagons, ladders, stripped fence rails from nearby farms and iron bars made up the haphazardly constructed barricade reinforced with the bodies of the Union cavalry. Burnside carbines, sabers, blankets, and haversacks had been thrown in the street in what appeared was retreat.

"These men were routed earlier," Wilhelm said.

"Not surprised," Cobb said. He pointed with a gloved hand. "Look. Those are Hampton's colors." The white palmetto, a shorter type of palm tree with a white crescent moon on a field of indigo blue of South Carolina rippled and flapped defiantly in the distance. "Stuart ain't far then. Hampton's boys are some of his best." He gestured hastily. "These boys here, greener than grass." The booming of cannons started in successive blasts like a drummer from the heavens. *Boom, boom, boom. Doom, doom, doom.*

"Horse artillery. Damn." Smoke swelled into a cloud lingering among the forest on the other edge of the town like a reluctant fog.

Brick, wood, and glass, burst from the side of a three-story building, pieces raining down onto the street. A man with two women and three children raced around the side of a house. The man ripped open cellar doors; they disappeared as they raced down steps to take cover. The man reappeared, peered around and slammed the doors closed.

F Company turned west on the main street and they traveled through the town toward Farnsworth's right flank. The 7th Michigan had taken their place along the ditch of a road. Most of the men knelt down with their Sharps carbines. The 7th Michigan was a saber regiment like the 13th meaning that most of the better equipment for firefights went to the other three regiments, the 5th, 6th, and 1st Michigan Regiments. On the other side of the road, the fourth men of their units held the horses for the dismounted troopers. A few of the mounts nervously tossed their heads at the sound of cannon, giving the handlers a difficult time keeping them steady.

Wolf's company galloped hard, passing the 7th Michigan down Gettysburg Road as they stretched between that and the Littlestown Road. The air reverberated as two cannons unloaded their ordnance from the woods across a scorched field, targeting the newly arriving 13th Michigan. Wolf instinctually ducked his head with every thunder clap of enemy cannon. The bugle sounded the call for dismount.

"Hurry now, boys," Cobb said, hopping from his horse. Wilhelm had already dismounted. The men followed suit, parting with their horses.

Sweaty hands wrapped around his gun and he pulled his carbine along its strap, unharnessing the weapon.

Wolf shoved Billy's reins to Private Lent who was on the verge of peeing himself. Rubbing Billy's nose for a moment, he said, "I'll be back, boy."

He hobble-ran for a copse of trees with the other troopers, passing through tall, tick-ridden, uncut pasture to get there. He laid down on the dry ground and crawled prone in a bed of pine needles, holding his carbine out in front of him. He couldn't see much from their vantage, brittle yellow grass rising hundreds of yards out, the canopy of green treetops further away, and they weren't going to hit anything without the enemy being a lot closer.

Only soft encouragement from the noncommissioned officers could be heard between cannon fire. The troopers lay and waited for orders.

"Keep those heads low, boys," Cobb said.

"How do they know where we are?" Roberts whispered next to Wolf. It was as if raising his voice would draw the deadly fire upon them.

"Does it matter?" Wolf said.

"Suppose not."

A shell popped down the line, shaking the trees nearby. The men ducked down deep into the pine needles and dirt, covering their heads with their arms. It was the only thing they could do. Hope that when the shot exploded over your head that the fragments would miss completely or, if you were unfortunate enough to get hit with shrapnel, that it would hit your arms instead of your face and neck. Not that one couldn't bleed to death from taking a flying piece of metal to the arm. That was unless it was solid shot, much better used against closer ranks of men, but if they did send a non-exploding shell their direction it could remove a head or a limb even easier than an army surgeon.

"Was just thinking for next time. Maybe we shouldn't just run at 'em.

Maybe sneak around more."

Wolf looked over his arm at his friend. "You're telling the wrong soldier." He waited a moment as a shell hit a tree nearby splintering fragments of wood, showering the men below. Wood dust enveloped the men and someone coughed down the line.

"You men sound?" Wilhelm asked.

Quiet affirmations came from the troopers.

"Maybe you should be in charge?" Wolf said to Roberts.

"I don't see how we could be in any less of a mess."

"Me neither."

Most shots harmlessly sailed overhead, detonating over nothing or smashing into trees, or crashing into the earth instead of their intended targets.

A shell burst over a platoon of the 7th and cries erupted from their line. Men wailed in agony. Wolf couldn't see them, but he could hear the cries of pain. The sobbing and calls for help. The cries for their mothers. The woeful sounds of shredded men filled in the booming gaps of the tiny one-sided cannon battle raging unchecked along the Federal line.

"Steady, men," Wilhelm whispered. "No need to fret."

Franz breathed hard next to him, sucking in dust and coughing. His curly blond hair dampened with sweat. "Father."

"Quiet now, son. No point in being afraid. We can't control where their cannons fall."

Time ticked by and the men were submitted to the enemy cannon for over an hour until the rattle of a caisson and horses caught their ears. Soldiers drove four horses pulling a single battery behind them. The drivers pushed the big-boned animals to their limit in an effort to get the artillery into place.

"Pennington's Battery," Cobb said with a smile. "Hip, hip, hurrah!"

The men lifted their voices into a cheer as more guns were rushed into place. Finally it was time to give the enemy a taste of their own misery.

"He trained under Captain Tidball. He'll quiet those pups down."

The battery rattled and rolled into place nearby. They unlimbered six 3-inch ordnance guns.

Cobb hushed as he watched them prepare their cannon, as if the enemy cannon could locate him if he spoke louder. "They're rifled, barreled cannon, meaning they can shoot accurately much further. Like a rifle, the shell spins out of the barrel, meaning it is much more accurate than those smoothbores the rebels got. Made of wrought iron too."

Wolf eyed him, not understanding the difference between wrought iron and brass or regular iron. But the black wrought iron reflected the sun, tall, four-foot wheels on either side.

"They won't overheat," Cobb said.

Each gun had its own eight-man crew comprised of a sergeant, who was in charge, a corporal who managed the caisson and another corporal that was the gunner, and five others. The others were assigned varying support tasks and each man was trained to perform the tasks of the others in case of battlefield casualties.

One artilleryman dunked a long staff with a sponge on one end, hard, blackened wood on the other, into a bucket of water and swabbed the bore of the cannon, making sure no sparks would prematurely detonate the charge in the heat.

"Six hundred yards. Prepare an eight-pound shell," shouted one of the corporal gunners.

"Fuse, three seconds," shouted the other at an artilleryman by the caisson.

An artilleryman shoved a charge bag of gunpowder down the barrel and used a rammer to drive it down the tube to the end. One man kept his thumb over the vent making sure no sparks or embers prematurely discharged the gun. Another private loaded the shell, ramming it to the end of the tube wedged near the powder. The gunner removed his hand from the vent and stuck a pick inside, piercing the powder bag. He then placed a primer in the vent attached to a lanyard.

The gunner sighted the cannon in by adjusting the angle of the barrel. The crew stepped away from the gun hands covering their ears.

"Fire," barked the sergeant, his mustache drooping from the sides of his face. An artilleryman ripped the lanyard and the cannon roared smoke and fire and death.

Wolf couldn't help but put his head down as the ground quaked beneath him. The artillerymen repeated this process over and over, and the rebels dueled the federals back and forth for hours. As Wolf listened to the cannon duel, he was thankful the enemy had found a new target even if it was his own men.

The men lay prone in the hot Pennsylvanian summer sun and Wolf grew almost immune to the artillery battle, like an encroaching thunderstorm on a summer night. The 6th Michigan had reappeared from its scouting and took a position along their flank, centering the 13th between themselves and the 7th. If he listened hard enough between the cannon fire, he could hear men yelling across the field like faint gray ghosts whispering from afar. And both parties were perfectly happy allowing the cannons to do all the work.

As the sun began to shift from directly overhead to the west in a hazy, blistering, blue sky, the pounding of hooves traveled down the road. Guidons from the brigade and of the individual regiments rippled behind Custer. The general jumped off his horse near the cannons and grabbed a Spencer rifle off his saddle. He ran for the trees holding F Company and crouched down with Captain Peltier.

"You know, Captain, I'm tired of all this back and forth. Let's push these Rebs back. Get your boys blooded."

Surprise etched the captain's face. *Why would a general be crouching down with a captain when he had a host of regiments to lead?*

"What's he doing here? Doesn't he know he's a general now?" Cobb said.

They studied the young general with intensive scrutiny.

"It looks like he wants to lead from the front," Wilhelm said.

Rolling for a better look, the sergeant snorted. "Won't be a general for long like that."

"No, he won't," Wilhelm said.

The ground erupted into a geyser of dirt, dust, and metal near one of the cannons and men went down. Custer ducked his head and pointed. "Get those men help." He marched over to the line of F Company laying in the copse of pine trees. Wolf peered back at the general, removing his arm covering his head.

The flaxen-haired man looked down at his men. “Looks like you men are well acquainted with the dirt. Let’s get acquainted with our enemy. Follow me.”

CHAPTER 18

June 30th, 1863
Hanover, Pennsylvania

They crept from the trees at a crouch. The men had been ordered to remain silent as they stalked directly toward the enemy batteries. Over three hundred men from the 13th and 6th Michigan Regiments in more or less a line began the grueling covert movement toward the rebels.

The ground covered them for almost half their march. Grass swayed in the field. It was waist high and varying shades of brown, tan, but mostly green. The slender strands engulfed the men with soft stalks as if they were lazily propelling them closer to the rival guns.

When they overtook a small crest, staying hidden became even more important. Wolf struggled across the wild grass-laden field, putting most of his weight on his healthy leg. With every step, the three hundred men crawled, ran, and snuck closer to the Confederate battery.

The sun was relentless blanketing the men in sweat. Brows glistened, coats were different hues of darker blue, and faces reddened into shades of pink to bright strawberry among them. Wiping his forehead, he stayed crouched in the long grass. He cursed his wet woolen coat and pants now, they took every opportunity to itch and scratch, capturing the heat from the sun.

Franz tripped and fell and Gratz hoisted him upright. Cobb waved them forward, trying to keep the line intact. With every step, the enemy cannon magnified in volume, commanding the field while Pennington's guns diminished, growing softer until it stopped altogether. Custer had ordered them to stop the barrage twenty minutes after the men had covertly entered the field and Pennington had followed his orders closely.

As Pennington's battery grew silent, a cheer clamored from the rebels that he could distinctly understand. The command to halt filtered through the men. Cobb signaled them with a flat palm to lay prone in the grass, waiting for the signal to open fire. The rebels were close enough to hear distinct words.

"Get those shells on up!"

"Quieted them boys down, didn't we?"

Men laughed. "Hurry now!"

Time daunted the Union soldiers. Pre battle brought all manner of feelings, none of which Wolf knew were normal. *Will I fight well? Will I be harmed? Will these be my last moments on God's earth? If I fall, how will father know? And Josephine and young Abigail? Who will spare them the news? Would they write his name in the paper? Was it worth it?* He thought about what it meant to take a man's life. The bible was explicit in its condemnation of taking the life of your fellow man. He'd shot at the enemy, but he hadn't taken a life. Maybe that's all he would ever be is a supporter, a man of the line who fired but somewhere inside him he knew he wanted to miss so he missed. Or he would kill and have to carry that burden along his shoulders like a bow yoke the rest of his days. Whatever war of conscience that went on his mind, he took strength from his brothers around him surely feeling all the same things.

After a terse tuck of his chin, Wilhelm said quietly. "Get ready. We're about to attack. Make sure that pistol is ready for when we get close." He felt himself gulping and turned to Bart, who'd found himself next to Wolf. Pointing at his pistol, he said. "Make ready."

Bart's face poked through the grass with a nervous grin. "Ready."

"Pass it along," he said, pointing.

Bart turned away, whispering the message to Wheeler and it was relayed from trooper to trooper down the line.

"On his mark," Wilhelm grunted.

"On the general's mark," Wolf whispered to Bart. The round-faced man nodded. "Yes."

Wolf could feel every nerve in his body and his stomach flipped and flopped like a barrel rolling unevenly down a hill. The battle was almost upon them. A real fight. Not a chase through the woods, but real combat, stuff that filled the newspapers. If this was what he'd always wanted, why was he so nervous? He turned back to Wilhelm. "How will we know the mark?"

"All hell will break loose. Aim for the men on the cannons. If they get canister shot loaded, they'll carve us up quick and we'll wish we were back among the trees."

Wolf's Sharps carbine was loaded with a single shot. His Colt held six-shots. Percussion caps were in place. He could fire seven shots without having to reload. Not that he could hit anything with his pistol from this distance. He touched his ammunition pouch for his carbine. Open lever. Slip in cartridge. Close breech. Half-cock hammer. Place percussion cap. Full-cock hammer. Take aim. Squeeze trigger. Repeat.

He took a deep breath waiting for the surge of violence. The grass was drier than it should have been and it crinkled beneath him. He wiped the salty sweat from his eyes, trying to clear his vision, the liquid stinging them. His gut churned and the wait took on a world of its own, time stretching in anticipation. His heartbeat pounded visibly in his chest. The turf smelled fresh laying in it, but the pungent, rotten egg, sulfuric smoke shrouded the air from the continuous cannon fire throughout the afternoon.

The rebel cannon fired another series of rounds on the silent Union troopers across the way. Whoops and yells of taking it to the enemy sounded from the men working the guns. War was even easier when they didn't fight back. Wolf wasn't sure it could be called war then, just slaughter.

Custer knelt in the knee-high grass. His broad-brimmed hat poking out along with his Spencer rifle placed to his shoulder, eye aiming as if he were on a wild safari hunting a giant elephant. His rifle banged and smoke puffed from the front of the barrel. He worked the lever and hammer quick and fired again before Wolf could blink.

"Get 'em, boys!" the general shouted. The three hundred men bounded partially upright, keeping low profiles. With his powerful arms so as not to struggle with his leg, Wolf pushed himself standing. Taking his thumb, he fully cocked his Sharps hammer and took aim at the startled artillerymen. They had no choice but to try and load their cannon faster. An artilleryman ran for the canister shot, disappearing toward a caisson wagon, holding the devastating anti-infantry load out.

Custer had already fired two more shots before Wolf had fired one. The Spencer rifle was new, and its abilities far outmatched the muzzle-loader and even the Sharps carbine. It was a repeating rifle, the seven rounds loaded into the stock of the weapon would be fed into the firing chamber by cocking the weapon's lever. It took out one of the main steps that a Sharps wielder had to take, which was opening the breech and placing in a cartridge.

Gunshots rippled from their loose line of formerly hidden troopers. To Wolf it sounded like a string of firecrackers popping off. He had no idea if his first shot hit his mark. He operated as a frantic steam engine, his hands moving seemingly disconnected from the rest of his body with mechanical repetition.

A sporadic volley went out. Carbines were much faster than the muzzle-loading rifled-muskets of the infantry and a sustained rate of fire far surpassed most of even the best rifleman's abilities.

Three of the men surrounding the cannon went down. One man cried out, but the others became the silent dead. A man dragged his brown-coated partner away from the artillery piece. A rebel sergeant sent more men forward. The new rebels desperately tried to adjust the cannon's aim downward against the close proximity enemy troopers.

Wolf couldn't hear them, the gunfire was too loud, but he knew they would be calling for canister shot, metal balls, scrap metal, or iron shrapnel to shred the dismounted cavalryman to bloody ribbons.

His hand flipped open the lever, a thin piece that acted as a trigger guard, then went for his cartridge pouch. The cannon continued to turn, a behemoth with a vicious punch. Some of the men around him had gone to pistols but at this range it was futile.

"Drive them off, boys!" Custer shouted.

Wolf's hand fumbled around the pouch, his fingertips were numb like there was no blood left inside his veins. The linen-encased cartridge felt oddly wet in his hands. He shoved it into the breech of his barrel, flipping the guard closed. It trimmed the tail of the cartridge, leaving exposed gunpowder on the top of the breech box. His hand went back to his sardine box for percussion caps. He placed one on the metal nipple. The hammer audibly clicked beneath the pad of his thumb so when he squeezed the trigger the hammer would slam into the cap and create the spark needed to combust the powder and linen, igniting the majority of the gunpowder and propelling the lead bullet from his carbine.

Squinting an eye, he focused his aim, making the irons flatten in his vision. Four men loaded the cannon, hurriedly prepping the gun with frantic grimaces plastered on faces.

Wolf squeezed the trigger. His carbine fired and smoke spewed from the barrel. It drifted upward, mixing with the cloud fogging in the air. The man ramming the bore collapsed onto the cannon. The scalding barrel seared his skin, but it didn't matter now because he was most certainly dead.

The rest of the artillerymen retreated before the withering fire, a man clutching his back before disappearing into the underbrush. Wolf couldn't be sure if he was the one that fired the shot that killed the rammer, but that was his intent. *No man will call me coward.* One rebel artilleryman gripped his leg in pain and the two others wrapped arms around him, dragging him for the timber.

Custer's voice rose through the gunfire. "Let's take those guns, boys!" He rushed forward with a pistol in either hand. Wolf drew his pistol as they neared the six-pound guns. They were focused on capturing the enemy cannon, not the rebels that marched between the trees like gray wraiths.

A ripple of thunder came from the forest, as if it were uprooting itself and coming to life. Men in blue around Wolf crumpled onto the ground. The smoke drifted toward the sky, swirling around the trees, engulfing it in a whitish gray like the wisp of a ghost soldier.

Then came a noise the likes of which Wolf had never heard, both terrifying and unsettling like a horde of banshees or wild Huns that rose out of the forest like an unholy choir of the dead. It was as if the depths of Hell had opened, revealing all the devil's tormented denizens at once. The yell cut through the dismounted cavalrymen, sending them into a timid standstill. Wolf peered down their position. Men looked to one another, unknowing of what hostile force awaited them.

"Hold that line," Wilhelm shouted. If he was scared, no one would ever know. He held his carbine lowered in front of his body ready to give a salvo when called.

The rebels gave another high-pitched whoop like a volley of bullets into the courage of the Union men. A soldier turned and ran.

"Steady now," Custer said. He pointed backward. "Stop that man. None of my men are cowards." A sergeant barked at the trooper's back and pointed his carbine at him. The cavalryman stopped in his tracks and slunk back to the line, finding his spot again if only to have a slightly rearward position of his fellows.

Custer shoved one pistol in his belt while he reloaded the other. He shook the rotary of his revolver to remove an errant paper from the cartridge. Replacing them, as well as percussion caps, while eyeing the trees for the encroaching enemy. He finished and duel drew his pistols, aiming them at the murky timber behind the unmanned rebel cannons.

Shadowy forms materialized from the gun-smoke mist that clung to the ground and trees in the sulfuric man-made mist. *Devils or men?*

They turned into armed devils. Gray coats covered blood-red shirts beneath. A flag billowed and rippled as the man carrying it waved it menacingly at the Yankees. A blood red star on a sable field with the crimson words: *Mortem Tyrannis.*

They whooped like animals as they marched toward Custer's men, sending shivers down Wolf's spine. That call would be something that he would remember until his dying days.

"Red men?" Bart barked. His eyes scanned the trees frantically.

"Rebels!" Wolf yelled.

Bart blinked, taking in the enemy before him. "Yes."

The man leading them could have been Custer's antithesis. His brown curling locks hung from beneath a gray, folded slouch hat to his shoulders. An ample mustache and goatee framed his mouth and pointed from his chin.

A maroon sash wrapped around his hips and a red blouse puffed from an open gray jacket. His saber flashed in circles as he led his red-shirted men forward.

Undeterred by the enemy, Custer shouted, "Let's give them a nice volley, boys!"

The red-shirted rebels came to a halt in the trees, loading guns, still hooting like wild Plains Indians.

"You heard the general," Captain Peltier shouted.

Cobb spat, "Where's Wells? Why is the captain issuing these orders?"

"He was with Moore last I saw," Wolf called back.

"No point in worrying now. Get that gun up." Wilhelm brought his carbine to his shoulder, taking aim.

"Ready, aim."

Wolf pointed his pistol toward the shrouded gray men. Bart sighted his carbine. Berry struggled to get a cap on his carbine nipple, his rotund fingers fumbling.

"Fire," Peltier commanded. A weak report from the men went out. A gray man evaporated in the fog of war, but the rebels stood their ground like a smoky wall. Yells picked up as if they could smell victory. They'd been spared and now would show their enemy a response in violent kind. A loud volley rippled forth, adding smoke and lead to the air.

More blue disappeared now in the open field with no surprise. The right flank of the 6th Michigan started to break as dismounted gray cavalrymen swung around the trees flanking them, slowly sealing off any option for retreat. Blue-coated troopers turned back for the safety of their line and horse artillery.

Without the buffer of the 6th Michigan, the 13th began to lose its nerve. In ones and twos, the men turned and ran.

"Hold your ground!" Wilhelm screamed.

Another man wailed and went down into the grass, grasping his leg. Wolf stayed in place, reaching for a reload. He bared his teeth, as the chaos swirled around him. And then they broke. The avalanche would not stop until everyone was overrun or dead. The men melted around him.

"Fall back!" Custer screamed.

Men turned and ran for the four hundred yards back to the safety of the Union line. Wolf joined them in the retreat. He hobbled, lagging behind the other troopers in the sprint for safety. He felt an arm wrap around his shoulder lifting him. Custer's mustached face puffed near his. "Didn't know you had a bum leg. Next time we'll keep you on top of a horse." He twisted behind him and fired his pistol three times.

"Yes, sir," Wolf said between breaths. He tried his best to keep his composure. He knew it would be a long run. Wilhelm emerged next to him wrapping an arm around his other side and gripping the waist of his pants.

"I got him, sir. Carry on before they overtake us."

Custer twisted, looking behind them. "They don't have the guts."

Breathing hard, Wolf joined him, glancing back. The red-shirted men watched them retreat not leaving the relative safety of the timber. The flanking rebels had shifted their line back into cohesion with the others as to not expose their flank. Cannoneers reclaimed their threatened prize.

Wolf's leg ached fiercely by the time they reached the 13th Michigan line. The men gasped on the ground, watching the rebels in the distance with wary eyes.

"They come?" Bart asked. He sucked in air through his nose and slipped a cartridge into his Sharps carbine.

Wilhelm's mustache flared as he breathed. "No, boy. But they might change their mind so load 'em up."

Wolf knelt and shook the pistol, checking for any clogs and reloading it. Custer stood watching as the Confederates limbered their artillery. The threat of losing their battery had been enough for the enemy because the day's fighting was coming to a close. Pennington showered the withdrawing rebels with a few going-away shots, but they faded into the timber and he did not want to waste ammunition on trees and rocks.

The cavalrymen of the 13th Michigan fell back in line to take stock of their first true engagement. Scouts were sent to watch the rebels and ensure they weren't up to anything nefarious and the day quickly surrendered to the night. And the men slipped into an exhausted sleep.

CHAPTER 19

July 2nd, 1863
Four miles from Hunterstown, Pennsylvania

F Company of the 13th Michigan sustained five casualties from the Battle of Hanover. Three dead and two wounded. Wolf had heard the 6th Michigan had it much worse, over a dozen men injured or killed. Brigadier General Judson Kilpatrick had moved his cavalry division north of Gettysburg in an attempt to shadow Stuart's movements. He'd wanted a fight, but instead chased phantom armies for an entire day.

"Think we'll chase ghosts again today?" Roberts asked. He munched a succulent apple, crunching away with his mouth open.

"I thought for sure we'd catch Stuart," Wolf said.

The company sat in formation in the morning heat awaiting orders. It was summing up to be even hotter than the first. The 13th Michigan waited for hours in the sweltering sun. It battered the men, burning their skin red. The worst part was knowing that the longer the day went on, the hotter it would become.

"I ain't surprised," Cobb said. He adjusted his hat back so it covered his neck. "Back to the old days. Stuart and his Invincibles riding circles around us."

"Maybe we'll catch them today?" Franz chirped.

"Wouldn't count on it. Battle's that way." Cobb pointed toward Gettysburg. "Got almost his whole army there. Fulton over in A Company heard that Lee's got his entire army there too. Shaping up to be a real scuffle. Never thought the Old Snapping Turtle had it in him."

"It's like we're playing second fiddle to the real show." Wolf draped his sash around his neck trying to shield himself.

Cobb glared in his direction. "Better to be a second fiddle than a dead fiddler."

"Bugger a fiddle. I'd rather be at home on my farm. This weather depresses me," Van Horn said. "I'd rather just get this over with. Win or lose the war today. Then we can go home."

Wilhelm twisted his curled mustache. "Were it that easy, my friend. I'd be right there with you."

Van Horn glanced at him, but didn't say a word. His mouth settled into a gloomy discomfort.

Impatient hooves stomped the ground in restless boredom matching their riders. Captain Peltier walked his horse down the formation. "F Company, we're headed to scout the south of Hunterstown. Cobb's unit had luck last time. Let's see what we can find this time."

Cobb dipped his head and removed his hat. He grumbled to himself. "No damn luck, if you ask me."

"Any sign of Stuart, you get a rider back to command. Godspeed, gentlemen," Peltier said.

"Men, let's move." Cobb waved his black top hat and the detached unit followed him into the woods south. They spread in a single file line and they walked their horses through the rolling hills populated with dense timber. The green leaves of the trees provided the men cover and the dominating sun even appeared to oppress the wildlife of the region. Not a fly flew and the troopers stripped jackets from torsos in an attempt to stay cool. No crows called. Only humid mugginess embraced them as kin.

The heat didn't relent, even as it crossed into mid-afternoon. There'd been no sign of anyone as they scouted the countryside. A storm of cannon from Gettysburg sounded off like distant thunder, threatening to engulf them with terrible rains at any moment.

"Halt, men," Cobb said. A small creek bubbled nearby, cracking the forest in two halves. The troopers dismounted. "Let's get those mounts watered and canteens filled," Wilhelm said.

Wolf led Billy over to the brook and crouched down to fill his canteen while his horse greedily lapped water with a long tongue. "Thirsty fellow, huh, Billy?" The horse didn't answer, and he patted the animal's sweaty flank.

The cool water felt refreshingly terrific on his parched throat and red face. Wolf took another swig and wiped his mouth, letting the fluids rejuvenate his overheated body.

Cobb pointed a finger at him. "Wolf, Franz, and Roberts. You take watch."

The unit centered itself in a small glade and began building a fire to warm food and coffee.

Sharing a look with Roberts, Wolf sighed. It was the worst being on the sergeant's shit list and any undesirable task always fell on them. The men tied their horses and grabbed their carbines for their trek.

Wilhelm gave them a weary grin. "There'll be a cup for you boys when you return."

"And bacon?" Franz said with a smile.

Wilhelm's demeanor softened with a glance at his son. "I'll see what I can do."

The three troopers marched into the underbrush, dragging their feet. A general disgruntled attitude cloaked the men with the extra duty.

"You ever remember it being so hot?" Roberts asked as they walked. He slapped at a mosquito buzzing around his neck.

Wolf's brace squeaked with every step. "No. I can't imagine Hell being hotter than it is out here."

The distant cannon reverberated like marching giants. "Father said it was cannon, but I can't believe it," Franz said. He eyed the distance with fear.

"Don't see no clouds," Roberts said.

"Your dad seems to know these things," Wolf said.

Franz stared off in wonderment. "How many do you think could cause such a rumble?"

Roberts scratched his head. "I'd say ten or twenty."

Franz's eyes envisioned the battle. "Must be hundreds of 'em."

"And we're stuck riding around miles away. Looking for a command that's probably already there. Where's the honor in that?" Wolf said.

"Well, I saw one real close yesterday and that was enough," Roberts said. "Trying to keep me'self in one piece." He gestured out toward the storm. "They can keep 'em over there."

"Don't you want to take the field? Win the day? Be a hero?"

Roberts shook his head no. "I do not. I'm perfectly content being what I am. Cavalry and alive."

"This could be the war. This very battle. I want to be in it."

"You signed up for the wrong service then. We're cavalry. Scouting, spying, and protecting the flank," he said, as if the thought cheered him. "Ours isn't to fight pitched battles. That's the infantry."

"Not a few days ago, we were on the field in a real fight." Wolf made sure to leave out his trailing thoughts of doubt and fears of fighting, those parts were better left unsaid like they didn't exist.

Franz chuckled with a musical hint to his voice. "Berry had to have dropped his gun three times."

The young men shared a laugh at the expense of their large Polish friend, lazily navigating over and around fallen logs.

"The general likes a fight. He'll find us another one. You can be sure of that."

"Well, maybe it's better he doesn't," Franz said. "Better to be cautious than charge headlong into a bullet."

Wolf shook his head. "Going toe-to-toe with the bastards is the only way to show them our worth. If you don't fight, no one will respect you."

"I'm no coward. I stood with everyone else in the battle line. But, that doesn't mean I like it."

Wolf eyed his curly haired friend. He'd never considered him much of a fighter, but he'd held with the rest of the men. That said something about a man. When he was willing to stand his ground, knowing the enemy was going to lay a volley of screaming lead into the men around you. Knowing that one of those bullets could be calling your name. "I know, Franz. Just don't be shy about it. It's much harder to stab a man fighting than a man running."

Franz removed his hat, fanning himself with it. "You're right, Johannes. I should be more brave. You think this is a good spot up here? Looks like a road up yonder."

Studying the land, Wolf gave the other two men orders. He had no rank over them, but it came naturally and they listened. "Roberts, you want to take the right, I'll take the left, and Franz you can be in the middle." It was better to surround the weaker part of their party and give him a bit of extra courage. "If you see something, signal the others so we can get word back to the Sergeant. We're spying. No fighting."

"No need to remind us," Roberts said with a smirk. He tossed an oblong green pear in the air and caught it, walking to his spot. Franz gave Wolf a cheerful grin and followed Roberts down the natural line of trees.

Wolf meandered the other way. When he reached a suitable distance, where he could see them, but would have to shout, he settled in. He jabbed his boot at the undergrowth avoiding a vine of plants he thought was poisonous. He leaned against a tree and used it to lower himself down to the dusty, dry earth badly in need of a rain shower. He took his carbine and set it on a nearby log and scanned the terrain.

The distant storm ebbed and flowed as if it couldn't decide which direction to go. One minute it grew loud, the next it shrank to a whisper. Before him, a small country road zigged around clusters of trees. An acre of browning clovers, that could be used to feed their horses and other livestock, ran down the timberline. It was a decent spot for an ambush, not that they would be fighting today. All the fighting was being done in Gettysburg. Their mission was to only observe and get word back to the 13th so the brigade could take action against their elusive opponents.

Wolf pushed his forage cap up onto his head and rested back on the tree trunk behind him. Flicked an ant, tore some leaves from a nearby plant, and tossed them. But he couldn't fight it. His eyelids dipped in the waning heat and he let them close while he rested, relying on his ears to do the scouting. *Just for a moment. The other two can watch.* He slipped and fell into a hard sleep and the boom of gunfire ripped him from the realm of dreams. He squeezed his eyes closed tight for a moment, trying to gain focus and glanced down the tree line for Franz.

His comrade knelt crouched down on one knee. He held his carbine in both hands, but wasn't aimed in. Standing with a bent back, he tried to see what Franz was looking at. Wolf snatched his carbine as two shadowed riders turned their horses in circles on the tiny dirt road.

One of the riders slumped on his horse's neck while the other held a pistol in one hand, reins in the other, as he searched for the shooter.

Wolf hobbled down the trees to the field trying to get closer to Franz. The massive rider capped his pistol three times and spurred his charger in the direction of Roberts. He pushed his horse hard, swiftly bringing it into a gallop. Covering the short distance in seconds, he reared his mount, pointing his gun down at the dismounted trooper, who looked tiny by comparison, almost like a child.

Roberts struggled with his carbine. Wolf couldn't tell if he'd dropped his cartridge or a bullet was stuck in the bore, but he was not firing his weapon. Frantically, Roberts's hands worked, tugging, pulling, and trying to find a way to get his firearm functioning again. The rider pushed his formidable charger into the underbrush within feet of Roberts.

"Run," Wolf said to himself. He limped down the line of timber hurrying toward his comrades. Foliage and tree branches blocked any kind of shot.

Roberts held a hand in an attempt to yield to the towering rider.

"Please, sir."

The horseman had broad shoulders and a long torso. His beard was full, wild and hung down to his chest, and his bearing was one of utter confidence. He was a man who knew he would be respected by sheer size alone. This was different. It wasn't just domineering physicality, it was class too. He had a proud, confident demeanor, like a man of great wealth. Wolf recognized yellow stars on his collar. The rider sat tall in the saddle, pointing his weapon at Roberts, waiting for something. It was as if he were in a Roman gladiatorial arena waiting for the emperor's verdict, life or death.

That's an officer. If we could capture an officer, we would heroes, he thought. Franz turned Wolf's way, his eyes alight with fear.

"Shoot him," Wolf called. Franz nodded dumbly and started to stalk toward the man, steps fragile and hesitant, but didn't fire upon the rebel officer.

Roberts stared from below. Fixing his weapon was of no use, the man had him dead to rights. He dropped his carbine and held up both his hands in surrender. "Please."

The officer said something, but Wolf couldn't hear him from his distance. Roberts shook his head no.

The broad rebel raised his pistol just a fraction and shot. The weapon capped off and Roberts sank to the ground.

"Roberts!"

Franz stiffened, his back gone rigid. The gunshot awakened him from his trance. His carbine shoved to his shoulder; he fired too quick. Smoke puffed into the air above him.

The officer calmly stared down the trees, locating his next victim. He kicked his horse's flank and galloped toward Franz.

Fumbling to reload his weapon, Franz's hands shook.

The carbine took its place at Wolf's shoulder. *Not today.* But the officer closed the distance so fast, he thought he'd merely ride Franz into the dusty ground.

Wolf squeezed his trigger and his shot sailed low of its target. The rider's horse shrieked in terror and tossed him into the browning clovers. The officer stretched out his hands to brace his fall and impacted the field with a roll. The horse crashed into the ground and slid. The injured animal rotated to its back, hideous screeching gnawing at the nerves of the men.

With a scrap of metal on metal, Franz drew his light saber, gaping at the downed enemy officer.

"Kill him, Franz!" Wolf shouted.

The officer's head moved and he was half sitting. He coughed, shaking his head as Franz brought his blade down near the officer's chest.

"Yield," Franz said.

The officer rolled and managed to release his long, straight, heavy saber. He lifted his straight sword, deflecting Franz's blade away. The officer spun around and slashed near Franz's belly, driving him backward.

Wolf continued his hobbling, hastily reloading his carbine as he neared. A bullet whistled by his ear, thudding into the tree behind him and he ducked as an afterthought. The officer's wounded companion bore down on him, still clutching the side of his horse as if every step equated to horrible pain. His face was covered in freckles and strawberry blond hair stuck out from beneath his hat. His revolver reported again with a flash and Wolf dropped to a knee. The rider closed in and Wolf couldn't wedge the linen cartridge in the breech.

Wolf dropped his gun and drew his pistol. The two combatants fired at one another in an excited frenzy, until both guns went dry. Each man clicked his empty pistol, caught in the repetitive fury of a fight.

The horse veered away from Wolf and galloped for another twenty yards, until the rider slipped from its back and collapsed on the ground. Whether or not it was Wolf's bullet didn't matter, the man was down.

The ring of metal on metal caught Wolf's ear and he turned back when he heard a cry. The rebel battered his heavy cavalry sword over and over into Franz's saber, like a blacksmith flattening hot metal. The young trooper fell onto his back, overcome by the rage of the giant. The rebel yelled as he beat his blade with a violent wrath.

With every strike, Franz became slower until the enemy's sword bit jaggedly into Franz's neck. Wolf's jaw dropped. His friend had been cut down before his very eyes.

The rebel officer stood for a moment, his chest panting, his eyes brimming with violence like a wild animal. Wolf stopped his reload, letting his gun find its holster. *Not both of them. This bastard.* His blood surged to his face. His belly filled with the nervous excitement of taking it to a rival, but this was different. If he lost, this man would certainly kill him and he didn't care. He didn't care how big the bastard was he went up against. He only cared for revenge. He drew his light saber and charged.

As quick as he could manage, he rushed the officer from his flank and swung his sword savagely at the man's head. The rebel half turned into the strike, but it was too late as Wolf's blade caught him atop the skull. The officer reeled away in shock. "For Franz!" Wolf swung again and the officer deflected his blade with ease, throwing Wolf's blade to the side. Blood trickled down his enemy's face and soaked into his beard with a glistening red.

"You killed them!" Wolf yelled.

The officer's voice came like a deep boom. "This is war, boy. Men die. Boys die easier."

Wolf jabbed the point of his saber, trying to pierce his breast. Easier to kill by stabbing than slashing, that's what Wilhelm had told them. The broad man stepped back with surprising agility and slapped the back edge of his saber hard onto the top of Wolf's wrist. Pain shot deep into the bone, shivering along his arm. His arm froze. Unable to obey commands. The dampened sound of the saber hitting the clovers signaled his rapid defeat.

A soldier without a weapon was a naked man. Defenseless, he stood awaiting his judgment. His pistol was empty. His carbine lay somewhere in the field. He stared at his hand in disbelief as the feeling started to return. Running wasn't an option. He would easily be overcome by the athletic commander. Wolf didn't bother to raise his hands. No use in asking for mercy from a man you just tried to kill.

The brutish officer pointed his sword at Wolf. The tip hovered near his neck threatening to end him.

"Better to die on my feet. Even if it's to you scum." Wolf spit on the ground. He'd lost fights, but never one with his life on the line.

The officer did something Wolf didn't expect. He smiled. Blood ran down the side of his skull and trickled into the crevices of his thick beard, a broad grin on his thick lips. "Damn glad they ain't all like you, but won't matter soon because this war is about to be finished." He laughed and took his other hand and brought it up and beneath his slouch hat. He rubbed his bloody fingers in front of his face. With a flick of his wrist, he flung the blood away. "I should kill you for what you done to my horse. That was a first-class mount. Cost a pretty penny."

"I should kill you for what you did to my friends." Franz's body was limp, an unmoving form on the ground.

"We all lost friends in this war. That's what war is, losing your friends, your brothers, your fathers, your sons. The goal is to make you lose more than me. Then the war will be done."

Wolf shook with rage and met the tall officer's dark eyes. The officer regarded him coolly, like he was disciplining a little boy, unimpressed at best.

"Tend to your friend. You can die another day." He lifted his sword from Wolf's neck and turned around and grabbed the reins of his comrade's horse.

"You're making a mistake. I'll get you one day."

The officer pet the animal for a moment, soothing her startled nerves. "No, you won't. You'll be lucky to come out of this war alive." His words were soaked with confidence, like he'd seen the future and knew the fate of every man.

Wolf eyed Franz's carbine. *If I can grab that gun and fire quick, I might catch him off guard. That will show him. If he can bleed, he can die.* Wolf lunged for the gun and rapidly brought it upward, setting his sights on the hulking officer.

The rebel didn't pay him any heed. He continued to soothe the unsettled beast.

"Boy, that carbine won't fire, so don't waste your time."

"You lie," he spat. His finger touched the trigger, expecting it to give beneath him.

"No, I don't. Look at it."

Wolf's eyes peered down at the weapon. His hated enemy was correct. No cartridge was loaded in the chamber. With a flick of his wrist, he flung the lever out. The officer hoisted the body of his fellow soldier on the back of the dead man's horse.

Fingers scraped the edge of Wolf's cartridge pouch, fumbling for a linen-clad messenger of death.

The officer turned and eyed him with disapproval and shook his head. "Charles was a good lad." He marched the horse quick for Wolf and raised his straight double-edged sword, swinging it down hard onto the barrel of the carbine. *Clank!* A spark leapt in the air. The carbine somersaulted from his hands and the officer slashed his blade across his face. The tip bit, not deeply, but lacerated his skin, stinging like fire.

In shock, Wolf lifted a hand to his cheek. Thick blood bubbled from the wound, trickling down to his jaw.

"I told you not to waste my time. Enough blood's been spilt."

Weaponless, Wolf held his cheek with one hand, watching the man with hate.

With the grace of a man born in the saddle, the rebel steered his new mount near Wolf, pointing his sword at his neck. "Stop trying to think of ways to kill General Wade Hampton and tend your friend." His eyes went from fierce to sympathetic. "He's almost gone." He watched Wolf for a moment, the steeliness of war creeping back in his dark orbs. "Not afraid to die, are you?"

Wolf stood silent.

Shaking his head, Hampton said, "This war has gone on too long." He let out a high-pitched whoop that seemed too high for the gruff man's voice, and spurred his horse away. Dirt kicked into the air, masking his retreat back to the road. The horse's hooves thumped and they disappeared.

Wolf turned to his friend. He bent down. Blood had pooled in Franz's mouth, running down his cheek like a crimson stream. It wetted his blond curls and stained his boyish face.

"Franz," he whispered. "Hang on. We're going to get you help."

"Papa," he managed to utter.

"He's coming." Wolf looked out into the woods, searching for comrades. "Help!" he called out.

When he turned back, Franz's eyes were glassy like they were marbles instead of flesh and blood. Wolf pleaded his case with a corpse. Angry tears flowed down his cheeks, stinging his facial wound until he heard the sound of boots crunching through underbrush. He glanced into the timber and blue-coated men emerged from the trees.

"He's dead," he muttered to them.

Wilhelm's erect form shoved through the others. He dropped his carbine and fell to his knees. He grabbed his son by the collar and pulled him close.

"Franz. Boy. Wake up," Wilhelm whispered. His voice grew harsher and more distraught with every passing moment. Franz's arms tumbled to his sides, lifeless. Wilhelm squeezed his son, gripping his head as if he were cradling the boy as a baby to sleep. Tears rolled down the father's face and he hushed German words upon his dead son.

Wolf stared at his hands drenched in his comrade's blood. "He killed them," he said below his breath. He shook his head in disgust at how the man had disarmed him with ease and slaughtered his friends like they were chickens.

The other troopers spread out, taking position along the tree line, peering out at the road with carbines in hand.

"How many, Wolf?" Cobb hissed. He pushed his black top hat up on his head in an attempt to see better.

"There were two."

"Where's Roberts?"

"Hampton shot him."

Cobb gave him a questioning side glance. "Who's Hampton?"

"General Wade Hampton, sir."

Keeping himself close to the ground, he urgently stepped around Franz next to Wolf, his short-whiskered face nearing his subordinate's. "You mean General Wade Hampton of Stuart's command? Be clear."

Everything was a daze and the green-leafed timber was a hazy mass of forestry. "He was hulking, dark beard and fierce eyes, his hair curled around the edges of his slouch hat. He wore three plain gold stars on his collar.

"No wreath around them?"

"Ah, yes, they had a wreath."

"The Brute himself." Cobb shook his head to the sounds of Wilhelm's sobs behind them. "He got Roberts too? Dammit."

"He shot him before he fought Franz. I took a shot but only killed his horse."

"The giant must have been pissed." Cobb reached out and grabbed Wolf's shoulder and squeezed. "You stayed alive. That's all we can ask." He took his hand and turned his private's face in his direction. "Lucky to come away with only this scratch. Not many do against such a foe." He half stood and pointed at Franz. "Collect him and find Roberts."

CHAPTER 20

July 2nd, 1863
Hunterstown, Pennsylvania

With the discovery of General Hampton's South Carolinians, Sergeant Cobb and his remaining men returned to report their findings to the 13th Michigan command. The squad's mood was soured by the loss of Franz, but was lifted a fraction by the revelation of Roberts back at the camp. He'd run the whole way, only sustaining a gunshot wound to the wrist from a somewhat chivalrous Hampton.

When they'd reached the column again, they heard that elements of the 6th Michigan Cavalry had already engaged with rebel cavalry in Hunterstown, a small town filled with decaying buildings built almost eighty years earlier. The Confederates had ceded the village to the federal troops and the few buildings brimmed with General Kilpatrick's cavalry division led by Custer's 6th and 13th Michigan Cavalries.

A two-story red-brick inn held a cluster of horses and General Kilpatrick's 3rd Division Cavalry Corps flags. Wolf led Roberts to a house that had been taken up by Union surgeons as a makeshift hospital.

"Give me your hand," Wolf said. He helped the trooper to the ground. Roberts held his wrist with a bloody rag wrapped around it gritting his teeth. "It hurts so bad."

"I know. We'll get you help." They walked up the steps and knocked on the door.

A man dressed as a butcher answered. Gore soaked his apron. His white sleeves were cuffed at his elbows and his hands were dyed red. When he pushed his glasses higher, he streaked blood onto his sharp nose point. His muttonchops hung off his jaw.

"What?" his voice was hurried and worried with a slight British accent.

"Sir, he's been shot."

The butcher scrutinized Roberts. "Looks well enough to me."

A man screamed from another room. It was gut-punching, as if he were in the process of disembowelment.

Another man in a tattered blue uniform stepped from behind him. "I need to go. I need to go," he stammered. Eyes that couldn't focus darted around the town. He shoved past the butcher and bumbled outside.

The man watched him escape. "Gary, Jesus. I told you to watch him," he yelled back over his shoulder.

"Sir, are you a doctor?"

"I'm a bloody surgeon and I'm busy. What do you want?"

Wolf took Roberts's arm and held it to the surgeon's face. "He's been shot in the wrist."

The surgeon sighed and gestured for them to enter the house of horrors. "Come in." Piercing screams echoed off the wall. "Somebody find me some morphine and chloroform." He pointed back into another room. "Wait there." A nurse mopped the hallway, smearing all manner of fluids. She regarded them with sad orbs for eyes.

Roberts and Wolf entered a room with a dozen other men and took a seat in the corner. Shot, gutted, shattered, and broken men littered the floor around them. All wore the blue of the Union and all were mangled. One of the men sat with his back along the wall. A bandage covered his head and eye. Scarlet seeped from the white dressing.

"Who you with?"

"Custer's Michigan Cavalry Brigade."

"I heard 'Old Death' is from there," the soldier gestured with his chin in the surgeon's direction. "We're the remains of 157th New York." A man in the room moaned and another cried tears flowing down whiskery cheeks.

"Luckily, you won't have to see the fighting like we do. Prancing around on your ponies. Bunch of bowlegs."

Wolf narrowed his eyes, sensing his contempt. "We seen some."

The soldier looked down at the ground, holding his knees with his arms. "No, you ain't. Not like what's going down in Gettysburg. Smooth-cheeked Barlow thought it was a marvelous idea to move his line onto a small elevation in the land. Not a bad thought unless you're creating a bulge in the line." He coughed in his hand and his eye squinted in pain. He waited a moment, digesting his torment. "First it was the Baron von Gilsa's men that got flanked. Then Ames's brigade. They broke quick. Then it was our turn." He shook his head in disgust. "The 157th was supposed to do our own bit of flanking. We marched up Carlisle Road parallel to the rest of our boys and wheeled around to do the flanking of Doles's Georgians. 'Cept when we marched out, Krzyanowski's brigade had already been shattered like a brittle twig and the other two runnin' left us alone and surrounded. They was on either flank and our front and they poured lead into us like they was shootin' turkey. Didn't take long before we collapsed. Four hundred and thirty-one men went out there. I don't know how many of us are left, but I'd say more than half of us are gone. The entire XI Corps is on the run."

Wolf gulped. An entire corps was shattered in a few hours. Things did not bode well for Lincoln's boys again as what was becoming bloody routine work.

"Roberts," the surgeon said. He waved him into another room. Both the men followed in dread. They sat the short thief in a chair and he clutched his arm as if they might steal it. The surgeon snatched a barbarous rag and wiped his hands on it. Pale hands and feet overflowed in a nearby bucket. A crimson-drenched bone saw lay haphazardly on the table.

"Get those off," the surgeon said, pointing to Roberts's makeshift bandage.

Two aides lifted a body from the table and carried the patient from the room. Wolf didn't know if the man was alive or dead, only that he wasn't moving.

"Put your arm on the table." Roberts apprehensively did as the surgeon asked.

"What are you going to do?" Roberts asked.

The surgeon grabbed his forearm and squeezed. "Does that hurt?"

"Ow, doc."

"How about there?" His eyes were magnified on the other side of his glasses.

"Yeah, I got shot."

The surgeon made him place his injured limb in the air. He poked around the exit wound. "You did well stopping the bleeding."

Roberts gritted his teeth and growled.

"You'll be okay." Wolf tried to comfort the man by giving his shoulder a squeeze.

"I bloody well know that," Roberts snapped.

Clapping his hands together, he finished his inspection. "Can you move your fingers?"

Roberts moved his thumb and front two fingers.

The surgeon released him and wiped his face with the back of his permanently stained hands. "Your bones aren't broke so that's good. I don't see or feel any bullet fragments and I don't see a reason to take off the hand today. We'll bind it and hope you don't get an infection."

"Take my hand?" Roberts held his hand up and stared at it.

The surgeon raised his eyebrows. "I could take it as a precaution? It'll be quick."

Roberts paled. "I'd rather keep me hand."

The surgeon ignored him prepping a bowl of water. "You might not have much use of it, but at least you'll still have one for now."

The surgeon poured water around the wound and scrubbed it with a rag. Roberts groaned loudly. Then he bound Roberts's wrist tight with a bow.

"Try to keep this clean. No dirt. Change the bandage when you can."

"Do you have extra bandages?"

The surgeon snorted. "If it turns black, I take it off. Now, get out of here. I don't have time for small talk."

The young men nodded. "Thank you."

They escaped the charnel house and breathed a sigh of relief as the door closed behind them.

"Horrible in there."

Roberts nursed his arm. "You're telling me. He wanted to take my hand."

They untied their horses and questioned ranks of blue cavalry until they found the company near the edge of the small town.

Gray-headed Shugart waved them over. "God be praised, you're all right. Let me see the wound."

Roberts held out his arm for inspection.

"Try and keep it clean and I'll be sure to pray for a quick recovery."

"How's Wilhelm?" Wolf asked.

The elder Quaker turned, viewing soldiers over his shoulder. "Hasn't said much. We laid his son near the church for burial."

Wolf steered Billy to the tall, mournful corporal. "Wilhelm."

The aged corporal slowly turned toward him. His eyes were red-rimmed and simmered with angry sadness, even his mustache seemed to droop with pain.

"No son should die before his father."

Wolf nodded fiercely, feeling his gut churn with anger. "No, they shouldn't."

The first sergeant walked his horse down the company column. "Company, we are about to ride in support of the 6th. Looks like our friend, Wade Hampton, has turned around to face us like a man."

"Did he say Hampton?" Roberts said, cradling his wrist.

Grim determination filled Wolf's eyes. "He did." And he knew Wilhelm heard him too. The men didn't say a word. They knew revenge awaited them and sooner than any of them could have expected.

CHAPTER 21

July 2nd, 1863
Near Felty Farm, Pennsylvania

The regiment started to move at a shrill bugle call of advance. They rode only a half mile before they ran into elements of the 6th Michigan along the road. Companies of the regiment had taken cover on a western ridge, dismounted under a wooded area while a single company stood in the lane, still upon their mounts like they'd been forgotten to be issued orders.

The 13th Michigan took their column to the eastern ridge on the other side of the 7th Michigan. While the 7th was also on foot, the 13th held its position mounted, mobile and ready for rapid deployment. With a quick command, they could support any of the flanks or surge where the fighting was heaviest.

"He's just waiting for us," Cobb said. He looked nervously at their flank. "It's gotta be a trap." He pointed. "See. I don't like it. This is how we get done in."

"Quit your croaking, Sergeant," O'Reilly said from behind.

Cobb muttered under his breath about his bad feelings for the place.

Green corn with tawny tops and pale caramel wheat fields stretched between the adversaries on either side of the lane. A two-story maroon-brick farm perched near the Union troops along with a three-story stone barn. Another smaller red-brick farmhouse was situated near the Confederates, almost as if these two farms represented the divided nation.

The road sloped at a slight incline until it reached the mounted gray troopers leering from across the way. In the trees on their flanks, dismounted cavalry was positioned behind split log fences, rocks, and trees. It appeared to be a quality defensive location, providing protection to the rebels from any sort of credible attack.

"Any move we make will be at a disadvantage. Those troopers will hide and blast away at us. Not good ground. No sir. There be plenty of the bastards too."

The sergeant was right. Looking out, it was clear that hundreds of Hampton's men held the woods and road, most of his men waiting near a curve over a half mile away. Wavy heat emanated from the ground as if it competed with the sun to see which one could cook the men into biscuits first.

"Over a thousand?" Corporal Shugart asked, his beard quivering as he spoke.

"Looks to be," Cobb said. He rubbed his bristly chin hard. "Maybe if we get some cannon going. Loosen them up before we engage. It's the only way." He turned and looked back toward Hunterstown. They knew Pennington was with the column but would have to traverse to the front in order to make himself a player in the fight.

"Steady men," Lieutenant Wells said as he walked his horse by.

"Always brave words," Van Horn said.

"Always behind," Wolf finished.

"Quiet in the ranks," O'Reilly said, following the lieutenant.

The short Irishman always seemed to be hearing something from the men, knowing their issues and angst before they became anything more than a soldier's complaints.

Down the line, the black and red guidon with the golden wolf flipped and fluttered like a rippling stream.

"Will you look at that. Pure suicide," Cobb said, pointing.

Along the contested route a company from the 6th Michigan walked their horses. The day was beginning to fade and their sabers didn't reflect the sun anymore than tarnished silver.

Wolf watched Wilhelm for a reaction. He didn't say anything, only passively observing the troopers with indifference. His face even looked like he longed to join them, for surely death was better than knowing that he'd never see his son again.

"The Boy General," Roberts said, pointing with his reins.

"Where?" Lent asked hurriedly.

"There, in front."

Sure enough, an officer led the company in a non-regulation black coat and pants and broad-brimmed hat with golden curls resting on his navy collar. The roughly fifty cavalrymen hastened their pace to a trot.

"Why aren't they spreading out?" Lent asked the men around him.

"Road's too narrow," Wilhelm said. "They'll die." The words fell from his mouth with yearning to join them.

The company maintained an almost perfect column as they galloped to their deaths, Custer at the head.

Meanwhile, Pennington and Elder's batteries were arriving. One could hardly tell if they were Union or Confederate at this point. Some were shirtless, others wore only shirts, a few wore regulation caps, but the rest wore civilian headwear: straw, felt, bowler, derby, and farmer style, showing no uniformity and the broadness that the civilian volunteer brought to the field. A slender man directed the battery and the artillerymen unlimbered their horse artillery with practiced efficiency, trying to not gawk in horror at the charging horsemen.

At almost three hundred yards, Custer's sword went level with his shoulder and they shifted into a full gallop. The Confederate horsemen stood their ground, having amassed past the farmhouse. Ranks upon ranks of Hampton's cavalry. The South Carolina palmetto whipped defiantly in the breeze, unfazed by such a brazen display of bravado. Or was it saluting the men it was about to send to the next world?

Volleys rippled from the trees like five-hundred hammers striking nails at once. A few horses and riders went down into the dirt but the barely fifty horsemen kept riding.

"Dear God," Shugart said, looking up at the sky. "Protect our brave warriors, for they do your good work."

The Union cavalryman ignored the deadly bullets and soon the rebels were committed to fight an enemy that should have withered and fled before them. With the crash of flesh on flesh, steel on steel, man on man, Custer speared the company into Hampton's ranks. The tiny roadway forced the men into instantaneous melee fighting. Then the next rank of men crashed into them. And the next rank. Men and horses wailed alike, the horses the worse of the two.

The riders cut through the first ranks of rebels and barely slowed as sabers swung wide and pistols blared their violent song. When Custer hit the second rank of rebels, he had significantly less men and his charge lost all steam. The blue and gray melded together as one tried desperately to kill the other in the madness of close combat.

Wolf's heart gushed with the brave glory that Custer must have had to lead such men. He watched the black-hatted indestructible Custer's saber dance until he toppled from his horse, disappearing in the chaos.

"No," Wolf whispered. "Not him." Not the man who had led with such fearlessness. The bold general that led from the front, not asking his men for anymore than he'd give himself. Not the man that gave them hope.

"He's down," Cobb said. He ran a hand over his horse's mane. "Only a matter of time. We always lose the good ones." He looked around. "Just be thankful that wasn't us."

Shaking his head, he said, "No." He touched the sash at his neck, running his finger over the emblazoned wolf. "Not today." His spurs scraped his horse, jolting it out of formation. Billy tossed his head in annoyance but obeyed.

"Private!" Cobb shouted at him. "Get back in line."

"No!" He spurred Billy into a gallop.

Wolf's saber screeched from its sheath. He held it in the air, curved and bright. "To the general." He didn't bother to see if anyone followed him. Billy moved into a gallop and Wolf clutched his saber at an angle as he charged the fray of swirling blue and gray horsemen.

Billy's hooves chewed green corn stalks and dirt, tossing both alike. Wolf leaned tight to Billy's neck, avoiding flying corn while making himself a smaller target for whistling bullets. Dismounted rebels took shots at him as he pounded over the field, but he kept his distance, praying that he was a quick enough moving target to avoid a bullet.

More rebel horsemen were pushing in on the sides of the Union company, threatening to envelop them, precipitating certain annihilation. Wolf drove Billy right into their backs. The rebels didn't notice until he was beside them, screaming and slashing like a madman.

He sliced a horseman's upper back as he raced by the man. He had no way of knowing the man's fate as he blurred by. With a wicked backswing, he brought his saber across his body, cutting into a buckskin-clad thigh. The rebel hollered in surprise, pushing his pistol and hand on his wound trying to hold his blood inside his body. Billy led him even deeper into the horde of dueling cavalrymen.

Dust and gun smoke enveloped everything in the fog of war. "General?" Wolf called out. He spun Billy in a circle. Gunshots echoed around him. The clash of sabers chanted a metallic melody. The cries of wounded men and the desperate gurgles of expiration filled his ears.

A rebel with a flat-brimmed hat forced his way in front of Wolf. "Die!" He fired a pistol and flames screamed from the barrel, but his shot missed. He cocked his thumb over the hammer again.

Wolf swiped at him with his blade, swooshing air.

A trooper in blue crashed into his opponent and the rebel fell from his horse. More Union horsemen joined him, shooting and slashing with sabers. Sergeant Cobb's black top hat disappeared in a swirl of sabers. "To victory!" he called as he passed by.

Wilhelm was there. His face was a twisted thing of rage and hate. As if he'd become some sort of unstoppable machine. His sword flashed with speed and utter precision. Killing was the only result. Men collapsed in his wake. His horse seemed to know exactly where to go without him directing it. He hacked a man three times in the neck and whirled backward and flicked his saber into the chest of another man who bellowed as the blade bit deep.

Wolf prodded his horse toward the center of the fighting. He traded saber strikes with another rebel and the man disappeared. Coughing in the dust and smoke, he scanned the ground. A man in black lay on his side and Wolf's stomach leapt in fear. The general was trapped beneath a fallen animal. Custer fired a pistol around him, avoiding the trampling hooves as they ran by. Wolf steered Billy at the man. The horse slipped on the body of a fallen trooper, but kept going.

"Sir," Wolf yelled at the general. The general spun and pointed his pistol at him. "Bloody hell, trooper."

A rebel rode hard at the general, his saber drawn. Yanking the reins to the side, Wolf put Billy between him and his fallen leader. The Confederate horseman sneered with missing teeth as he jabbed at him like his sword was a spear. The tip jabbed to his right, missing his body. Wolf twisted in his saddle one way, dodging, and then the other. He swatted a third thrust from the rebel and lunged with his saber, piercing the man's chest. It was as if the man's body resisted every inch of the blade, instead forcing it to grind slowly. The Confederate's eyes gaped in shock.

"Ja!" Wolf ripped his sword free with a flourish of fresh crimson spraying into the air. The rebel's head rolled backward and he slipped from his saddle.

"Sir, hurry." Wolf offered his hand to the general. They clasped fingers and he tugged Custer from beneath his dead animal. He blew hard out his nostrils, fluttering his mustache, and took his arm, using it to swing behind Wolf with ease.

"Fall back!" Custer yelled.

Wolf yanked Billy's reins leading him out. Custer fired a round point blank into a rebel horseman. The man cried and clutched his side.

"Come on, Billy," Wolf urged. The horse's pace increased in speed and they navigated falling horsemen. They galloped back toward the Union lines. In chaotic cluster, the troopers hightailed it to the safety of their own men. Billy sped across the field, spit flying from the corners of his mouth, lips smacking, and down the road leading back to Hunterstown. They only relaxed when surrounded by Union men.

Colonel Gray of the 6th Michigan peered disapprovingly at the general riding double with Wolf. He had a neatly trimmed beard that was more silver than anything else and clear tell-all eyes. He removed his cap and wiped his sweaty brow.

"By God, man, do you have a death wish?" Wolf wasn't sure who he spoke too.

Custer patted him on the shoulder, breathing hard. "Fine scrap, huh, lad?"

"Yes, sir. Love. A. Scrap." He lowered his head in exhaustion and relief, having survived the fight. Disbelief at the sequence of events shocked him into an unblinking state.

"Brave ride."

He didn't know if the general was referring to himself or to his intervention that surely saved the man's life from capture or worse. Custer dismounted from behind Wolf, favoring a leg.

"Just a bruise. Get me a new horse." Aides ran to get the general a new mount.

Gray looked up at the sky. "Surely, we aren't going to charge them again? My A Company broke on them."

An aide led a new mount to Custer. He soothed the animal with his hand and looked over at a starry-eyed Wolf. "That's better. No, Colonel Gray, but we've drawn the angst of the enemy, so let's give them a little taste of Northern lead, shall we?"

Gray nodded his head in acknowledgement of a superior. "It'll be a pleasure, sir."

Rebel soldiers followed hard on the remnants of the single company that had so fearlessly thrown themselves into the rebel ranks. Enemy horsemen pushed their horses to the limit, pounding the earth with rapid hooves, but Pennington was waiting.

"Canister shot!" called Pennington. Artillerymen carried cylindrical canister shot back to the guns. Each tin-cased projectile was dipped in turpentine to prevent corrosion and filled with roughly twenty-seven lead or iron balls, like wicked walnuts of death, and packed with sawdust to create more cohesion inside the shot. This particular shell was sealed on either end with a wooden disc and a bag filled with gunpowder in the rear. When fired, the iron balls would propel forth, shredding entire blocks of men as if they'd been peppered with a giant shotgun blast.

The 6th, 7th, and 13th Michigan Regiments awaited the rebels, eager to deal their own deadly barrage, most dismounted behind tree cover. The rebels charged, horses bounding for them, but with thunderous booms they withered beneath the iron canister balls of Pennington's six guns. Rapid volleys from the dismounted cavalrymen quickly turned the Confederates around and they fled back toward their lines in disarray.

Custer pushed his mustache back up to his nose in thought. "I think we gave them a bit better than we got." He turned toward Pennington's battery. "Well done, sir."

The slender man tipped his hat with a smile. Custer turned his horse toward Wolf and stuck out his hand. "I'll take a Wolverine over a Reb any day of the week."

Wolf eyed the gloved hand hesitantly. He wasn't supposed to interact with a general on friendly terms or as equals. They were far above his station.

"Shake my hand." Custer gestured down at his hand with his chin.

Wolf took it, gripping it, unafraid. "I disobeyed orders, sir."

Custer smiled. "Haven't we all?" He released Wolf's hand and raised his chin. "Thank you for disobeying orders, Private." He squinted at Wolf, judging his character. The night rapidly approached the opposing sides with equal embrace and a grayness was gently veiling the field. "Private?"

"Private Johannes Wolf, General, sir. F Company the 13th Michigan."

Custer narrowed an eye. "Private Wolf. Hmm. You were the boy that brought me the message the other day. I'll see that your commanding officer knows my appreciation. You and your men." He turned away, reliving the battle. "It could have gotten sticky without you." He didn't speak for a moment. "Very good." The general had put the issue to bed.

Wolf's unit waited nearby, bloodied and dirty men.

A big smile split Bart's chubby, bearded cheeks. "Yes."

Wilhelm's eyes were flat as if he'd died already.

Custer put his hand to his forehead and saluted his men. "Well done, lads!" Wolf returned the salute.

"Let's find our company." Wilhelm said, giving the general an unenthusiastic salute. The small group of riders walked their horses back to the 13th Michigan and Hampton's men vanished into the night.

CHAPTER 22

July 2nd, 1863
Two Taverns, Pennsylvania

The men journeyed through the evening. Exhaustion hounded them and Wolf dozed in his saddle. One could not really sleep atop a horse, only partially so, the sway of the animal could put one into a deep trance-like state, especially the exhausted cavalry force marching through the night to Two Taverns.

Two Taverns was a hamlet between Littlestown and Gettysburg consisting of two rival taverns. Rumor trickled down the grapevine that Kilpatrick's pursuit of Stuart was cut short and his division had been recalled back to Meade and Gettysburg where an epic battle was teetering in the balance. The men were too tired to express any fear or excitement.

They crossed York Road, then followed a dirt pathway roughly seven miles until stumbling into the small village in the early morning. The two taverns sat across the thoroughfare from one another, filled to capacity with officers. The Dancing Lass was run by a grumpy Irishman who didn't allow colored folk inside, while The Mule was owned by a Dutchman who didn't allow the Irish. This dusky morning, they accepted all Union men.

"Keep the horses saddled," Wells said as he passed the men. "We must be ready to depart at a moment's notice." He turned his horse around in a short circle. "Which ones are part of Sergeant Cobb's unit?"

Wilhelm raised a tired hand, his back still straight despite everything he'd been through in the last day. "We are, sir."

Wells eyed Wilhelm's corporal chevrons with a slightly higher level of trust than any of the privates. "Gather the men that charged out of command today after being told not to do so."

"Yes, Lieutenant."

The men already knew who they were. They'd been there. One of their number hadn't returned. Sergeant Cobb was none of the men's favorite. He was a lech and a drunk. But there was a bit of fondness for the jilted sergeant, one that Wolf knew the men would miss even if only in the heat of battle. Truly, it had been a miracle more of them hadn't been slain in their attempt to save the general.

The few men formed a grim, tired line.

"First Sergeant O'Reilly," Wells called out. The tall lieutenant glared at them with apparent disgust and lack of discipline, towering from his horse's back. It was more than discipline, it was their station in life, and Wolf was sure that nothing they could do would elevate them in the haughty lieutenant's eyes.

The regiment wasn't bothering with tents, a true bivouac; they just collapsed on the ground to sleep in the grass beneath trees with haversacks and bedrolls as pillows. The midnight weather was pleasant enough. Only the faint buzz of mosquitos to drone the men to slumber.

The short first sergeant marched over to the men. He looked like he'd recently awoken from a half-day's sleep, well rested and ready to pick a fight with a tiger.

"Poorest discipline I've ever seen," O'Reilly said. "Riding out like that. Very well should have been killed, each and every man. Death wishes, all of ya. Then our company would be down a dozen men." He shook his ruddy cheeks in disapproval. He peered at Wolf with a tiny twinkle in his eye that evaporated with stern command. "I would have had Sergeant Cobb court-martialed for such conduct, leading you men out like that, but alas, he has gone to be judged for his sins at the pearly gates. And they were a plenty. Suppose if it wasn't a bullet, it'd been the French Fever." He stomped his foot on the ground. "Not too hot down there is it?"

The men were too tired to laugh, but a tiny smile formed on Wolf's lips, remembering their sinful sergeant.

"Men," Lieutenant Wells said, cutting in. Wolf tried not to roll his eyes away from the junior officer. His smooth cheeks and educated demeanor gave him away as a rich enlistee with not much in common with a rank and file man, a true blue blood. "You must follow orders. I totally concur with the first sergeant's assessment. This is a punishable offense. Your actions threatened the entirety of our company and command." He tersely shook his head. "And each and every one of you followed the other like a pack of dogs wishing to die." He collected himself. "I cannot comprehend why, but these orders are coming from the general himself, and I cannot disobey them."

The lieutenant removed a piece of paper from his jacket. Tiny fires gave weak illumination, the darkness stealing any light, and the note hovered near his eyes. They were missing precious sleep, for who knew what the next day would bring with the enemy so close.

"Corporal Berles." Wells gestured at the man. Berles held his back like he had a steel rod for a spine. He appeared weary, but not tired, like he could run ten miles with a snap of his fingers. Berles stepped forward. "Sir."

"In the absence of a sergeant, you are to be bestowed the field promotion of sergeant. You will maintain the same unit you were with before. I would like to say that while the First Sergeant has intimate knowledge of this company, I advocated against this promotion based on the previous insubordinate actions you've taken."

"Thank you, sir."

Roberts snickered and Wolf averted his eyes in mirth.

Wells blinked for a moment, deciding whether or not the erect German was mocking him.

O'Reilly corrected a smile on his lips. "Attention, lads. Let's get this done so I can get some damn sleep. Quiet."

"Yes, let's." Wells continued to stare down at his paper. He appeared to be having a hard time coming up with the right words.

Wolf closed his eyes for a moment shut-eye threatening to take him while standing.

"Private Wolf," the lieutenant said. He eyed the men, not knowing which one of the grubby enlisted men was which.

Wolf's eyes snapped open. *Dear God, what now?* "Yes, sir."

Wells's eyes went back down to the paper. "You must have done something right today, because you are promoted to corporal in Sergeant Berles's place. Step forward."

Wolf strode out of line. The first sergeant approached and looked up at him. "Two along each arm. Not too high." He handed over four cloth, yellow chevrons and clapped Wolf's back. He paced back to Berles and gave him an additional chevron for his sleeves.

"You men have been rewarded today, but the colonel will have order. Is that understood?"

Wolf's smile could not be stopped. The soldiers all spoke loud. "Yes, sir."

"You men are dismissed," Wells said with an irritated wave of his hand. "Come, First Sergeant." About facing, the lieutenant pretended the men now didn't exist.

O'Reilly winked at the men and followed the junior officer. "Carry on."

The two disappeared into the camp.

The newly appointed sergeant's promotion appeared to mean nothing to him. His voice croaked a harsh whisper, "Night."

The men watched him disappear under a blanket, kicking off his boots to get comfortable.

Talking to a man about this lost son wasn't something Wolf knew how to do. How did one broach the subject with the wound so fresh? He didn't even know how to feel about the loss of his friend. A sense of guilt filled the void. Should have done more. Never should have left him alone. Should have told him to run. Every replay of the scenario left Wolf embittered to the outcome because in the end nothing changed. Franz was still dead. Hampton still free.

Roberts smacked his back joyfully. "First battle and already promoted. Fast track." The short man gave Wolf a mock salute with his uninjured hand.

Raising his chin high into the air, he said. "Now, go dig a latrine, you lowest of the lows, Private. You disgust me with your private ways."

"Don't you go turning into Wells on me."

"Not a chance."

"Say, how about we hit a nip of the old bottle instead and celebrate?"

Roberts gave Wolf a mischievous smile and pulled out a thick, unmarked bottle.

"Where'd you get that?"

"Cobb ain't gonna drink it."

"You stole it from a dead man?"

Black eyebrows narrowed. "Look, Wolf. The man's dead, trust me, he would have wanted it this way. It honors him. And besides my wrist is killing me. I need something to stem the pain."

Wolf sighed with a smirk. "Uncork that."

Roberts stuck the bottle in his mouth and ripped the cork free and spit it out.

"You don't think you'll need that again?"

Roberts took a swig shaking his head. He grimaced for a minute as the fiery liquid burned his throat. "Nah. I think you and me can take care of this."

Wolf took a drink of the foul liquor and almost lost the contents of his empty stomach. He coughed and handed the bottle back to his comrade. "That man must have been drunk all the time. That's wicked strong."

"Pretty sure he was," Roberts said. He tipped the liquor back. He spit some out as a rider barreled at them, hastily shoving the bottle behind his back.

The horse exhaled loudly, chest heaving.

"You," the horseman pointed at them. "Is this Kilpatrick's command?"

"Yes, sir. Well, only a portion. This is Custer's brigade."

"Where is he?"

Wolf stood tall, it was almost impossible for him to make out anything other than horses and men, but he knew the 13th Michigan was in the middle of the column and Custer was with the 6th near the front.

"He'd be further up the way from here. He's camping with the 6th Michigan."

"Thank you." The aide spurred his horse back into stride.

"I wonder what that's about?" Roberts said.

"No idea. Nobody tells us anything."

"Sometimes it's better not to know." The bottle emerged from behind his back. "It's best."

The young men laughed, trading off on the bottle into the early morning.

CHAPTER 23

Early Morning July 3rd, 1863
Stuart's Headquarters, Pennsylvania

Hampton knocked on the door to a simple two-story farmhouse off of York Pike. The cicadas and katydids screeched in the light of the full moon, singing night songs in the trees. He was tired, but felt it the most in the backs of his eyes. The combination of the war, the days in the saddle, and the fact it was well past midnight all made him feel like a man twice his age. He removed his riding gloves one at a time and tucked them into his belt. He didn't suspect he would get much sleep tonight.

The door was opened abruptly by General Stuart's aide-de-camp, W.W. Blackford. His eyes spoke volumes of weariness. Hampton figured this was the position they were in after three years of fighting, wary and tired.

"William," Hampton said with familiarity. He knew the bushy brown-mustached man well and would treat him as an equal in the after-hours meeting with Stuart.

William nodded his head in respect. "General."

Hampton removed his black slouch hat and made sure his straight sword didn't catch the doorway on his way inside. He was surprised to not hear the soft strum of the banjo or the laughter of an eligible bachelorette or even a widower on occasion seeking an audience with Stuart.

Keeping his voice softer than was accustomed to him, he said, "How'd the meeting with Lee go?"

William's dark brown eyes darted toward the dining area in the next room. "Not well. He sent Sweeney and his banjo packing not long ago." He lowered his eyes in shame as if he'd betrayed his leader and superior by sharing his weakness.

Placing a hand on Blackford's bony shoulder, he said. "Didn't want to Jine the Cavalry tonight anyway." He waited a moment, judging the man before him. "All can not be lost."

Blackford's face went sour as if he'd fed him lemons. "I don't know if this battle can be salvaged."

His hand squeezed his slender frame. "Nonsense. Nothing is so bad that we cannot prevail."

The aide nodded his chin a fraction.

"Let me see our Knight, maybe I can talk some sense into him."

Blackford led him to the next room. Their boots echoed off the wooden floors. He stepped to the side and gestured with a hand toward Stuart.

The Knight of the Golden Spurs, "J. E. B.", and Beauty to some, stood at the end of a rectangular, sturdy farm table. He wasn't a short man, nor nearly as tall as Hampton, but there was an air of presence about him that came with success on the battlefield as a young commander. An aura that had receded since the last time he'd seen him. A gold star was pinned to his gray slouch hat. A sable ostrich plume stuck from the side and it lay on the table as if thrown in haphazard dismay. His gray jacket's brass buttons were all undone. A red flower on his lapel drooped.

He glanced at Hampton with youthful eyes that held disappointment. Brown hair held perfect form and his beard, which was far bolder than a man of his age should be able to grow, made him look more refined than he was.

Rubbing his mustache, he said. "Marse Robert is not pleased with us."

Hampton gave him an open-palmed salute. Even as a senior in age, he was not in rank. "I heard as much, sir."

"He thinks we've lost him this battle and, with it, the war."

Each word was a barb in Hampton's soul. Never in a million years would he believe that Stuart or any man in his command would be responsible for failing the Southern cause. All their men were true, bold warriors of the South, committed to winning this ugly war. They'd already sacrificed so much. He'd dug well into his bank accounts to outfit men for the struggle and, with the blockade, his business back home plummeted into stagnated returns. It was much more than the lack of his management, he had quality men to take care of his business and his wife was more than capable. *Everything rides on our winning the war.*

"With all due respect, he must be mistaken. We've only done what he's asked. We've always served him well and he's never been wanting."

Stuart studied the map of the region unraveled on the table. This was enemy territory and not ground they were familiar with. It was no Virginia. "He believes we left him blind and now he is committed here." He stared at the map as if it would whisper to him the secret to victory.

"We came as fast as we could. We had to circumvent an entire army to reach him."

Stuart shook his head. "Not fast enough. I offered him my sword."

"Dear God, Jeb, don't be silly."

Stuart continued to scrutinize the paper terrain. "He told me it was a lesson and, while my honor is intact, I have much to prove." He glanced at Hampton noticing the bandage wrapped around his skull. "It's not bad is it?" He blinked, he deeply cared for his men and his fellow commanders. That made the men love him. "Don't pummel me with more unwelcome news."

Hampton instinctually brought a hand up to the side of his head. Stuart's words were harsh. He did them no good sitting the war out and neither did Hampton. It would take their whole effort to overcome the Yankee hordes. They did not have the time for incidents of honor or injury. "Yanks been gettin' more brazen, but it's only a scratch."

Stuart ran his eyes up and down Hampton, deciding for himself if his subordinate told the truth. "Glad you are sound. I'm going to need you tomorrow."

Hampton stepped closer to the table to get a better view of the map. The Union forces were spread below the town of Gettysburg and the corresponding ridges and hills like a reverse, upside-down J if one viewed it from north to south.

"They're dug in good down here." Stuart pointed at Round Top and its adjacent companion. "Longstreet tried them there today. Thrashed the Yanks in the wheat field to the peach orchard and pushed them all the way back to Cemetery Ridge, but no further." His eyes bounced to Hampton's. "He was repulsed."

His words were a sanitized version of they'd been ground up and lacked proper reinforcements to stage another assault, therefore not reaching their objective. "Pete must be livid."

"Rumor has it, he wants my court-martial." Pain laced his eyes. The young general would rather have been bayoneted through the heart a hundred times than lose the faith of his superiors and peers.

"Speak no more. Nothing will come of it."

Quietly, Stuart nodded and cleared his throat. "We've been turned back here." He tapped a circular elevation named Culp's Hill near a creek. "Ewell's got a fresh brigade, so he'll see if he can fold them in the morning, but Lee said they could be heard chopping wood and building solid fortifications at the top. I doubt we will have success there."

"Not if they are dug in like a tick."

Stuart skimmed over the paper, dropping a fingertip. "But here is where Marse Robert thinks he will succeed." His finger tapped the map near the center of the line. *Pat, pat, pat.*

"That's a lot of open ground they'll have to cover to reach that point." Hampton shook his head, he was beginning to see the desperation that was about to be unleashed on the third day of battle.

"Who's leading?" His eyes regarded Stuart.

"Longstreet's in command, but the divisional commanders are Pickett, Pettigrew, and Trimble."

"They are reliable."

"They are. He's going to warm them up with over 150 cannon and send their eleven infantry brigades from four divisions—over thirteen thousand men—to mount a frontal assault on Cemetery Ridge. At the same time, Ewell will strike Culp's Hill in simultaneous assaults." Stuart tugged his beard worriedly at the map as he lived the battle in his mind.

"Sir, did you try to dissuade him of such course? Surely there is a better way."

Stuart gave him a weak smile. "We were not in favor of making recommendations."

Hampton sighed, studying the map again, shaking his head. A flash of anger crossed him. "He will get them killed. It won't matter. I could defend that breach with a couple hundred men and two batteries. And look here. Do the Federals have batteries on Round Top? What about Cemetery Hill?" He took the side of his hand and ran it at an angle. "They are going to rake them with artillery on the flanks, from the front, and that's all before they get within striking distance of a Federal infantryman. Then here." He pointed at the line of Federals. "What's going to stop these units from marching forward and flanking ours? Nothing. It will be slaughter of the highest degree."

The young general shook his head, eyes distant. "He feels he has no choice. It's the only place he hasn't attempted to dislodge them. If he can smash their center, we can fold them up. Their army will be destroyed. Then all we have to do is march to Washington and capture the despot Lincoln."

"If he can break them."

"If we can break them."

"Us?"

"We can redeem ourselves yet." He slammed his fist on the table. Another uncharacteristic behavior for the Knight of the Golden Spurs.

Hampton watched him, worried. *Is this the beginning of the end? Is this where we unravel? Destroying ourselves from within?*

"I'll not have him thinking bad of us. We will win his favor back."

This young man had shown poise, composure, tact, and brilliance on countless occasions. To watch him act so rashly and fueled off emotion struck Hampton as out of character.

Stuart's eyes spoke of danger to be contradicted. "Pickett is to be the hammer, we are to be the anvil. He wants us to attack their rear. This will split them in half at the center and cause chaos throughout the entirety of Meade's line. They'll break and then it's off to the races."

Slowly, Hampton nodded. It wasn't an overly complex plan. It was a common tactic if the forces were amassed in the correct places. He could visualize the troop movements in his mind.

While gray-clad soldiers marched forward across the grassy fields in desperate glory, all the Federal soldiers would be shifting and preparing to defend. They wouldn't notice the five thousand cavalry, on paper more like thirty-five hundred able men, charging into their backs. Sabers swinging, pistols blazing, the Southern knights would slaughter their artillery and any units recovering within the safety of the rear.

Blue-coated men in the front ranks would turn and begin to worry as they heard the fighting and calls for help in the opposing direction. A direction that was supposed to provide safety. Their commanders would look worriedly behind only to find thousands of mounted men charging. Panic would wash over them like a tidal wave. They wouldn't have long before the terror would take their men. Cannons gone, the rebels would march unmolested until they engaged the infantry, but the Union men would be torn, which enemy should they face? The dread of annihilation would grip them; it would hold them indecisive until it was too late. Then the real slaughter would begin. Thousands if not tens of thousands would be captured and Lee's sweeping tactical victory on the third day would be a strategic one as well.

Even if there was a modicum of victory from the infantry assault, the flanking cavalry assault would prevent a coordinated retreat. The Unionists would be forced to either wing, breaking down into pockets of defeated men. They would be surrounded and completely destroyed.

Most likely those pockets would surrender without delay; with no supplies and reinforcements, it would be the only way to save their skins. Congress and Lincoln would call for Meade's head, further throwing the enemy into chaos.

"It has promise."

"Marse Robert thinks it will end the war. And if he thinks this will finish the Northerners, then I do too."

Hampton was slightly more reserved than his commander, but he didn't doubt that both he and Lee thought this could be the most pivotal battle of the war.

"Then we will not be deterred from reaching the Federal rear."

Stuart's eyes hardened and he could see glory and redemption and newfound favor. "We will follow up this road. There's cavalry, I believe, under Gregg here at this intersection. Not much." He bent closer to the map so he could read the fine print. "Low Dutch and Hanover roads. They will be swept to the side and we will have a clear shot at Meade's rear."

Hampton let a smile spread on his face, masked by his unruly beard. "That we can do, sir." Federal cavalry had been easily handled in the war. Even though Northerners had access to countless quantities of horse flesh, of which rebel troops were required to provide their own mounts, they were still bested by the Southerners.

The main difference was that the Southern man was a natural quality equestrian, with ingrained soldierly traits, while the Northerners never had the same aptitude. This was exploited by the rebel leaders who knew how to win. It seemed every other month the Northerners were ousting one another and Lincoln would be promoting a new general to lead the Oppression. They'd rather stab one another in the back than win the war.

"Lee wants us to drag the net, in case Ewell can dislodge their right flank. If he succeeds, we will corral them back into Longstreet's assault. We will alert him we are in place by firing four shots. One in each direction. Then our attack will begin. We won't have much time to reach the rear. Those infantry have about a three-quarter mile walk. "

"It will be done, sir."

"I don't like being outside his favor." Stuart's mustache worked underneath his nose in irritation. "Let's redeem ourselves. We strike hard and fast."

Hampton smiled. "Hard and fast."

CHAPTER 24

Early Morning July 3rd, 1863
Two Taverns, Pennsylvania

Before the sun cracked the horizon, the 13th Michigan was breaking camp.

"Up and at 'em, boys," Wilhelm's voice cut through the humid morning darkness. Grogginess laced the men into a stupor. With only a few hours of sleep, they rose like the dead, slow and rigid. "Johannes, come hither."

Wolf rubbed his eyes, smacking dry lips and a dusty mouth. He clawed at his canteen, guzzling as much water as he could while the new sergeant stared at him.

"Sir." His head had a slight pound to it from the drinking the night before. He wrapped his gun belt over his light-blue trousers and tucked his white shirt into his pants.

"Give me your jacket," Wilhelm commanded. His uniform was fine and proud, not like a grieving father but of a career soldier who knew the importance of appearance. His forage cap shadowed his face; his mustache was curled in a circular fashion. His weapons on his person all in proper order.

Wolf stooped down and snatched his jacket handing it to the new sergeant. Wilhelm scrutinized his haphazard appearance.

"You got a housewife?"

"No, I'm not married."

Wilhelm didn't smile. His eyes held a sadness but still a father's love. "A sewing kit. Next time you get to a sutler, pick one up. They're good for patching clothes or wounds."

Roberts rolled to his side, mumbling. "My gosh darn arm is smarting today."

"Get some clean bandages on that," Wilhelm said, without looking at the man. He sat on the ground sewing Wolf's corporal stripes onto his sleeves in the retreating darkness. Every few threads, he placed his face close to the coat, making sure the chevrons were straight.

When he was finished, the men had tended their mounts and prepared to go. Wilhelm handed the coat back to Wolf. "You probably won't need a coat today, but the men need to know who to look to on the field." He nodded his head. "Put it on."

Wolf took the jacket, slipping his arms inside.

Wilhelm lifted his chin, then brushed his sleeve, eyeing the stripes. "It will do until we can get one of the women to look after it."

"Thank you."

Wilhelm gulped and stuck out his mustache, covering his emotions.

"I'm sorry about Franz."

Wilhelm reached for Wolf's shoulder, squeezing it tight in a strong hand. "Nonsense lad, you and me both know that this wasn't the place for him." He sucked in air through his nose. "I never should have let him join. I have to live with that."

"He was a patriot who took up arms for his nation in her time of need."

Wilhelm's bottom lip pushed up on his upper. "I know he was. God took him instead of me because he was pure of soul." He shook his head. "Such a sweet boy."

Wolf's own guilt was returning without the alcohol to hold it in check. "I tried to save him."

Water surrounded Wilhelm's eyes, threatening to fall, but they refused to let a tear make flight. "I know you did, son." The word son seemed to hang off his tongue, turning to ash in the father's mouth. He closed his eyes for a moment in silence and gave a weary smile. "There'll be time for that later." He turned toward the other troopers. "Come, men, we have a long day ahead of us." His voice was grave and his words were more as a reminder to himself than his small unit.

"You heard the sergeant. Let's get mounted up," Wolf said to the men. And they clambered atop their mounts and waited for orders.

The sun rose above the horizon in an orange flame, adding an early heat to the Pennsylvania humidity that tried to drown the soldiers in sweat. Roberts tapped his canteen, staring at the hole, hoping for more water. Droplets of perspiration were already running down Wolf's back, dampening his wool coat, and his headache was unrelenting in its pounding.

Farnsworth's brigade had marched out before dawn and Custer's brigade waited to follow the column toward the Round Top to support Meade's left flank.

Wolf assumed his position on one of the flanks and Sergeant Berles took the other. Bart and Roberts were in the middle. The company guidon fluttered in the soft morning breeze, red over black with the golden snarling wolf's head. It represented the unit and their small place in the much larger command. They stood in the company and in turn stood in the regiment. There were five regiments and Custer's men numbered over two thousand. A formidable force.

"Did you hear about Rock Hill or High Knob? I forget which. It was next to the Round Top." Roberts asked.

"No," Wolf said.

"A great battle was fought there. Longstreet's men charged the hill five times and each time three regiments threw them back." He paused.

"And then what?"

"We ran out of ammunition."

"Were they routed?" It was an obvious question. One couldn't fight long without ammunition and, against a determined enemy, surely they would be overrun or forced to retreat.

Roberts chuckled and burped. "No! At least that's not what Rogers said in B Company. You see, their colonel is a real learned fellow, some sort of professor or doctor, I dunno. Chambers or Chamberlain. Anyway. He had those boys fasten bayonets."

"They charged?"

Roberts's horse moved beneath him and clopped its hoof to shake off a fly. "Ran those rebels right back to Richmond. We're headed that way now to run support for them."

"You think they'll strike there again?" Wolf said.

Dan smiled at them. "We will be good."

"Won't matter, boys. If they strike, we'll fight. I have no doubt of that with the Boy General in charge."

"You growing soft on him, Wilhelm? That almost sounded like a compliment," said Roberts.

Wilhelm tersely shook his head. "I didn't say that, but the Boy General does know how to find a fight."

"That he does," Wolf said with a half smile. Custer gave him an ounce of faith in their leadership. The general may have led some ill-fated charges, but there were flashes of bravery that showed the rebels they weren't scared. They weren't cowards or pigs for the slaughter. Not everything was a foregone conclusion of defeat at their hands and that little bit of faith was infectious. The men could feel it.

The bugle sounded the advance and the men breathed a collective sigh of relief. The waiting wore them thin. Then again, that was a soldier's motto, hurry and wait. The column trudged ahead at a walk. The long rank of blue meandered down the road and veered away from the others north and east while the rest of the regiments went south.

As Wolf's company took the bend in the route north, he watched the slowly disappearing Federal troopers. "We're splitting the division?"

Wilhelm eyed the other elements of the division melting into the landscape in the other direction. "I'm sure there's a reason."

Three miles north, they linked with another brigade of horsemen. The sun dangled low in the sky, like a yellow pendulum reaching for midday supremacy over the land. The distant echo of cannon-thunder dissipated into the air and the orders were given to get comfortable.

The 13th Michigan dismounted along a stretch of road. Every fourth man held the horses for three other men. Troopers handled their carbines and took their place along the lane, staring out at clovers and wheat. Leafy verdant trees surrounded the field and the land rose in the distance. A log cabin farmhouse stood beneath a heavily wooded ridge stretching almost a mile away from the elevated road.

"Surely this isn't where the Rebs will strike," Van Horn said.

More dismounted troopers in blue spanned along the route that ran perpendicular to them. One could catch glimpses of them in between trunks and shrubs.

"As good as place as any," Wolf said.

"This is Hanover and Low Dutch Roads," Wells said, as he inspected the men from horseback. "We are in the distant rear of the Federal lines."

"Bugger that. The fight clearly ain't here."

"Why's that?" Wolf asked. He imagined a fine battle in the fields and didn't see why it couldn't happen. Even if the thought made him nervous. "Could be a fight."

"Cannons are somewhere else."

Wolf took a seat in a ditch along with the other troopers.

"Keep watered, boys. This is promising to be another hot one," Wilhelm said. He removed his forage cap, running a hand through his wet hair.

Wolf took his father's sash and used it to dab his face. He gulped down tepid water from his canteen, trying to stem the heat and his headache, cursing his celebration the night prior.

Roberts plopped down next to Wolf. "Plenty of excitement by my watch. Nice fields. Mosquitos to swat. No cannon balls to evade or bullets to dodge."

Wolf gave a short laugh. "Suppose it could be worse. I just want to prove that we're soldiers. You know? Show 'em we can fight."

Roberts nudged him. "I'd rather sit here, nice and safe. Eat this here apple. I'll split it with ya." He handed Wolf an apple and he halved it. They quietly munched in the heat. Juices flowed from broken red flesh and Roberts licked his fingers.

"Is that Farnsworth?" Wolf gestured at unknown men lining the Low Dutch Road.

"What's that flag say, Roberts?" Wolf asked.

The small thief shaded his eyes under his forage hat and squinted. "3rd Pennsylvania and 1st Maryland."

"And that there?" Wilhelm insisted.

"Can't tell whose command."

"Not Farnsworth. Why did they take us from our division?"

"It's not for us to speculate, but I'm sure the Boy General had his reasons."

"Won't matter. More picket duty either way," Van Horn said. His long face glistened despite the dourness that laced it, as if he hated picket duty worse than the heat. And the men sat under a hot, hard sun and watched the field grow to the tune of distant, cloudless thunder.

CHAPTER 25

Morning July 3rd, 1863
East of Gettysburg, Pennsylvania

Custer cantered toward a large white command tent with his orderly in tow. In the early morning dawn, a couple of pickets recognized him and allowed him into the small camp. He dismounted Roanoke and limped to the shelter, his leg purple from his fall. His belly bubbled with the decision he'd made in the early hours of the day.

He stepped inside the tent and removed his broad-brimmed hat, running a hand over the brim. It was closing in on a hundred degrees in the late morning sun. Each day the heat seemed to get worse, threatening to burn out both men and horses before they even engaged the enemy.

A man stood, using an appropriated card table to hold a map. He was tall enough to seemingly need to hunch over in his command tent. His beard was long like an ancient biblical patriarch and mostly dark brown, and his hair was brushed over the top of his head in neat fashion. Unlike Custer's fair locks that matted to the top and sides of his skull.

Custer's dashing uniform was covered in tan dust and soil from fighting and the long march, where the 2nd Division of the Cavalry Corps commander was clean, pressed, and fresh, as if he hadn't seen a lick of combat.

"General Gregg, sir," Custer said and offered a salute, crisp yet with a sense of confidence in the general's presence that belonged to a man of many more battles and many more years his senior. Over the last few skirmishes, he could feel the men swinging in his favor, including a few of his regimental commanders who had been passed over for advancement by Pleasonton.

Gregg acknowledged Custer with gaping eyes that indicated a man under immense stress. He sighed, staring back down at the map. "They're here. I know they are. Lee has tried everything. Why wouldn't he try to ride around our rear and pin us in like a fox in a henhouse?" He gestured Custer to come forward, joining him.

"You ran into Hampton's men here?" Gregg asked. He pointed at Hunterstown.

"We did, sah. We gave them a hell of a fight, although my mount was killed in the charge. Fine horse. True shame."

Gripping his long beard with nervous energy, Gregg spoke. "Stuart has been a thorn in our side for a long time. He was always a clever boy at West Point, but I never thought we would face one another in the field." He glanced at Custer. His eyes were set forward on his brow, giving him a perpetual tired look to his face. His nose was well proportioned and narrow. "Never thought we would be fighting against them. Only side by side." A tinge of sadness crossed the general and, as if he realized his momentary lapse may make him appear soft in front of a subordinate, he squared himself away.

He'd been known since he took command of the 2nd Cavalry Division to be a man of unflappable judgment, never rattled in the face of a fight as long as he was directing the battle not leading it. Some whispers said Gregg feared a violent death, but his ability to move his units into the right place at the right time quieted the men and solidified respect.

Custer knew that was the difference between them. He would lead from the front any chance he had. They came for war and if there was no glory in war then why fight it? Some thought him too young, but leading could only be done from the front. "Sir, my men have taken Hanover Road in conjunction with the other elements of your division." He waited a moment.

"Good. Jeb's out there. I know he is."

"Kilpatrick's been requesting my brigade return to his command." He hesitated, he knew he'd directly disobeyed an order from his commanding officer to respond to the pleas of another superior officer. It provided him with a level of protection from scrutiny, but he'd only been in charge of his brigade for a few days and his lack of following the chain of command could be seen as a slight or even open insubordination, but he'd followed what he thought was the right call.

"I will handle Kilpatrick. You will hold until McIntosh and my cousin Irwin can get their units into place." He drummed the map with his index finger. "Hanover and Low Dutch Roads hold the fate of our rear." He encircled just below the town of Gettysburg. "We've been pushed into an upside-down J. Lee's tried us here." He pointed at the right. "We barely held and he tried us here." He gestured at two well-defined hills. "Round Top and its spur. Nasty fighting there. Among the rocks, we slaughtered each other. The men are calling it Devil's Den."

"Pleasonton thinks Jeb's going to come over Wolf Hill, but it's filled with rocks. Jeb wouldn't bring his mobile cavalry over a craggy bastard like that. Not a single mount would survive. Hell, infantry would struggle to get over the top." With sad eyes, he eyed Custer carefully. "You aren't the only one to *ignore* orders today."

A grin curled on Custer's golden mustached lip. "Sir?"

"Pleasonton wants me back near Culp. Greene's got a strong position and breastworks on Culp's Hill, along with proper support. The rebels aren't going over Culp's today. The first day, they gave us a run. Now we're entrenched."

Cannon boomed miles away, as if a response to the Union effort in the fading morning.

"I will delay sending word that I'm staying put. Always better to ask for forgiveness than permission." Fire lit in his eyes. "This is the place. We're going to protect this intersection. Low Dutch connects to Baltimore Pike. Baltimore Pike is the gateway to our rear."

"We will be happy to assist. If there's a fight, my boys want to be in on it." He swept locks behind his ear.

"I never doubted your valor. Lee will go all-out today. He's gotten a fresh division to throw into the fray. If he can remove us from this field, he can claim victory and the press will love him for it."

Custer regarded him coolly, his first week as a brigade commander proving the most interesting of his young career. "We will hold the intersection as long as you need."

"I know you will. My division will shift units to relieve you, but until then, you are acting in the field. You can direct as you see fit." His buggy eyes judged him for a moment. "I must continue to adjust our forces to ensure success. You understand?"

"It is an honor to lead, sir."

The smallest of smiles parted Gregg's giant beard. "You did the right thing heeding my orders. Remember, today is the day. If we hold, we will have a great victory. If we're routed, the war may very well be over."

The thought that a single battle could win or lose the war felt foreign to Custer. He'd only just gotten in command of a brigade composed of his Michigan boys. Even if he was from Ohio, he always considered the Michigan regiments to be his very own. He'd only wanted to lead a single Michigan regiment and, through the leadership shake up that seemed to happen on a monthly basis, he'd acquired a general's star.

"We will carry the day."

Gregg lifted a hand in salute. "Carry on, General. I will see you when this is over."

With more snap than was necessary, Custer knuckled his forehead. "Sah," he said with strong conviction.

He pushed the tent flap out of his way. The dominating sun momentarily blinded him. His orderly waited, holding the reins of both horses. They galloped back to Hanover Road. His mind itched with the drums of war. His war was only beginning and this could be the final overture.

He turned toward Joseph. "This could be the war."

"Sir?" the young man said.

"We will either carry this day in glory or fade into history as the men who lost the United States of America."

***

Soon after he reached the intersection of Hanover and Low Dutch, more of Gregg's division was beginning its deployment, slowly trickling in to hold the intersection north of Baltimore Pike. The plan was for Custer to hold the intersection until the bulk of Gregg's Division could deploy.

McIntosh's brigade would arrive first and take Custer's place at the intersection, relieving Custer to rejoin Kilpatrick's and never see a lick of fighting by the day's end. It was encroaching on midday and, by the time he reached the left southern flank of the Union army, the battle would be waning with the light of day.

A man whipped his horse toward the general. "Sir, I come from Major Weber."

The grizzled trooper with sunken eyes appeared to have not slept in twenty-four hours. If Custer learned anything from the last few days, it was that intelligence on the location of the enemy was equally as important to bravery or numbers. He'd been caught off guard a few times as he led charges. He wouldn't let that happen again. Major Weber and two of his companies were sent to scout the area for enemies.

"Go on."

The trooper pointed toward Cress Ridge, thickly covered in green and brown timber. "Sir, those trees over yonder are filled with rebels."

"Filled?"

"Yes, sir. Further south we saw no less than a thousand of Fitz Lee's men whose line had drifted out of the forest. Rebs weren't even bothering to hide it."

"Well, I'll be damned. Gregg was right." He smiled, he might actually get to make a play in this war that made a difference. He turned to Joseph. "Get word to Alger and the 5th. I want skirmishers out in this field. Go now, the enemy is upon us."

His orderly spurred his horse and dust clouded as he galloped along the roadway toward Alger's men.

In fifteen minutes, dismounted troopers marched through the lush wheat and clover fields lapping at their legs, Spencer rifles in hand. They marched spread out with spacing between the men, not in a thick shoulder-to-shoulder mass of infantry. Their job was to be flexible and delaying, to move quick, provide a buffer between the forces, and hopefully draw the enemy into a position that he could exploit.

The Spencer rifles in their hands would ensure they had a distinct advantage over their opponent. The weapon had only been recently issued to Union troops. The rebels didn't have anything like it and Custer preferred it that way. Whatever tipped the scales in their favor. That was why he hadn't sent the 13th Michigan. They were green and had only Sharps carbines. A suitable weapon for cavalry, but not nearly as dynamic as the Spencer. Seven shots without reloading. True battle-changing power.

A cannon boomed from the other ridge. He shaded his eyes to see better. It came from near Rummel Farm. His blue regiments followed his lead, turning and staring toward the forested ridge. Thirty seconds later, another bass explosion was heard, but this one seemed more faint. *Do they not know we're here?* No shells flew overhead and no balls sailed at his men. Custer couldn't help but cock his head to the side in uncertainty.

His regimental commanders and their officers were trickling to him for orders. Colonel Moore eyed the ridge with beady eyes. "What are they doing, sir?"

"I don't know," Custer said. He scanned the trees, waiting for an answer. The 5th Michigan continued to march over the farm, preparing for impending contact.

Thirty seconds passed and another cannon was fired, this one too was faint, as if it were pointed in the wrong direction.

"Are they fighting someone on the other side?" Moore said. His voice may as well have been a chirp in Custer's ear.

"Hmm. Lieutenant." Custer waved another messenger forward. "Find McIntosh. I need to know exactly how far away they are from supporting us."

"Sir, yes, sir." The young man sped away in a dusty whirlwind.

Cannon exploded from the other ridge. This one was aimed in their direction. The shell exploded over the 13th Michigan taking cover on the Hanover Road. Men cried out as hot shrapnel rained down upon them.

Gray-clad men emerged from the trees dismounted, guns in hand. A flag waved the enemy onward. *Who do we have here?* Custer hastily took out his field glasses from its hardened leather pouch on his saddle. He brought the heavy glasses to his eyes. His vision zoomed in. The man waved the blue state flag of Virginia, causing him to smile.

"Jeb Stuart. We meet again. Ready for another scrap, are we?" He let his field glasses drop. "Then that's what you'll get."

CHAPTER 26

Noon July 3rd, 1863
East of Gettysburg, Pennsylvania

General George Custer left his men in position of the intersection while he waited for McIntosh's brigade to arrive. He'd stretched the 7th and 13th Michigan along Hanover Road and placed Pennington's battery directly at the angle, blocking movement toward Baltimore Pike.

He then moved the 5th Michigan with their Spencer repeating rifles into a skirmish line when the rebels had made themselves known in force. If this was to be the place for Stuart to test the Union line, he would be running his men into some excellent firepower. He put his brass-encased field glasses to his eyes.

Gray, all shades of brown, butternut, khaki and tan-clad men had been seen in the distant woods, most on horse. Two of Stuart's batteries lay in heaps of worthless scrap metal and wood, many of the artillerymen casualties of Pennington's precise and rapid fire.

He withdrew the glasses. He'd been onto them all morning, waiting to see where they concentrated their forces. None of it mattered much, as he was to be relieved by McIntosh soon freeing him to rejoin to Kilpatrick's 3rd Division near the south of the line.

The pounding of horses' hooves captured his attention. A thickset, bearded colonel with an entourage of junior officers steered toward Custer. He halted his trotting horse nearby.

"General, my men are coming up." He inspected the field and Custer's brigade with an eye of a man who knew soldiering. "That's a fine body of men you have." He had a plain face on heavy cheeks and his hair retreated from the front of his head even as he attempted to comb it in a way to cover the missing pieces.

"These are my Michigan boys. Hearty and true. Colonel McIntosh, it's good to have you on site."

McIntosh gave a quick salute and glanced over his shoulder. "I don't see why Gregg is so fixated on this junction. Looks plain enough." A column of his men were emerging from Gettysburg. They flowed back into line along Low Dutch Road.

"I think we'll have enough of them here for a battle." He pointed.

Tiny specks of men and cannon were setting up along Cress Ridge. Pennington was giving them a thrashing with his 3-pound ordnance guns. Smoke dissipating from bursting shells.

"Can you get your men up with my 5th? They can't disengage without support."

McIntosh stared intently at the farm fields that sprawled out before them and even harder at Cress Ridge. "There's enough rebels over there for a fight?"

"I think you'll find those woods full of rebels."

Briskly McIntosh nodded. "Lieutenant, send word to Major Beaumont, tell him to move the 1st New Jersey up quick and link with the 5th Michigan." He turned back to Custer. "I would hope you wouldn't fully withdraw until Irwin arrives."

"Wouldn't dare."

McIntosh's lieutenant held his place. "I beg your pardon, sir, but Major Beaumont has already been informed twice to move his regiment forward. McIntosh's healthy face turned red like a beet.

"By God, I will ring his neck myself. Damn them, bring them up at a gallop!"

The terrified lieutenant nodded furiously and turned his horse toward the 1st New Jersey.

McIntosh's blood pressure was high, veins bulging beneath a white collar.

He shook his head for a moment before looking back at Custer.

"This isn't the first time Major Beaumont was slow to fulfill his orders."

Custer nodded, he'd been around men like that before. Men that lacked the fortitude for a quality fight.

McIntosh pulled at his collar trying to loosen it. "When we are up, I'll send word."

"Thank you, good man," Custer said.

McIntosh spun his horse and galloped back down Low Dutch Road away from the intersection.

Thirty minutes passed and the day moved solidly into the afternoon. McIntosh's regiments were taking their time arriving and Custer grew worried. He'd already taken another rider from Kilpatrick asking him to hurry south to rejoin with his proper command. He wasn't looking forward to rehashing that conversation with his immediate divisional superior, but the situation dictated otherwise. If he pulled his men out before McIntosh and Irwin Gregg were fully deployed then he would not only risk his own men's lives in a hasty withdrawal, but the defensive position they now held.

"Lieutenant," Custer said.

He waved a young man toward him. "Get to McIntosh and ask him how much longer before he can take this field?" If he didn't make haste back to Kilpatrick, his short brave stint as a general would be in jeopardy.

The lieutenant gave a quick salute and galloped off to find McIntosh. Custer warily watched the rebel lines. With a yell, rebels were pushing through the Rummel Farm and engaging his men despite the effectiveness of repeating rifles. The firecracker bangs of the skirmish popped in the air. He could see a regiment of McIntosh's there with them. If Stuart put much more pressure, he wouldn't be able to depart the field.

The sun hammered down on him as he waited for reinforcements. His black jacket and pants were already soaked through. He undid a canteen from his saddle and took a long drink of the lukewarm water. His horse, Roanoke, adjusted its feet beneath him. He dismounted, cupping his hands to give the horse water. He patted Roanoke's neck, flecks of perspiration misting in the air. He walked over to Pennington's battery.

The booming of his battery dominated the stifling afternoon. Pennington wiped his brow below his kepi when Custer reached them. His ears stuck out from the sides of his head like a bat and he only sported a newly formed mustache and goatee sprouting from his face. He wasn't much younger than Custer. The lanky lieutenant gave him a tired salute.

"Nice shooting."

A mischievous smile crossed Pennington's lips. "First shot hit one of their guns squarely in the muzzle and our second went through a wheel. The rest of that battery left the field in minutes." He'd systematically dismantled the opposing artillery.

"No finer shooting has been done. Prepare your men. Soon we will be disengaging and traveling south. I want your guns poised for another engagement there."

His artillery commander blinked then eyed the treed ridge holding the a sea of Confederates masked by timber. "Seems like there's plenty of the bastards here to deal with."

Custer followed his gaze. "I don't make all those decisions. If it were up to me, I'd see the rebels thoroughly whipped before we left this field."

"General Custer, sir," came a shout from behind.

A junior officer saluted, peering from above, blotting out the sun. "Kilpatrick is respectfully requesting you rejoin his division. The matter is urgent. He is preparing to dislodge rebels in the south."

Custer pushed his mustache up onto his nose as he thought and let out a sigh. "We will join him as soon as this position is secure. You have my word."

The young man nodded, urging his horse away. Custer watched his back as he disappeared in the other direction. Conflicting orders from two superiors, one, his actual superior who was in his chain of command and the other, a desperate, but quality commander who'd foreseen this battle that was formulating like a coming storm before him.

His messenger came back from McIntosh. "Sir, the last of McIntosh's regiments are in place and Irwin Gregg is getting close."

"Close ain't in place." He studied the field again. His position wasn't bad. A clash was brewing here. Pennington ripped another shot onto Cress Ridge.

He sighed. There were more things to a career than a glorious battle and, if he was going to survive this war, he needed to protect his career like an exposed flank.

"Get word to Alger. His men are to start disengaging from their skirmish."

Crisp salute found the junior officer. "Yes, sir." Dust billowed as the young man galloped to find the colonel.

Custer wiped his nose then slapped Roanoke's neck. "You good, old fellow?" he asked the animal. The horse kept its head down, conserving its energy. "Sure you are, old boy." He swung himself back in the saddle.

"Fine work, Pennington. Keep fire on them until Alger's men are disengaged. Then you can limber up for our southern march."

Custer walked Roanoke back to the intersection of the two dirt roads east of Gettysburg. He eyeballed the long line of his troopers. They'd waited all morning while the rebels had arrived, thinking there was to be a fancy scrap. "No more than a bloody skirmish with some fabulous artillery work." He'd make sure Pennington received high marks for his performance. A brevet promotion to captain would be coming in his near future.

"Colonel Moore and Colonel Mann, get your columns pointed south. We're to rejoin Kilpatrick."

"Yes, sir." They said in unison. They rode off to their commands. His regiments formed rank in rows of four troopers. After fifteen minutes, they started to walk their horses past him and away from the skirmish.

The ground began to shake beneath him. Men glanced around in fear. Trees quivered, leaves trembling. The air vibrated under the assault. Not the way it did with charging horsemen, but the way it did during an angry storm with rolling thunder. He turned and looked behind him. It was an immense, violent storm, but it didn't reside in the sky. It was man made and meant to destroy.

"Sir?" Joseph, his orderly, said.

"That's a cannonade like we've never heard before."

"Sounds like it's just over the next ridge."

"It does." He could imagine the fire bursting from muzzles, smoke blanketing the fields in the terrible beauty of men at war. It was as if the gods themselves were battling in the heavens, but it was men here on earth causing such a fierce storm with enough power to make the land shake and the heavens roar.

He recognized the divisional flags of General Gregg coming his way.

"Sir, look," Joseph said. He pointed out to the field.

A host of cavalry was forming along the flank of McIntosh and Alger's 5th Michigan, threatening to ride down his dismounted troopers. He put his field glasses to his eyes. Virginia flags whipped in the hot sun. Deep blue with the state seal at the center holding the Roman goddess Virtus standing with sword and spear over a fallen tyrant. "1st Virginia?" A veteran unit filled with excellent horseman heralded as one of the best of the south.

A quick calculation of numbers danced in his mind. There are more men in those woods than we can handle and my men are about to get swept three-quarters of a mile into the dirt.

Gregg galloped all the way to Custer. His patriarchal beard had blown to one side and he readjusted it to the center of his chest.

"General," Gregg said, his forehead glistening.

"Sir."

"Where are your men going?"

"Sir, I've received two requests from Kilpatrick to rejoin him in the south and I fear that I will be punished if I ignore him again. McIntosh has fully deployed and Irwin is arriving. I can leave this field to their capable hands."

Gregg shook his head emphatically. "I beg you, sir. Do not leave this field." He thrust a finger out at the Confederates forming their line. "This is the battle. If you depart now, I fear we will fail. Stuart will march to Meade's rear."

Custer judged his superior with vibrant, cool eyes. He'd already followed this man's orders, creating a rift between him and his commanding officer. This was his fourth full day in command of a brigade and he'd been asked to make a choice between the conflicting orders of two commanders. Reputation. Reprimanding. Even court-martialing were at stake. He didn't think it could go that far, but if Kilpatrick failed and wailed up the wrong tree to Pleasonton or even Meade, Custer's career would be short lived. His relationship could be soiled with the man that promoted him when so many other more senior officers were deserving of the task.

But General Gregg was right. This was shaping up to be a fight and he wouldn't back down with it so close. General Kilpatrick may be facing his own battle, but this was becoming a key juncture in the Union defense. The linchpin in protecting the rear which could cost him his career if he was wrong. He pushed out his mustache beneath his nose as he gritted his teeth and turned his horse back toward the skirmishing men.

"Joseph, get word to Moore and Mann. Get their regiments back here on the double, countermarch. Tell Pennington to prepare to hammer those horsemen's flank with canister. If they get this far, make them pay."

Custer gave Gregg a winning grin. "You know, sir. If we're wrong, my rising star will fall before it has risen."

"I would see to it that they know it was me directing you." His eyes were weary and bulged a bit, but they told Custer that his efforts would be sincere. Also, his kind words would most likely be overlooked if he was wrong, impacting both of their careers, but the newly made general's the most. The reality of the situation was, if both Gregg and Custer's assessments were incorrect and the battle wasn't here, he would take the blame and fade into oblivion.

It was all a risk he knew he had to take. The Virginians were preparing to charge. They had formed an ordered and proper rank. A man trotted down their line calling to his men. Sabers were drawn, glinting with the sun.

"What say you, General?"

"Hell yes, General! I'm always looking for a scrap." He kicked his horse toward his column of men as Gregg breathed a sigh of relief and the Virginians swept over the field with a terrible yell.

CHAPTER 27

Afternoon July 3rd, 1863
East of Gettysburg, Pennsylvania

Near a fence of Rummel Farm, gunfire rippled over the 5th Michigan's dismounted troopers. They were pinned down, struggling to disengage with the men in front and about to be crushed by a flanking cavalry charge.

Wolf watched as Custer galloped in front of his reserve regiments, his hand in the air. The 13th trotted along with the 7th Michigan, hastily countermarching back to the intersection they'd guarded all day without action.

Custer shouted. "To me, men! To me!" His horse whinnied as he led it down Wolf's regiment, trying to find a formation in disarray. Dust choked the men. The sun battered them relentlessly. Captains and lieutenants attempted to force them into ranks.

Both regiments were woefully depleted of fighting men, never reaching full strength. The 7th was only outfitted with ten companies and the 13th with six companies. Together they maybe had a full-strength regiment accounting for casualties, illness, and low initial recruitment.

Two whole regiments of Virginian riders were moving from trot to canter, about to drive down the dismounted line of the 5th Michigan and ride them into the ground, churning them into dirt and bone.

"Carbines away, boys. This is going to be a saber fight!" The men hastened to shoulder their carbines on straps and draw their sabers at the sergeant's order.

Wolf drew his light saber. The call of steel releasing from iron scabbards echoed down the line like a raspy metal snake uncoiling. The curved cavalry sword felt oddly light in his hand. The leather on the handle felt right, worn enough and blooded, but not ancient. Horses shuffled into and out of rank, riders trying to keep them in check. The nervousness of the riders permeated from their steeds.

"Steady now!" Wolf stared down the blue line, eyeing the men around him. The sergeants and corporals centered the privates in formations. The regiment stretched along the Hanover Road in a long row. Peltier was centered in front with his bugler. Wells centered his platoon and Little centered on 2nd Platoon.

Behind them waited another row of men. Two long rows of horse flesh, metal, and man, ready to charge. He strained to see the 7th Michigan but they were there too. In the same skittish position as their sister regiment.

Sabers appeared small in the Poltorak brothers' hands. Roberts was nearby, reins wrapped around his injured wrist. He gave Wolf a nervous smile, his dark eyes reading the enemy. The look on Van Horn's face was ready to spit fire and old Shugart's lips moved as he whispered prayers under his breath. Lent's cheek trembled and his eyes darted back and forth watching the rebel cavalry thundering across the field. Wilhelm was focused, attention on the charging enemy encroaching on the 5th Michigan with extreme violence.

"Lent," Wolf said.

The young trooper stared at him wide-eyed and blinked. "Corporal?"

"Remember why you fight."

Confusion spread across Lent's face and he gulped.

"You fight for the men at your side."

Lent nodded, his shoulders shivering.

Custer pulled his horse to a stop in front of his depleted regiments next to their captain. "It doesn't matter who you are or where you're from, those are your brothers on that field." His saber screamed as he removed it from its scabbard. It glinted in the sun as he pointed it at Alger's regiment. They bore down on the men, ready to ride them into the ground, slice them to ribbons with sabers, and shoot them in the backs as they turned to run before the equestrian prowess of their foes.

Custer's nose flared and his eyes grew wide with the potential delight of battle. The men felt the energy from him, feeding their own internal flames.

Wolf glanced at Wilhelm.

An eerie, cruel fire composed of red violence and green vengeance danced in his eyes, alight with the prospect of killing those that had slain his son.

"Those men intend to run your brothers down. Now let's go show the enemy what Hell looks like." He turned his horse around with his saber high in the air. His voice filled with certainty, he yelled. "Sound the forward march!"

The bugler placed his instrument to his lips, blaring a short tune. Down the line, other buglers sounded their horns. The horses' hooves clopped the ground as the two regiments walked into the pastures. Dust caked both man and horse, saturating the air. The company guidon held by First Sergeant O'Reilly fluttered casually as they walked. He opted to carry the guidon in this battle, taking his place in the ranks.

Custer prompted his horse to a trot and then straight into a gallop. Lifting his saber high in the air, he called out to his men. "Come on, you wolverines. Charge!"

The bugler's cheeks puffed out as he belted out the same monotone tone in succession followed by high-pitched shrill notes indicating to all the men to charge.

"Ja!" Wolf yelled. The regiment spurred their horses into a gallop and the thumping hooves turned into a growing storm of thunder. Cavalrymen whipped their animals onward, keeping pace with their brothers in arms.

The dismounted troopers in the field gave a volley into the charging rebels and turned to fall back toward McIntosh's line. The two full rebel regiments swarmed through the dismounted men not fast enough or wounded. A cluster of troopers took refuge in the log cabin farmhouse and surrounding barns.

The gray horsemen surrounded the barn and house, peppering it with pistol and rifle rounds. The Southerners expertly began the process of rolling the dismounted troopers back toward the Low Dutch Road. It was a mixture of corralling the 5th, slaughtering the resisters, and capturing those too tired to escape. Dismounted Union troopers threw their weapons to the ground, raising hands in the air. All while the 7th and 13th built into an angry storm.

Custer's men chewed farmed earth beneath their hooves. Tossing clumps of dirt high into the air, they were a tempest of violence coming on with feverish energy. The dismounted troopers from the 5th Michigan, 1st New Jersey, and 3rd Pennsylvania, still in the field shifted their remaining line to give room for the descending regiments. Battle calls were made from the charging troopers. The regimental flag flapped in the wind and F Company's guidon whipped as the horses hit full stride across the field still in tight formation.

The 1st Virginians had seen them now. They wheeled with confidence and proper order, maintaining their composure with few gaps that rapidly were filled. Kicking their mounts to a gallop, they adjusted to meet the charging Northern horsemen.

On the flank of the mounted men, the 7th Michigan took a withering volley from Chambliss's dismounted troopers. The green unit swerved and changed course. Screams carried from the tired lungs of both men and horses alike as they were driven into a fence made of stone and wood, disrupting any sort of order they'd maintained.

Rebels waited on the other side pouring lead from pistols and rifles into the horsemen. Men, mostly no older than eighteen, crumpled from their saddles as the bullets struck their bodies. Wolf tried to ignore the calls for help as men were cut down with the scythes of war. The 13th had its own bulwark to climb, except this was man and horse.

The gray and brown wall ahead of them accelerated until the cavalries were almost upon one another. One could see their faces now. Wild angry eyes, beards drenched in sweat, open mouths calling for blood, sabers and swords raised at their enemies, pistols in hands, and battle glee.

Wolf made eye contact with the rebel directly across from him. This would be the man he would be closest to when the lines struck like a titan clapping two monstrous hands, one blue and one gray together. His horse was brown, not dissimilar from Billy. His beard was coffee-colored but his chin was streaked with gray, the wind forcing it against his neck as he rode. The man's nose was bulbous and although Wolf couldn't make out the color of his eyes they stared through the Union men as if they didn't exist.

The rebels pointed pistols as they encroached within fifteen yards. The Federal cavalry leaned close to their mounts, shrinking their bodies and merging into one with the animals to avoid the death whistling overhead. Pistol fire sprinkled from each side, not enough to slow the charging forces.

"For the Union!" Custer shouted.

The mass of men and horses collided with a booming crash of flesh on flesh and the chaos began.

CHAPTER 28

Afternoon July 3rd, 1863
East of Gettysburg, Pennsylvania

Men howled as sabers were thrust through bellies and breasts. Horsemen were thrown from their mounts, disappearing into the smoke and dust. Horses piteously screamed as their bodies were smashed into one another at the urging of their riders and legs were snapped in the collision.

Wolf swung his saber over Billy's neck at a rebel aiming a pistol at him. His curved blade caught the Confederate diagonally across the front of his face, sliding through flesh and cartilage. He felt the blade stop on the facial bones of the other man, but his force was already slashing the saber through. The gash split the rebel from his forehead through his nose. His eyes rolled into his head and his horse kept going, jostling the stunned man.

Rank after rank of riders whipped past them. Wolf tucked his arm in tight to his body for fear that his saber would be ripped from his hand or his arm from the socket. Private Lent took a bullet through the cheek, a jagged exit wound on the other side. He made a muffled cry as he tried to hold his teeth and tongue inside his mouth.

A pack of blue drove into the gray by the force of their charge, but were slowed by the bodies of a slower yet larger force of gray.

A rebel swiped at Wolf with his sword, the blade reflecting the sun like a deadly beam of light. He barely parried the blow, brushing the saber to the side. Another rebel aimed a pistol at Wolf and Roberts's horse crashed into him, sending both riders to the ground.

Wolf spun his mount in a circle, the air filling with smoke, dust, and the coppery smell of dying. It all nipped at his watery eyes. His platoon fractured to the flanks, losing cohesion.

Swordplay danced among the cavalrymen as they broke into individual battles. Horses circled one another as the men dueled above. Wolf spurred Billy toward a cluster of men and he rammed his saber into a rebel's back, penetrating his gray coat into the muscle beneath the shoulder blade. The man arched in pain, lifting his head backward, his hat toppling from his head. With a yell, Wolf yanked his blade free.

Breathing hard from the effort, he yelled. "Wilhelm? Bart?"

The faint bugle call of rally was sounding. It cut off halfway through, and filled in with the clash of metal swords and the crack of pistols.

The flap of the company guidon caught his eye. Red, black, and gold whipping back and forth in the air. "Come on, Billy. Ja." His gelding increased pace weaving around sword and horse alike.

A rebel charged him. Spit flew from his mouth as he screamed, "Die!" He pointed his gun point blank at Wolf, the barrel shoved within inches of his face. Wolf grabbed his arm with his reins. Billy whinnied as the men struggled for the weapon. *Bang. Bang.* The pistol fired off shots as they wrestled for the weapon. The rebel was ripped from Wolf's hands and thrown from his saddle. He pushed himself off the ground, but Bart turned his horse around in a circle and the horseman was replaced by muffled cries.

Wilhelm pierced a man's breast with his saber. "To the flag, boys," he yelled at his men. The Polish brothers rallied closer to Wolf and Wilhelm and, as a collective, they forced their way toward the flag. They kicked their horses onward in a chaotic fury. The company guidon dipped.

"No!" Wolf screamed.

He pointed the Polish brothers forward. "To the flag."

They pressed into the throng of men surrounding the red and black company colors.

First Sergeant O'Reilly used his flag as a staff, hammering it downward on the oppressive mass of Confederate horsemen pushing and shoving to get the troop's standard. It was his reminder of home. F Company's small piece of honor. The greatest shame that could become a unit was the loss of their standard.

O'Reilly was shot in the chest, blood escaping and flowing over his blue uniform like newly formed crimson waterfalls, yet he clung to the guidon with fierce determination. He arched his back in pain and another rebel jammed his saber into O'Reilly's belly, doubling him over in death. The bearer still held the flag in a white-knuckled grip even as he faded from life on the double, still in the saddle.

A gray horseman fired another shot into O'Reilly's upper chest and the first sergeant tipped out of his saddle, relinquishing the guidon to the rebels.

Wolf released his pistol from its holster and shoved the reins into his hand holding his saber. He fired into the rebel holding the flag victoriously high in the air. The Confederate flinched and the flag fell from his hands.

Wilhelm struck a mighty blow to the closest rebel's head and the cavalryman's horse took him away in a daze. More rebels saw the flag was almost in their possession, crushing in. Wilhelm grabbed the flagpole from the dying rebel. An open coated gray lieutenant was trying to gut the sergeant with repeated jabs of his saber that the sergeant deflected in haste.

"Wilhelm, flag," Wolf shouted, holstering his pistol. Wilhelm turned to him eyes ablaze handing the flag off. Wolf was now the target of every rebel within striking distance.

A faint bugle trumpeted far away as it cried a quick and shy tune of retreat. A victory cheer lifted from the rebels as they saw their chance. Their enemy was being mangled and ready to run. The 7th Michigan had been cut to ribbons along the fence. They'd valiantly tore the rails down and charged the Confederate artillery, but had suffered great casualties.

The 13th Michigan was being overwhelmed with their colors threatened. Alger's dismounted troopers were making their way back into the cavalry that had displaced them only minutes before, putting pressure with well-aimed shots in their flank, but the regiment was at risk of being enveloped and destroyed by the enemy.

Wolf swung savagely with his saber left and right and left and right in a madness that bubbled inside him.

One of the Polish brothers took a slash to his thigh and Van Horn's hat partially deflected a saber swing. Blood ran down his face.

Wilhelm used his horse to create separation. "Retreat, men. Back to the road."

Wolf turned his mount in a circle trying to tell which way was back to safety. A rebel jabbed at him with a sword. Wilhelm's blade hacked the rebel's arm, cutting through sleeve, flesh, and bone alike.

"Ride, Johannes."

"Come on, Billy!" Wolf cried. As a disorganized knot, the troopers raked their horses with sharp spurs for the safety of Hanover Road. Bullets whizzed by as the dismounted Confederates tried to score hits upon their flank.

As he neared the Union line, he could see small groupings of cavalrymen trying to reform. Companies of the 7th stood together, brutalized men having been bravely beaten.

The artillery blasted upon the flank of the swooping rebels.

Wolf's men reached the beaten-down road baked in the heat and he tried to catch his breath. His saber was heavy in his hand, the lightness disappeared with the exhaustion of combat. His mind had a heightened aura surrounding him, almost a sense of euphoria. Billy's chest heaved, sweat drenching his coat, but he calmed as they stood watching the two forces regroup.

Bloodied and battered Union men he didn't recognize, began to rally around him. Men from the other companies. Men breathed hard with wide-eyed stares still filled with the fury of battle.

Wilhelm was there, blood droplets splattered his face and clothes, his sword resting on his shoulder as if he were about to go on parade. "Form up, men. We must be ready in case they try us again." The orphaned troopers regrouped into a short line around Wolf. "You're looking good, men. Find a spot. Get your noncommissioned officers on the flanks."

A trooper pointed and shouted. "More come!" He spied north of Cress Ridge.

Wilhelm squinted, watching the gray men scrambling to stay in rank, forward. "Eager bastards, aren't they?"

The entirety of a brigade marched for the critical intersection that the men now regrouped on, even larger than the last charge. Thousands of polished sabers reflected a blazing midday sun, blinding those who dared stare. Their line was tight and well composed, as if the men had marched this way from birth.

Men from the 13th and 7th trickled back to the intersection like lost prodigal sons. "Wolf," shouted a man on foot. Roberts stumbled in out of breath. "Lost my horse." He'd run almost a mile back to the safety of the Federal lines.

Wolf pointed at a stray mount. "Over there," he directed the man. Plenty of horses rejoined the ranks without riders, the beasts skittish and scared from the gunfire and cannon, but searching for the soothing words of a rider.

Roberts sprinted for a spare mount.

Only a few hundred men struggled to regroup. Nervousness somersaulted in Wolf's gut. The rebels marching their way numbered in the thousands. They were going to be ridden into the ground and chased from the field. *Are we the only ones left?*

Sergeant Berles exhaled hard. "Don't worry, boys. We're just scattered, our men will return. It's going to take some time to get everyone reorganized, but the boys will rally to the flag." Wilhelm eyed Wolf for a moment. "Keep that flag high where our boys can see it. Let the enemy know this is where they'll die if they want it."

Wolf kept the company standard high in the air. Wind took it now, tossing and beating the hand-sewn guidon as if it too wanted to see it fall, yet it didn't, Wolf's grip was fierce. They'd bled and died to ensure it stayed in their own hands and earned the honor of continuing to carry it. "Where's the lieutenant?" Sergeant Berles said.

The men didn't know. "Sir, I saw him that way," a trooper said.

"Get him," the Sergeant commanded, then to Wolf he said, "Keep that flag up so the lieutenant can find us." The men around him stifled a chuckle.

"The captain?" Wilhelm asked.

"Captain went down near the barn," shouted a man with shaggy black hair.

"We'll find him later." They knew he meant dead or alive, but each man hoped their captain was alive, for he was a good-natured fellow who offset the poor judgment of the colonel.

A pack of men trotted to the flag. Lieutenant Wells gestured out at the reforming regiment. "You men, what are you doing?"

"Reforming, sir," Sergeant Berles called out, eyes focused on the enemy.

"We must retreat, Sergeant. You can see Hampton brings the 1st North Carolina, the 1st and 2nd South Carolina and more men to bear!" Wells pointed with a white-gloved hand. "You men fall back. We'll be crushed." The troopers hesitated, the battle between their noncommissioned officer and platoon officer coming to a head in their minds.

"We are reforming, sir."

Wells's boyish face grew fearful. "You. You see them coming. We cannot stand against that." He got closer to the Sergeant. "This is suicide. We won't have a command left if we continue to fight here."

"Other men continue to fight here."

Wells's head bounced back and forth. "But we're not them."

Hampton's Confederates moved to a trot, their formation professional and tight. Thousands of the war's most elite cavaliers building momentum to break and scatter the Union forces and rampage freely the rear of Union line.

The jingle of sabers and the pounding of hooves emerged from the intersection. The troopers turned to see the return of their golden-haired general. He rode at the front of a fresh regiment.

"Looks like the 1st Michigan," a pale young private said.

"They been in reserve all day." The blue-coated troopers' uniforms were relatively clean. Not spattered with the soils of war, blood, dirt, sweat, and tears, only the dust of the ride and shining brass buttons. They were Custer's most veteran unit and the air surrounding them reeked of murderous confidence.

Custer jabbed his long, fine, heavy, double-edged straight sword in the air. He pointed it at the remainders of the 13th and 7th Michigan Regiments. He cupped his hand to his mouth. "You men, hurry."

"You heard the general," Sergeant Berles said. He made eye contact with

Wolf, ignoring the sputtering of Lieutenant Wells. "You lead them, standard bearer."

Wolf dug a spur into Billy's flank, but he needed little encouragement. "Ja!" The horse moved to a trot and the pieced-together companies of troopers followed the flag back into the fray.

CHAPTER 29

Afternoon July 3rd, 1863
East of Gettysburg, Pennsylvania

The ground reverberated with the shockwaves of the cannon barrage that was fading fast. The manmade rolling thunder that trembled the earth for the last two hours was dying down and dissipating into the annals of history. Time marched against them. They needed to position themselves to threaten the Union rear and force them into chaos during Robert E. Lee's direct frontal assault.

Hampton knew immediately that if they did not break the Federal hold here they would have failed in setting the anvil for Lee's 12,500-man Southern hammer. His men sensed it too. He watched the backs of his cavalry riding down the unsuccessful Union charge, but the enemy hadn't broken here. Which meant they recognized the importance of this ground as well. Men always fought harder when they knew what was at stake.

He observed from the northern part of the field, directing the flow and engagement of his troops. Parts of his staff, Captain T. G. Barker and Captain Marshall Payne, were with him.

The backs of his men continued to get smaller as they ran the enemy down. "They're too far. They've gone too far." He turned toward Barker. "They'll be flanked."

Scanning the area where he'd last seen Stuart, he cursed. He couldn't see his commander, but he must have known it as well. *I have to stop them or they will be shattered.*

He put his spurs into Butler, his secondary mount. Galloping down the ridge onto the field of battle, he removed his hat and began waving it at his pursuing men. "Fall back to me! Fall back to me!"

He tugged Butler's reins, bringing the horse to a halt. The horse did an excited circle, hooves quick-stepping. Sharpshooter fire increased upon his men. Followed by a canister shot from the federal battery. The deadly iron balls could cripple an entire column of men in one blast. "Men, fall back to me!"

The Jeff Davis Legion and the 1st North Carolina were slowing beneath the fire from the 5th Michigan. Fitzhugh's Virginians were still in hot pursuit. He could sense the battle drawing them and him into its glorious and painful embrace. The jangle of sabers and clip-clop of horsemen forced him to take his eyes off his other two regiments.

Captains Payne and Barker joined him. He turned over his shoulder to see a thousand troopers had amassed behind him.

"To the general!" Payne shouted with a hand in the air. "For South Carolina!"

Hampton spun his horse. His mouth dropped a fraction. He wasn't a man used to being surprised and he prized himself on his calm and cool manner on and off the field. His men had formed a solid rank and had followed him. A mighty outfit filled with warriors and soldiers alike. Anger overcame his pride.

"You weren't supposed to follow, men! It wasn't time."

Captain Barker looked back worriedly. More regiments from Fitzhugh Lee's Brigade materialized from the woods, protecting the flank like the entire movement had been planned. Chambliss's men had seen Hampton's Brigade begin to march and, joining the fervor of seeing an enemy run before them emerged in force from the timber.

"Sir, we have them," Payne said, licking his lips like a wolf. There was a glimmer of ecstasy deep inside his eyes as if he reveled in the thought of death.

Hampton gave him a glare fit to turn man to stone. The captain's elite company of red-shirted men sat atop their steeds around him. His boys had a hostile look that even their horses embodied. Prime fighting men. Blooded and eager. Hampton clenched his jaw. Gunfire still roared on his other men that were flanked but holding near the Federal lines.

"We got 'em, general!" shouted a man.

"Let's send 'em runnin'!" yelled another.

"For South Carolina!" added a soldier. The calls of his men were filled with pride and honor and faith that their cause was just so they were destined to prevail.

Hampton blinked, taking in the cream of the crop of excellence in cavalry. These were superb soldiers, even better men, and they had come to fight. He swallowed his anger. It was too late for that. He must commit to an assault or all momentum would be lost. Time was against them. Lee's attack commenced, his men had willfully devoted themselves to this battle. So they must break through by sheer force of flesh and will.

He had wanted to lead a flanking maneuver on the overly committed Union cavalry, driving them from the field. He'd been close to flanking them a few times already, but it was no use now. His men were committing to the climax of battle.

His boys looked glorious in their gray, butternut, and brown, like a brigade of God's very own vengeful angels. *Give the boys wings and they could be an army of the Lord.* They sat atop horses tall, proud, and free. What more could one ask for in this world than to live valiantly as free men, not under the oppression of a tyrannical government seeking to destroy their way of life?

Dismounted Union skirmishers ran from the field. He could smell a victory here leading to an all-out race for the center of the Federal lines. He imagined his boys galloping, their whoops filling the heavens while fear occupied the enemy infantry turning their defense into a chaotic scramble to survive.

He could win this battle and take the third day. He removed his hat and waved it in the air. A flanking maneuver would have been better, but surely they would take them now. The sun beat down atop his head, filling his saber wound with warmth.

"Those boys over there are scared. They're ready to break." Hoots, hollers, yelps, and yells clamored from his men. They were joined by the gunfire from the field of battle with a distinct, primal part of humanity taking its place in the symphony of shooting. "Through that junction lies the Union rear." He twirled his hat. "By God let's take it!"

He placed his hat back on his head, setting it a bit to the side as to not rub the wound from a few days prior. He threw a gloved hand into the air and swung it hard in the direction of the enemy, like a salute on its edge, chopping the wind.

His men moved their horses to a walk, trampling smashed pasture that had been ridden over again and again this day, each charge beating the earth to submission. He gripped the heavy sword on his hip.

Finding a secure hold, he ripped his blade free from its sheath. A heavy straight sword that only a man of his stature could successfully wield. It shone in the scorching sun's heat, picking up its bright rays and glowing like the sword itself was alight, ablaze with God's glory. He turned back over his shoulder. "Keep to your sabers, men."

The scrapes and scratches of metal against metal dominated the air as his men drew swords and sabers from their scabbards. Their blades dazzled in the sun.

He dug a boot into his horse and it changed gait to a trot. The hooves beat the ground faster. The fuel of battle surged in his veins slowly. *Win or die*, flashed in his mind.

His men took up their war chant, whooping and hollering as they rode, excitement ebbing through them. As they moved into a canter, they sounded like a thousand screaming Indians mixed with a howling of coyotes and wolves and all manner of devilry between. The cheer rose in this throat, feeling the flood of violence filling his veins. He bellowed at the top of his lungs along with his men, and they prepared to water the earth with Yankee blood and win this war.

"Charge them, my brave boys, charge them!" he roared. And his men galloped their steeds for glory.

CHAPTER 30

Afternoon July 3rd, 1863
East of Gettysburg, Pennsylvania

The disorganized companies joined Custer and the veteran 1st Michigan. The 1st resembled veterans in more ways than one. As a whole, they were much older than the 13th and 7th Michigan Regiments. They had grown thick beards and wispy mustaches, drooping muttonchops and long-hanging goatees, but most importantly they held the realistic wariness of men who'd seen their fair share of combat. A charge wasn't going to lead to glory, but danger and death. Not the starry-eyed wonderment that had plagued Wolf only a week prior. He was beginning to understand what war meant and it was the ugliness of mankind on a bloody scale.

Custer eyed his men. "To me, lads!"

"Form a proper line, boys," Wilhelm shouted.

The men hurried to obey, lining their horses in a long row next to the 1st Michigan, supplementing them with man, mount, sword, and pistol. Wolf took his place at the center of the line, making sure to keep the guidon high in the air to be seen.

A horse forced its way next to Wolf. He turned to stare at Lieutenant Wells. The tall man held his saber on his shoulder.

"Don't look at me. That's an order," Wells said to him.

Wolf kept his face forward. "Yes, sir."

"As much as I think it's an ugly thing, it's my flag too. I'll not let it fall into enemy hands."

Wolf hid his satisfaction. If the lieutenant wanted to die with the rest of them, he had no means to tell him he couldn't.

The approaching Confederates were spreading squadron by squadron.

"Must be all Stuart has," Wells whispered under his breath. He walked his horse to the front of the line.

The horde of men gave the impression that the entirety of Stuart's command or at least all the available men at his disposal were on the move toward the battered Union lines. They didn't bother to hide in the timber now. Each additional rebel stepping onto the field dwindled the courage of the Northern horsemen like a sculptor chipping away piece by piece until a stiff wind could blow the dust of their courage away.

Men trickled into the line, but not enough. No reinforcements ran to aid them. No cavalry galloped to their support. However, they weren't without fighting men. Pennington's battery hammered at the enemy horseman. McIntosh and Irwin Gregg's brigades manned the Low Dutch Road, but if the rebels blew past Custer's men like a cool breeze, they could do little to stop them.

Roberts pointed, a shake to his voice. "Wolf, there's the Red Shirts."

Near the center of the oncoming cavalry, a company of riders had their fine gray jackets open to reveal red blouses. They wore broad-brimmed, black hats and held shining sabers and pistols, while they hooted terror from angry lips. Their flag waved in the air, a bloody star on a field of black night. He couldn't make out the words in the distance, but they were there. *Mortem Tyrannis.*

The battle calls of the rebels washed over the Union men with cold fear. There was nothing like it. It was basic and wild, men filled with an unquenchable bloodlust. Even surrounded by his brothers, it made him doubt their survival.

Wilhelm puffed air through his nose. His mustache twitched. "Screaming and hollering never won a war. Staying in ranks and striking true does," Wilhelm called at the men.

It steadied their battered nerves for a moment. The yelling rebels continued their ride across the field even as Union sharpshooters picked at their flanks.

Wolf narrowed his eyes at the center of Hampton's men, the Red Shirts. "Hampton's near." A fierce pang of fear, doubt, and regret filled his gut. They all swirled into an unsettling anger.

The general that had killed Franz. War or not, Wolf wanted redemption for the loss of his friend, but not as much as Wilhelm.

Wilhelm turned toward his small unit of men, his voice barking. "When we charge, you aim for there." He pointed with his sword at the black flag.

Bart frowned. Van Horn's face soured as he peered into the field of advancing horsemen. They knew what charging the red-shirted men meant. Those were the unbeatable Red Shirts. The cream of the Southern crop. In their exhausted, depleted state, they wouldn't last long in a one-on-one contest.

After weighing his odds, Bart nudged his brother. "Yes." A broad smile crawled over both their lips. "Yes." The two large men slammed fists together and yelled in Polish at one another.

They were soldiers.

"What the hell? Yes," Wells added with a nod.

They would fight.

"Yes," Roberts shouted.

They had their honor.

"Yes," Wilhelm snarled.

They would get their revenge.

"Yes," Wolf growled.

They would fight to the last man. Each affirmation linking the men together in a singular purpose to take on the determined enemy riding before them.

The rebels came on in fabulous, well-ordered ranks.

The horses stamped, sensing a charge.

The Confederates thundered louder than the booming cannon of Meade's line three miles away. The gray storm came to engulf the entirety of the Rummel Farm.

A slender, pale officer with colonel eagles on his shoulders walked his horse next to Custer. He coughed into a black-gloved hand and held his hand over his mouth in pain. He calmed his breathing after a moment and then lifted his chin in resolution. He appeared ready to topple to the ground at any moment.

Custer nodded in honor to the sickly colonel. Custer's mount, Roanoke, his iron-gray stallion, stomped the ground beneath him, smacking lips and pulling on his reins. Pointing his heavy straight blade at the rapidly advancing Confederate cavalry, he called to his men. "Those men want to end the war today. They want to ride over us and crush our troops holding the line. I say, not today. I say, today we show them that we're made of the toughest guts they ever seen! To glory!"

He turned Roanoke, his mighty steed, toward the oncoming rebels and twirled his blade in the air. The 1st Michigan along with the remains of the 7th and 13th Regiments followed him eagerly. The bugler sounded the advance and the troopers moved their horses to a walk. The gray rebel thundercloud raged across the farmland like a menacing hurricane of man, steel, and horse, preparing to smother their Union foes, their calls for battle growing more powerful as they closed in.

The bugle call was given for the quick movement from walk to trot and then a moment later from trot to canter and rapidly into a full gallop.

The wind tugged at the standard of F Company of the 13th Michigan. Roughly thirty-two inches high, seventy inches long, and a dove of thirty-one inches to staff. The red was blood-vibrant over the field of pitch black. The golden wolf head snarled fiercely against the ebony cloth. It said nothing else. There were no crossed sabers, as designated cavalry guidons were supposed to bear, nor numbers and letters of their unit and company. Only a golden wolf baring its teeth at the enemy. Today, the first sergeant had carried it, and he'd been butchered in their last charge. Now, it was Wolf's turn to bear the company colors. *Let them take it if they can.*

The ground churned beneath their horses. It was a race to reach the Southerners first, each trooper trying to gain strides on the general that charged so blindly into harm's way ahead of the rest.

Billy's chest heaved beneath Wolf as he galloped, his muscle flexing with each step of the horse's stride. The animal must be tired after the first charge and now Wolf was asking the horse to repeat his performance. Without a horse, Wolf would be ridden down. A crippled man with little future in the infantry. Billy was his lifeblood to war and he led him again into the Confederate swell surging over the pastures, knowing this could be their last ride.

Rebel yells turned to demon screams as the collision between the cavalrymen became a guarantee. It was normal to protect one's horse, but all the men knew what was at stake and fully committed to the charge.

Wolf found himself bellowing like a wild banshee, the wind whipping his flag and his clothes. The other men picked up the cheer, forcing it back upon the encroaching rebels. It was the only way a man sometimes could steel himself before putting his terrestrial body in death's harrowing sights. It gave him the courage to fight and kill another man, and if need be die with his head held high. And the opposing men braced for impact.

There was a fraction of a second before the two forces met that everything slipped into slow-motion. It was as if time and space stopped. The fierce, defiant screams of men, the quake of hooves, sabers outstretched suspending in the air, all captured Wolf's mind, holding it hostage. The man's eyes across from him were an almost sky blue. His teeth mostly white. His cheeks covered with a short, blond beard. The young rebel's saber veered downward and he closed his eyes at the last second as if it could protect him from the violence.

Wolf did the opposite. His eyes stared into the oncoming madness as the front ranks of mounted men slammed into one another with a mighty crack that was heard in the heavens. It sounded like a hundred-foot wave crashing into the shore or a line of timber falling to the earth. The opposing men were a struggle of oil and water, with only one rising to the surface. The rebel across from Wolf blurred by.

Horses toppled, men were thrown to the ground and sabers flashed as riders moved past one another. The second and third rows of men pushed into the front, but they had slowed down to avoid fallen men and mounts alike.

Like a fist to the gut, the Union horsemen punched into the Confederate line, folding them to the flanks. The 1st Michigan continued through the lines of rebels, cutting them, but the rookie 7th and 13th stalled within the rank and file of rebel horsemen absorbing the forceful impact of the Union soldiers.

A rebel in a butternut coat took a swing at Wolf with a saber, the blade splitting the air. He parried the saber strike with the flagpole, the enemy's sword shaving a piece free. He yanked Billy's reins to the side, away from the man. Another rebel in an open red shirt wrapped a hand around the flagpole in an attempt to steal the colors. Fire barked from Wolf's Colt as he shot into the center of the rebel's crimson chest.

The rebel flinched, but didn't release the staff as darker crimson stained his shirt. The horseman dropped his gun and used both hands on the guidon. Growling into the man's face, Wolf spurred Billy away, and together they dragged the man out of his saddle. The Red Shirt fell to the earth and disappeared into the bloody grass and dust.

Frantic seconds passed as Wolf scanned for members of his unit. Blue- and gray-clad men seethed in the chaos of war and the scintillate swipes of sabers. The 1st Michigan had reengaged the rebels on a flank. The booming of cannon ripped into the rebel rear, driving the horsemen deeper into the mass of Federal cavalry.

If the rebel horsemen could rout the cavalry in front of them, they wouldn't be subject to the canister shots from Pennington and Randol's batteries. They drove down even harder on their Union foes. The closer they pressed into their enemy the less likely the cannon would risk hitting their own men. And the pressure grew even greater upon Wolf and his comrades.

A glimpse of Wilhelm flashed. He hammered his way like a blacksmith through red-shirted rebels. He would be struck down separated from the men despite his singular blind rage. Wolf spurred his horse in the direction of the crazed sergeant.

Wilhelm chopped down with brute strength left and right, not caring as gray men fell to the sides or rear of his mount. Amidst the chaos, parts of the unit gathered around the flag. Soon a circle of battered comrades surrounded him, fending off rebels in single combat.

Bart and Dan wielded their sabers with overwhelming strength and little technical skill like they chopped down trees. Roberts kept his pistol in the air until a rebel ventured near and then he would shoot. Gratz had both saber in one hand and a pistol in the other. Horses danced in excited nervousness of battle.

Pushing himself with his stirrups, Wolf sat high in his saddle. Rebel ranks closed around Wilhelm like a tightening noose. Every second he vanished further, cut off from the main salient of Union horsemen.

A bullet whistled by Wolf's ear, forcing him to duck down.

"What are we doing?" Roberts yelled.

"Hold," Wolf said, watching Wilhelm.

The sergeant made for a giant man atop a burly bay horse. With a bushy brown beard and wreathed stars on his collar, Wolf knew it was Hampton. He wasn't sure if Wilhelm knew or if he only wanted to cut down every rebel on the field, but they were on a collision course.

Speaking briskly, Wolf said. "Wilhelm's too deep. He'll be killed. Follow me." His comrades nodded, wide-eyed, as Wolf urged Billy into the swath of gore that Wilhelm carved through the enemy ranks.

His comrades fired pistols into rebels and swung sabers with dead-tired arms. They came upon Wilhelm circling his horse around the giant, General Wade Hampton.

It was as if Wolf witnessed two heroes from the Trojan War, Hector and Achilles meeting in combat for the last time. Their swords clashed with such might the blades must be chipped, they took turns jabbing sharp points at one another, and the metal clanged as the men fought for savage advantage. Wolf aimed his pistol at the general.

A shout came from Wolf's flank, "Yank!" The man wore a maroon sash around his waist and a gray kepi atop his head. "For South Carolina!" the officer yelled and spurred his black horse. The Confederate held his saber in a pointed, striking position, the tip of the blade reaching over the top of his mount. He rode his horse in perfect form of an experienced equestrian.

"Thirteenth!" Wolf shouted and kicked Billy to a gallop. He dipped the company guidon as he clung to his horse's neck, wedging the staff underneath his armpit. Earth whisked airborne as the men charged one another. The wolf flag snapped in the air like an accomplice.

Just as they were about to meet, Wolf leveled the guidon staff directly with the officer's chest. The man's eyes swelled in surprise. Cracking upon impact, the jolt sent shivering pain through his arm like a bell being rung. He immediately bent over in agony and gripped his limb, squeezing his chest. When he removed his hand, his fingers were painted with bittersweet blood. He grimaced, smearing the fluid in his fingertips.

The Confederate officer kept riding, his mount tossing its head, mane fluttering. Wolf turned Billy, gritting his teeth. The officer wheeled his horse around, facing Wolf, ready to make another charge. His red-painted sword wavered in the air. Wolf held his broken flagpole with its jagged edge, his shoulder throbbing.

The rebel officer peered down and felt the guidon of F Company, 13th Michigan protruding from the center of his chest. Dropping his jaw, his sword fell. Both hands grasped the shaft in astonishment. "By God." He glanced at Wolf and blinked dipping sideways off his horse.

"Billy." Wolf goaded his horse in the direction of the fallen officer.

The officer rolled on his back. His blond goatee filling with sticky bittersweet that dribbled from the corners of his mouth. He stared at Wolf with glassy eyes. Removing his maroon sash, he tried to stem the blood fleeing his body. The blood and sash ran together as one seamless color of death. "I have your, your colors," he said in a Southern accent. His eyes dimmed as his soul left him.

Wolf bent down and gripped the shaft. Heaving with all his might, he dislodged the embedded pole from the man's torso. The sash came with it, saturated with wet redness. He removed the long cloth and tucked it around his neck along with his father's. He draped the flag over his saddle and tried to gain his positioning relative to his comrades.

General Hampton still fought Sergeant Berles in a duel of the ages. Blood poured from multiple gashes, trickling into his eyes and beard. Rebel horsemen slashed frantically, attempting to push Berles back in a heroic effort to save their general.

More Union troopers saw the gold stars on Hampton's collar and made for him. Hampton swung his heavy sword into a Union trooper's head, splitting his face almost in two, reminding Wolf of the watermelon-topped straw men. Except the man's exposed skull was white.

Hampton was a bear being hunted by a pack of dogs. Even if the dogs won, there would be countless casualties. He stabbed his blade through the chest of another rider, flinging him to the ground with brute strength.

Wilhelm was the bravest of the pack, a hunting dog unable to be deterred from his prey. He steered his horse back into the general, chopping at Hampton like he was a tree to be hewed down.

Spurring his horse for Wilhelm, Wolf pointed his pistol at Hampton. After parrying a series of pointed jabs from Wilhelm, Hampton momentarily glanced at Wolf. A flash of recognition crossed his face. The pistol in Wolf's hand banged with fiery revenge.

The brute of a general didn't flinch when the bullet entered his body, but he snarled instead, swinging his heavy sword at Wolf's neck. The radius of the swipe was made longer by his excellent reach, the point missing by inches. The wind from the strike sent smoky air awash over Wolf's face. For a brief moment, Hampton was alone. He howled at Wolf. Spinning his horse, fending blows from all sides, but the moment came and went when more of his men rushed to save him.

Rebels thrust between Wilhelm and Wolf, using their bodies and horses to block them. High notes of buglers sounded the call for retreat. More blue troopers crashed into the rebel flanks as platoons and companies of cavalrymen joined the fray stymieing the enemy horsemen.

The canister shot and carbine fire ate into Hampton's regimental wings. The bold charges of both McIntosh and Gregg's men added their weight to the struggle. Captain Peltier was back in the saddle atop his black mare leading another contingent of the 13th Michigan. They hollered at the top of their lungs as they crashed their horses into the melee.

The rebels turned their mounts and made a calculated retreat and the Union troopers watched them, for they were too exhausted and ravaged by battle to give pursuit.

An officer in a red blouse helped Hampton as they rode, propping the giant upright in his saddle. Wilhelm's chest heaved. He was covered with blood from head to toe. Splattering doused his face. He leaned his head back and cried a primal roar of agony. Tears streaked down his cheeks, cutting wet lines over his face.

"Damn you!" He shook his head, spittle around his dry lips. "Damn you!" He screamed at the retreating rebels.

"We did it," Wolf said.

The anguished sergeant peered at Wolf, noticing him for the first time. Wilhelm blinked, recognizing his fractured unit that remained. "Johannes, my boy. Bart. Roberts." He nodded to the men sitting on their horses the field a bloody mess of the fallen. "Where's Berry? Van Horn? Shugart?"

Bart shook his head no. It had been a miracle that anyone was still together. Clenching his jaw, he turned back to Wolf. "You still have the flag?"

"Yes, sir." Wolf held the guidon for him to see. Blood from the officer soaked the top of the flag along the right side, staining it a deeper shade of red. The sergeant hopped down from his horse and scooped a Spencer repeating rifle from the grass.

He motioned with his hand. "Give it here."

Wolf handed the standard over. The sergeant fastened the flag to the rifle and gave it back to Wolf. "Let them know we're still here." His eyes held pain and anger and a bitter glimmer of hope for revenge.

Wolf's hands accepted the gun, wrapping around the wooden stock. The wind tugged at the flag, but he held it tight and erect. The remains of the 13th Michigan clustered close. It didn't matter that it was F Company's guidon, it only mattered that it was one of their flags.

"Thirteenth!" Roberts shouted, raising his injured arm in the air.

"Thirteenth!" the troopers yelled around him.

Wolf squinted at the blood-stained, bullet-hole-marked flag. "Thirteenth," he yelled and hoisted the flag to the sky.

The cheers of the men encircled them. Men from the Michigan Brigade crowded in the farm field, shouting their joy of battle survival to the heavens as the enemy retreated.

CHAPTER 31

Late July 3rd, 1863
Two Taverns, Pennsylvania

Custer walked into the Dancing Lass tavern. The interior had a musty smell and a short Irish barkeep with a puckered face. A large table had been commandeered by his division commander, Brigadier General Judson Kilpatrick.

The general sat in a chair with his dark blue regulation coat unbuttoned, a sweat-stained white shirt underneath. Beads of sweat ran down his face. With the entrance of Custer, he licked his thin, pursed lips beneath a long beak of a nose that dominated his face. It was made to look even longer than it should with his short chin and massive sideburns. He gestured for his aides and officers to depart. The men made uncertain eyes at Custer as they passed.

Raising his palm in salute, Custer said. "Sah, General Custer reporting for duty."

Kilpatrick smirked and raised his eyebrows. He took a shot of whiskey and wiped his chin. "Reporting for duty?"

Custer kept his chin raised, the other officers watched him from the bar. He'd expected an ass chewing and the need to justify his actions. "Yes, sir."

Kilpatrick gave him a quick shake of his head. "*Now*, you're reporting for duty?"

Gulping down his guilt, he spoke. "Yes, sir. General Gregg required my assistance with his division, sir."

Turning away, Kilpatrick grabbed a leather pouch and pipe from his table. He stuffed tiny pieces of tobacco into the end and struck a match to it. Bluish smoke dissipated into the air swirling around his head. "He did didn't he."

Custer kept his mouth closed.

"Left me half staffed to carry on operations near Round Top. Not sure if you know, but rebels were active there as well."

"You had General Farnsworth's brigade, sir. He's a quality brigade commander."

Kilpatrick sucked hard on his pipe. Powder blue smoke puffed out of the end and he blew out the smoke from his nose. "You haven't heard?"

"No, sir." Worry clouded Custer. He glanced at the officers near the bar. The mustached Farnsworth was not among them. He was a peer that had been promoted a few days earlier at the same time as Custer. Although not as young, he was new to leading men at a brigade level, and he considered him a friend.

"He's dead, General. Killed in action."

"How, sir?"

"I suppose the regular way. Five bullets to the chest. He was conducting a charge to dislodge the rebels from their position. Very unfortunate sequence of events in the south, where you were supposed to be."

Custer blinked rapidly, taking in the information about his friend. "That is very sorry news, sir."

Kilpatrick stood and paced to Custer. He was short and shrewd with narrow shoulders and he had to stare at Custer from below. "I feel like we may have miscommunicated earlier when I asked you to return to our *division*."

"I do not understand, sir."

"You are under my division, General, not Gregg's. I give you orders, not him."

Eyes drifted down to his commanding officer. "Sir, Gregg is a superior. I am obligated to follow his orders. He never could have carried the day without my troopers."

"You follow my orders."

"But—"

"But nothing," Kilpatrick snarled, his lips curling beneath his nose. "You will follow my orders or you will be court-martialed for cowardice."

Anger boiled inside Custer's belly, but he suppressed it even deeper down. He'd led four charges from the front lines while Kilpatrick hid behind his brigades, directing his men into the slaughter with only his own reputation to gain. Cowardice was the last thing the men would accuse Custer of, he knew that much.

"I understand. Sir." Custer said the last word loud and clear. It was plain that this man would recklessly have his men charge into a fortified position and be slaughtered like lambs to try and gain prestige. The rumors through his camp had been correct. Kilpatrick had sent Farnsworth to his death. Was it for politics? Farnsworth's uncle had secured his promotion and was a prominent Republican, while Kilpatrick was a Democrat. Or was it pure ignorance of war? Or was it growing impetuousness? Regardless, it disturbed him, rocking his confidence.

None of it mattered because it was clear that Kilpatrick wasn't fit to lead a company of men into battle. His command style was the converse of Custer's. Custer raced his men to the front because their charge meant something, to hold Stuart's men at bay. Not a charge to dislodge a useless regiment of rebel soldiers with suicidal frontal attacks.

Kilpatrick's eyes seemed to read his mind. "Do you have something to say?"

His teeth ached as he clenched his jaw. "No, sir." He knew where any word of dissent would get him.

"I will have my orders followed from here on out?"

"Yes, sir." *Over my dead body. I will disobey every order if it is for the greater good of this Republic.* A strong tongue wouldn't keep him a general. Survive with honor. The young general silenced his inner resistance.

"Then you are dismissed. We have an enemy to track down."

"Be a pleasure, sir."

Kilpatrick blew smoke out his mouth and waved Custer off with his hand.

"Oh, general, I almost forgot."

Halting himself, he itched to escape the tavern. "What's that?"

"You are to lead my vanguard south. Lee will soon begin his retreat, and we're to snatch his baggage train."

Custer stiffened. "Sir, my men have been in quite a scrap. We have wounded. And they need a rest."

"The brave Custer timid?"

Custer's mustache twitched. "No, sir. The Michigan boys can handle it."

"Good. See that your men are ready. We are to fall into pursuit in the next hour. Near Monterey Pass is where we'll catch them."

"Sir."

Mountainous and rocky terrain, the pursuit would be a cavalryman's nightmare. He would have said anything to get away from Kill-Cavalry. His boots thumped the floor as he marched back outside, not making contact with the junior officer's staring at his back.

He double-timed back to his orderly. The sweet taste of a hard-fought victory quickly turned to smoky ash in his mouth.

Joseph held the reins of a new mount, this one was white. Three horses in a few days, poor odds, but then again he was still in one piece without five bullet holes in his chest. "How is Roanoke?"

The mustached orderly nodded eagerly. "He took a shot to the leg, but he won't be lame. He'll be back to the fight in no time. Jolly good fellow, isn't he?"

"He is a right old boy. Tough as nails, even on the mend."

Custer settled atop his replacement. His body was bruised and his muscles sore from getting trapped under his horse in Hunterstown. Pale gray rain clouds gathered to the southwest, the same direction Lee's command retreated for.

Resounding thunder rumbled in the distance, reminding him of the battle earlier, but this battle was being fought in the heavens and promised to hamper his exhausted men's progress as well as the enemy's retreat. The sky darkened at full tilt, a mixture of storm and rising night.

"Make sure he gets extra fodder while we move. I'd like to hurry the healing process of the tough old chap."

"The brigade is toughening with a few bouts under their belt."

A grin formed beneath his mustache. "Yes, they are." He encouraged his horse into a trot back to camp. "And we ain't done yet."

CHAPTER 32

Night July 3rd, 1863
Rummel Farm, Pennsylvania

The Union troopers made camp around the fieldstone Rummel Farm and their outbuildings. Campfire smoke wafted toward the heavens and the sky drifted from purplish-red sunset to night as the men cared for the living and dead.

The white barn that had housed rebel then Union troops had been peppered with holes. Miraculously, none of the buildings had been destroyed and the owner John Rummel was joyous to be reunited with his wife after he'd been captured and released by the rebel forces.

The Rummel Farm land had been nearly destroyed, their fields and pastures razed by the thousands of horse hooves, holes in the ground from artillery, and the errant gear from fallen men. The land appeared to have been chewed up and spit out in tasteless dissatisfaction.

The wounded had been collected; the dead were looked after and laid in pallid singular rows of crumpled and battered men forever at rest, silent, souls no longer on the earth. Their hands were folded over motionless chests and, when possible, eyes shut. They'd found a Union trooper from the 1st Michigan and a 2nd South Carolina soldier locked in a deadly final embrace, knives plunged in one another's hearts. Unable to be pried apart, the two soldiers were left to be buried together.

The screams of wounded horses had been dealt with early after the affair.

The high-pitched screeches made Wolf shudder and the men put down the injured mounts, leaving the heavy beasts where they'd fallen covered in blankets of black flies. News started to trickle in about the climactic battle that had taken place at the center of the Union line. The massive cannonade that shook the ground had been over 150 Confederate cannon pounding the Union middle before almost 13,000 soldiers marched over an exposed mile to lock horns with entrenched Union infantry.

The Confederates had charged with such bravery that men were still in shock that they had been so brazen, but the dead spoke volumes of their courage. A courage that couldn't keep those men alive against the heavy lead balls of canister shot or the Miníe balls of the Union infantry taking cover behind stone walls. Yet the rebels had made it over the wall, only to be driven back by reinforced Union troops. It was being said that Lee had broken his army on the center that day. Time would tell if that was the truth.

Custer's brigade felt much the same way sitting near their field of battle miles from the Union lines. Stuart had led his own charge that had been stopped with the flesh and blood of the Northern cavalry. Effectively, it had been a stalemate, but the rebels left the field in the Union soldiers' hands. Stuart had been denied his purpose and if that wasn't a victory for the men then it was hard to know otherwise.

Wolf hobbled among the makeshift camp of the 13th Michigan. He'd seen the elephant enough now to know it wasn't all guts and glory. He'd killed men for his country and seen men die for theirs. It was enough to hope that maybe this war was coming to a close. But he wouldn't dare embrace that hope, only focus on his men instead. It may take a hundred battles like Gettysburg to find an elusive peace.

Men laid in exhausted heaps in the shadowy dusk. The company guidon had found a new home on a new flagpole lifting it above the devastation of the field. It flapped in the night wind, marking their place in the brigade. In the dancing flames, the camp was quiet save for the sobs of men. While there had been much joy immediately after the battle, it was followed with a great sadness as the dead were discovered and the wounded tended to. Then exhaustion both mentally and physically weighed upon the survivors.

He crouched down next to Dan and handed him a canteen. "Thank you," he said, tired. His voice was soft.

Bart sat nearby tending Berry. Berry had been struck with two balls, one in his belly and the other in his shoulder. The broad-framed man laid in a frail, weakened state with a blanket over him like a giant, sick toddler, much too delicate for a man of his stature. Bart held his head up while he poured water down Berry's throat. The injured man coughed, water leaking from his lips.

The battlefield hospitals were crammed with thousands of the injured and dying, so the regimental surgeon and his assistants were tending the wounded as best they could.

Shugart sat near a tree and one couldn't tell if he was praying or sleeping. Van Horn slept on the other side of the campfire, white bandages encircling his skull.

Wilhelm walked to where the men rested, he'd been tireless since the culmination of the battle. He'd washed the blood from his face and hands and resembled less of a crazed monster and more like a weathered farmer beaten by the elements and life alike. He waved Wolf over with a fatigued gesture. "Let's see that wound."

"It's fine." He'd shoved the Confederate's sash under his jacket to absorb the blood and it had stopped the bleeding in time.

"Sit, boy."

"What about Lent?"

Wilhelm frowned. "He's at the hospital. It was a horrific wound." He paused for a second. "He'll prolly muster out." Wolf had heard the term thrown around a lot recently. Mustering out meant he would die. Their unit would have lost another and Berry was at least going to be left behind in the care of the sawbones.

"Off with it," Wilhelm said.

Gingerly, trying not to use his injured shoulder, he stripped off his dark blue jacket and was surprised at how red his shirt had gotten. For the first time in days, he was happy about the warm summer heat. He took the officer's sash and gently tried to remove it. Clotted brownish crust ripped and tore, sending pain emanating through his chest, and he gritted his teeth. Reopened, the wound trickled blood.

"Damn, that hurts," he said.

"It should. You took a saber to the chest."

Wilhelm used the officer sash to wipe away blood and pulled out his sewing kit. Without looking, the man called at Roberts. "Do you have any of Cobb's shine?"

"Ah," Roberts said, his eyes darting back and forth.

Wilhelm eyed the single thread. "Bring it over." Fearing repercussions from robbing the dead sergeant, Roberts passed the bottle over. With a slight hand, Wilhelm tipped the bottle back, pouring the fiery liquid on his shoulder.

The wound agonized with the sting of a thousand bees, stealing Wolf's breath. He sucked in air and grimaced. "Can I at least have some of that?"

The bottle sloshing, the sergeant handed it over. Wolf took a swig. "I think you were supposed to let me drink some first."

Wilhelm ignored him, probing the laceration with a finger, sending fresh pain through the throbbing wound. "This should work. It's not too deep." He carefully threaded a thin piece of string through the head of his needle. He leaned over the campfire and dropped the whole thing into a boiling kettle resting over licking orange flames.

"What's that going to do?"

Wilhelm stirred the water with a stick. "It's a stiff cotton thread so I'm going to boil it first, soften the thing up."

"Shouldn't we wait for the surgeon?" Wolf eyed the floating string with concern.

Wilhelm shook his head no. "They're busy and you can't have an open wound. It will get inflamed and you'll get sick. We stitch you up and the sawbones can look at it later." He took the cotton thread out of the boiling water with a stick and laid it across his knee.

"Why you boil it?"

"Don't know. It's just how I was taught."

Wolf took another drawn-out drink of the alcohol. It tasted like rancid fire down his throat, but the warmth in his belly let him know it was working.

The sergeant bent closer, his eyes bloodshot. "You ready, boy?"

Wolf took another swig and grimaced. "Yes."

Wilhelm stitched his gash closed, each prick of the needle on the split skin agonizing, but after twenty minutes, and a lot of wiping blood, Wilhelm leaned back and nodded. "That will do." He put cut cloth over the suture and wrapped the sash tight around the wound.

Wolf moved his arm a bit, rotating his shoulder. He clenched his teeth. It felt torn, but secure.

"Now give me your jacket." Wolf handed it over and Wilhelm stitched that as well.

A slender man emerged from another part of camp. He stood and watched the unit for a moment from the flickering flames as if he were afraid before he walked forward.

"Men," Wells said.

The unit peered at him. They were still unsure about their lieutenant, but he'd gained a small amount of respect by riding into the jaws of death with them. Wells lifted his chin high into the air as he struggled for his words. He cleared his throat. "I wanted to tell you that you performed well today." He nodded his head gravely as if he were wrestling with something to share in common with the men. He swallowed hard. "I know that you have lost men and have wounded. I'll leave you to that."

He turned to leave only to stop himself. A man in a gold-trimmed, black jacket almost ran into him. Custer stopped and glanced angrily over at the men resting. "Lieutenant, prepare your men for march."

Wells gulped and stood tall. "Sir, we've had one hell of a day."

Custer spun on him, his blue eyes flashed anger. "Aye, we have." He skimmed over the men. "You in charge of these men?"

Wells only thought for a moment. "Yes, sir, these are mine."

Custer glanced up at the company guidon. "I saw that flag. You must be 13th?"

"Indeed we are, sir. F Company."

"You men beat the piss out 'em." He nodded intensely at his boys. "Gosh darn, I never been more proud, but we're to put the pressure on the running bastards. I need you to give me more."

Wolf stood using his strong leg to overcome the weak one. "We'll fight, sir." He was acutely aware of his topless body and his disheveled appearance.

"Aye, sir. We got more fight still in us," Wilhelm said.

Custer peered over at the other dog-tired men. "And you boys?"

The rest of the unit roused to its feet. No man wanted to be seen as weak by their commander. Battered, exhausted, but not beaten, they stood and were acknowledged by their general.

The young general lifted his mustache on his lip. "You have a good platoon, Lieutenant. Hardy men, all of 'em."

"Thank you, sir. They are hardy, no doubt."

A sad grin crossed Custer's face. "Those are my boys. A shame we lost any." He nodded, accepting the men that were gone. "Those are my boys." He marched off into the night. "Back in the saddle, we go."

CHAPTER 33

Early morning July 4th, 1863
East of Gettysburg, Emmitsburg Road, Pennsylvania

The wagon hit a stone and lurched the left rear wheel almost airborne. It crashed back down and General Wade Hampton let out a rumbling groan. "Mother of God." His voice was drowned out by the creaks of wheels and the hooves of mules and draft animals.

He stared up at the white canvas encasing the wagon. The whole cart rocked and reeled, offering him no respite from his wounds. The men had laid down blankets for the general but they provided no relief from the rocky roads being turned to mud outside the wagon. His sleep had been fevered and painful. He brought a hand to his head. White bandages had been wrapped around his skull where the Union sergeant had sliced him with a ferociousness that Hampton had only seen a handful of times on the field of battle. The man had no concern for his safety, wading through Hampton's men without a care for his own life.

Hampton tried to adjust his hip. Pain radiated from the bullet wound. *Then that bugger from Hunterstown put a goddamn bullet in my hip.* The surgeon said it would stay inside him, which meant he just couldn't die from sickness.

He closed his eyes, trying to breathe away the agony ebbing from his head and hip. The enemy should have broken. Custer, that brash golden boy. They shouldn't have been able to withstand us. Not our full might.

The wagon ground unceremoniously over another rock. "God damn!" He glared back at the driver. "Can you keep this thing off the rocks?"

"Sorry, sir," mumbled his driver.

Captain Payne's face leaned in from the rear of the wagon. Rain pelted his gray folded slouch hat, running off the rim and dripping on to his horse. "Sir?"

"Nothing, Payne." He pushed his head back down, struggling to find a spot that wouldn't bash his head off the side with the next rock the wagon rolled over.

An injured man cried out from the wagon behind them. "Oh God, please let me die." The cries of the wounded had been by far the worst part of the agonizing journey. The calls of boys for their mothers. The sobs to be left behind. The pleas to be removed from the hellish wagons crammed with the dead and dying. He was fortunate to have his own wagon.

Payne peered at him. An odd tinge of concern hung in them. "We'll get them back, sir. We won't surrender. Never. They'll bleed if a Yankee boot touches Southern soil."

Hampton stared at the white ceiling. The casualties were escalating as they trickled in. Almost 20,000 and rising. *Dear God, when will this war end?* He shook his head thinking about the loss of life. So many had been extinguished by this war, a war he could ill afford to lose. Too much money had been spent, too many lives lost, and too much pain. His carriage swayed and he sucked in a deep breath, resisting the urge to cry out.

He could feel Payne's eyes on him. "Sir?"

"I heard you, Captain. We will prevail. We must regroup and make ourselves feared again. Strike from the shadows. Cut to their core. Every inch of ground paid for in their blood."

"Stuart sends his regards, sir. He was most troubled by your state and wishes you a quick recovery." He would always support Stuart no matter the cost. The young general had so much promise and a great tactical mind, but like all young men he needed the guidance of an experienced mentor to help him along. Although Stuart had many times his age in military experience, life experience made a man's judgment sound. He worried that his recovery would go slow. Every injury he sustained seemed to take longer and longer to heal, removing him from the struggle when they needed their generals the most.

"Tell him that I regret my absence." He gnashed his teeth as the wagon jostled his body, sending shooting pains to his back.

"I will send your regards, sir," Payne nodded and went to take his leave.

"Captain."

"Sir?"

"Remember why we fight."

"I will, sir."

"When this war is over, these men will be our brothers again."

Payne stared at him for a moment unblinking.

"They will be our neighbors."

"I don't care to have them as neighbors or brothers. My brothers are here amongst these fine men. I have no need to reconcile with such a people."

Hampton tried to control his pain by breathing air through his nose. He gulped down his suffering not wanting to show weakness in front of his subordinate. "Remember they are our brothers by virtue of our founding fathers, but we must prevail."

Payne lowered his head in deference to his commander. "I bid you adieu, General. If time permits, I will visit you in South Carolina."

"Godspeed, Captain."

Payne wheeled his horse around and trotted down the muddy road, his mount throwing up clumps of brown.

Hampton watched his captain disappear behind a long line of wagons. He worried what would befall the young captain being off of his commander's leash. *However noble our cause, at what price? Have I just unleashed a wicked man on the world?*

He arched his neck in discomfort and closed his eyes, trying to tune out the cries of the dead and dying from dragging him downward into despair.

CHAPTER 34

Late Night July 4th, 1863
Monterey Pass, Pennsylvania

The rain poured down on the men. They'd gone days without any respite from the heat and now all the precipitation came at once. The men were so saturated with water that the rain had nowhere to go, rolling off hats, jackets, and pants, soaking through their britches. Even their leather boots failed to protect them from the downpour.

Lightning snapped and crackled across the sky, spiderwebbing bright light upon the twelve men of the 13th Michigan.

Water flowed down the rocky path, developing a new stream along the side of the steep mountain gap. The crack of muskets and rifles permeated the cavernous darkness of the night. Occasionally, an exploding boom of a cannon would echo between the pass walls as the Confederates pummeled the troopers trying to gain access through it.

For over three hours, Kilpatrick had ordered Custer's brigade to assault the pass. Alger's 5th Michigan had been thrown back with the severe wounding of its lieutenant colonel and Gray's 6th Michigan shot back and forth in the darkness against rebels with superior elevation, only the muzzle flashes to give the position of the enemy away.

The entire column of cavalry had been at a standstill until a young woman dressed in a man's farming clothes had emerged from the twilight. The daughter of a local farmer, she had come to help the distressed Union cavalry gain advantage over the Southern invaders. She led Sergeant Wilhelm and his unit around the other side of the mountain through thick, leafy timber.

Wolf wiped water from his eyes. He knew they'd come closer because the gunfire increased in its drum-like volume. The ground shook as the cannon bass boomed again, quaking the land beneath their feet. The troopers were dismounted, fearing for their exhausted mounts more than for themselves as they slipped and slid up the trail.

The young woman stopped them on the path and crouched down. "They're 'bout a hundred yards through those trees," she whispered. She looked like a young boy with her attire, smooth cheeks, and gangly, slender body.

"Aye," Wilhelm said and peered hard into the looming greenery. "The rain will cover our approach. Wolf, take three men and continue through this timber. Wait six minutes and then attack. I'll see if I can get ahead of them and hem them in."

"Yes, Sergeant."

Wilhelm turned to the girl. "You have our thanks, but off with you. This is man's work. No place for a lady."

The girl didn't complain, but hurried back down the steep trail.

Wolf faced his crouching men. "Roberts, Bart, Van Horn. You're with me." Soaking wet, the men appeared more black than blue in the starless night as they stalked forward. Wilhelm and the others disappeared through the trees.

The mountain foliage was thick with roots, vines, and loose stone, and the men made difficult work through the rocky timber. Wolf drew his pistol, having to use his other hand to steady himself on coarse tree trunks and jagged rocks alike. His weak leg painfully complained as he toiled, and the brace squeaked. And the pattering rain turned to be a blessing as it masked the sound of his leg.

Each man drew his pistol, knowing that this would be a close quarters battle in the dark. As they crept closer, they could see the muzzle flashes from the rebels holding the pass. The crack of the percussion caps, the puffs of smoke, and the bursts of fire propelling bullets at the pinned Federal troopers below. Wolf waved a hand palm down and his men crouched, taking cover in the underbrush.

"Get that cannon loaded," shouted a rebel.

"We don't have any more round shot," complained another.

"Fill it with canister. We'll wait until they try to get through again and shred 'em to ribbons."

"Yes, sir."

Two artillerymen went about prepping their gun slowly. It was a single piece of horse artillery, a three-pounder, a slender gun, but here it could do the work of an entire infantry regiment, obliterating any man or group of men daring enough to try to rush the pass. On the flanks of the cannon, rebels sniped at muzzle-flashes from Yankees below.

"How many you count?" Wolf asked Roberts. The short thief covered his eyes, trying to block out the rain. "Two on the cannon. Two firing off the side of the cliff and the man issuing orders."

"Five?" Wolf whispered. He couldn't contain his surprise.

"That be five."

"Must be more." He tried desperately to see more rebels in the darkness. His eyes obliged him with shadows and shapes of devils and ghosts, but he could only discern the men that Roberts had seen. So few men had held the pass against an entire regiment. This did little to boost his confidence that the war had any chance of ending.

The cracks of carbines and bangs of pistols drew the rebels' attention. They all turned to stare at the other end of the small camp.

Shadows covered the faces of Wolf's small contingent, fierce determination lingering beneath the surface. They were ready to unleash a harsh violence upon their stubborn enemy. "Let's get 'em."

They raced from the timber with bent backs. They were the ghosts in the darkness. The hunters of the rebels. Not the other way around. Van Horn had slid within a few feet of one of the snipers before firing two shots in the man's back. The rebel dropped his rifle, grasping at his back and toppled over the edge, disappearing into the pass.

Wolf lined up a shot on the officer, steadying his aim. The dismal rain pelted him, mucking his eyes, but he squeezed the trigger anyway. The rebel bent awkwardly to his left as he was struck. A host of bullets hit the men on the cannon and they collapsed, sliding down the metal tube.

Wolf limped to the fallen officer. The man gritted his teeth and clutched his side in grievous pain.

"Sons of bitches," he spat. He breathed hard, like the rain was attempting to drown him, but he was trying to keep his pain under control.

Wolf bent down next to him. Creases of suffering lined the officer's face, that and a white stubble like a light snow. "Where are the others, sir?"

The rebel officer sneered with painful joy. "What others?" He hacked and coughed and then arched in torment. "Oh God! Christ."

"There must be at least a company of men here."

The pain subsided and the rebel wheezed a laugh. "You cowards. Five men. Hahaha."

"Where are the rest? We will get you medical aid, but we need to know." Lightning flashed as it snaked across the sky like silver cracks in the darkness, as if the heavens were breaking into pieces.

"We held you for hours with five men. Would I had a company, I could have taken on your entire army." He spit water from his lips.

"Impossible."

"If we had the high ground at Gettysburg, you would've been destroyed to the man."

Wolf stood, the realization that five men had stymied his brigade dropped like a pit into his belly. He had no doubt that, had the tables been turned at Gettysburg, the Union would have been bested as well, but that's not the way it played out. "But you didn't."

Watery blood seeped through his fingertips bubbling away on the mountainside. "We'll never surrender while any of us still live. You can bet on that, Yankee scum." The man writhed in pain and exhaled loudly.

They were joined by Sergeant Berles. "What'd he say?"

"There's only five of 'em."

"I didn't see any others."

"Five men held us for over four hours?"

"Aye." Lightning continued to crack and split the night sky with splintering yellow light.

"So few men kept an entire column at bay." He was flabbergasted and angry that so few men could be so defiant in the face of their triumphant forces. They should be running, not turning to give a staunch fight. The gunfire from below ceased as the cavalrymen realized that no more violence was being delivered their direction.

Now the thunder of hooves filled the air as squadrons of horses galloped through the cleared gap in the mountain. The storm would not relent and would continue its assault against the Union soldiers long into the morning.

CHAPTER 35

July 5th, 1863
Ringgold, Pennsylvania

The Union men ravaged Confederate General Ewell's baggage train that night. They'd swept upon the supply wagons like a whirlwind of blue demons, horns in all. Their vengeance was taken with bitter ferociousness. All the frustration from the nighttime pass on the few guards and teamsters whipping their mules and horses in hasty retreat. It mattered not. The wounded men inside the wagons cried out as they were overturned in the panicked attempt to escape.

The 13th Michigan was left in camp the next morning, finding themselves looking after almost 1,500 rebel prisoners, most sick or wounded. A loose guard was placed around them, but most were so damaged that it would be certain death for them to flee. Not that either group would have ventured far.

Wolf's unit sat around a campfire in the morning sunlight, drying out from the night before. The morning had been spent on quiet reflection over the chaos of surviving one the largest battle of the war as it settled into their minds and souls, becoming a new part of them forever.

Wilhelm sipped his coffee, his back to a tree, boots crossed. "They say it was the biggest battle of the war. Almost 170,000 men fought. The largest battle ever fought on this soil. At least until the next one."

Bart crunched a piece of bacon. "Yes," he said solemnly. He stared off, preoccupied by his brother Berry, they'd left in haste from Gettysburg. Dan's leg wound was good enough that the captain allowed him to stay with the unit.

"But Lee's escaping," Wolf said.

Wilhelm nodded grimly. "He is. I just don't think either side was prepared for this kind of slaughter. Hopefully the Americans won't become too fond of it."

Van Horn didn't say anything. He stared out blankly, drinking his coffee.

The regimental flag flipped and flapped by the command tent, along with the Michigan brigade flag. F Company's guidon was nearby, sitting tall on its new trimmed pole, the bullet holes and blood stain now a prideful part of the men's standard. The regiment had lost over sixty men through the last few days, over a hundred wounded. Almost a third of their small regiment was killed or wounded over a five-day stretch. A couple more battles like the last few days and they would cease to exist. A brief flash of service ending with boys feeding the ground all over the nation.

The men around him eating their morning meal were veterans in every sense of the word now, even if most were young men new to the military. They'd seen men struck down by all manner of weaponry. They'd seen their brothers die, locked in immortal struggle with other men that were so much like them, yet so different at the same time. Not quite the other. How could one's brother be the other?

General Custer emerged from his tent with a cluster of colonels and other officers around him. He walked from campfire to campfire, talking to his men and sharing a cup of coffee with them.

Colonel Moore was with him, his rotund bearded face and short neck stretching to get a look at them. "Attention," Wilhelm called out.

The unit stood on their feet; Bart helped Dan upright. Wilhelm gave a fierce, open-palmed salute.

"You, the boys from F Company. You rallied the boys for the final charge?" Custer asked, his eyes running over them like water. A motley crew of men and boys, no, no more boys. His eyes stopped on Wolf. "Seems that you men have been in the thick of it lately. Stand at ease."

The unit relaxed. "Yes, sir." A few of the men sat back down, still drying, fatigue in every muscle.

Custer took a sip of his coffee. "By golly, you boys were busy. My thanks to your hard fighting. Our foe is both determined and formidable."

"Yes, they are, sir," Wilhelm responded with tempered words.

Custer faced Colonel Moore. "You're fortunate to have such men under your command."

Moore's pudgy cheeks jiggled. "They are a special group indeed."

"We need more like them."

Moore bit his tongue holding a disgusted gaze. "I will be sure to pass your compliments down to Captain Peltier."

"Say, where is the good captain? I would prefer to give the compliments myself."

"He is overseeing prisoner duty, sir."

"Who was your platoon leader?"

"Lieutenant Wells, sir."

Custer turned toward Moore. "I believe I saw him yesterday. Good lad?"

"Very tall, athletic lad, sir. Sound mind and the men love him. I supported his commission from the beginning." It was clear that Moore was taking credit for the group's success through Wells.

While Wells had charged with them after some convincing, he wasn't truly leading them, that had been left to Sergeant Berles. Now that Wolf thought of it, he hadn't seen the colonel until after the drums of battle had settled.

A proud smile curled under Custer's mustache. "I'd like to see him again as well. Let's head that way. I'd like to see a few of the Rebs anyway. Enjoy your rest, Wolverines, soon we'll be back in the saddle."

"The general thinks we fight well," Roberts said smartly.

Wolf raised his eyebrows. "Much to the colonel's disdain."

"Bugger the colonel. We survived. Brave, stupid survival. Sometimes they're one in the same."

"You'd think he'd would show a bit more appreciation to the men who rallied the regiment."

"We're just beneath him," Wilhelm said. He drank more of his coffee. "Immigrants, thieves, and invalids." The last words stung Wolf. He knew that as long as he wore his brace he'd be viewed as an invalid, despite his will to fight.

But the unit didn't seem to care. They grunted in tired approval of their sergeant's words. They were growing used to being at the bottom and crawling their way out.

"We can thank God for his protection," Shugart said with a look toward the rounded clouds drifting aimlessly through the skies.

A puckered look crossed Wilhelm, as if he'd been cheated by God himself.

Shugart ignored him with calming words. "He will look after the boy."

Wilhelm stood, pointing at the old abolitionist. "He didn't do a very good job and now he's gone."

"God works in mysterious ways. There's a reason for everything."

Wilhelm's face twisted in anger, his eyes flashing hate. "He was a sweet and gentle boy. This war wasn't his war."

"Yet, he answered the call to serve mankind and keep this nation united."

The sergeant pointed a finger at the older man. "Shugart, don't you tempt me. It wasn't my boy's time. It wasn't. So don't go telling me God has a plan because if these last few days were a part of his plan then he's a cruel God."

"Man corrupts all, even his best-laid plans."

Wilhelm shook his head. "Then you leave God out of this until man has set this ship straight."

Shugart's mouth clamped shut and he averted his eyes.

Staring at his small unit, Wilhelm dared anyone to contradict him. "We survived. That's all. God didn't have anything to do with it."

Whether they agreed or disagreed, the men quietly continued their breakfast, not engaging with the angry sergeant and avoiding his ire. Wolf stood to relieve himself. He walked through the hastily made camp, haphazard tents, men lounging, picketed horses, and wagons to where the rebels were being held under guard. He thought about what Wilhelm had said about God not being with them. He thought about his father and mother and his sisters back home. He wondered if they breakfasted with fresh eggs, bread, and sausage. He wondered if they prayed to God for his safety and his soul in case he fell on the field. They must. He knew they must. For it was the only hope they must have, not knowing anything about his whereabouts or well-being. He wondered if his father would read the newspaper about this great battle and be proud that his son did his part. Peering at the Confederates, he knew that their families must be doing the same.

The Confederates bore shattered limbs and bandaged wounds from any number of man's death implementations on the field of battle. Shrapnel, bullets, saber slashes, and other impalements brought on from splintering trees. These men had been treated and bandaged, given fresh water and rations. Some would still die, their injuries too severe to come through. Others would be taken by the fever that came on a few days later, their bodies blazing with heat until they were overcome. A few were only prisoners, men caught in the wrong place at the wrong time, and they looked happy enough to be alive and fed.

Wolf walked by the prisoner rebels huddled around a fire.

"Heya, Billy Yank," a rebel called over. A bedroll was wrapped around his brown jacket, his brown hat pushed to the top of his head.

Wolf approached the cluster of men.

"You boys eat this good all the time?" He showed him a bowl he was using to sop gravy with a hard piece of bread.

"Sure," Wolf said with a laugh. "If you like hard tack and salted pork."

The sun peeped through the round, chubby white clouds that were now far away. Wolf was dry for the first time that he could remember.

"These boys got it easy," the rebel said. The men around him gave a stunted laugh.

"What unit you with, Johnny Reb?" Wolf asked.

"The 12th Georgia Infantry."

The rebels added their units to the list. Most of the men came from Alabama, Georgia, and North Carolina. It was fascinating to hear the men speak with their different accents, and for a moment he forgot his own even if it was slight.

The man eyed Wolf. "We were all under Old Baldy Ewell. Then you boys caught up to us. Now we're here."

A man with a bandage around his eye called over. "Where you from?"

"Michigan."

The man scrunched his nose. "Michigan." He repeated the word as if it were entirely new to him. Where's that?"

"Up north."

The Southerner nodded. "Suspected as much."

"'Bout as far as you can get and still be in the United States."

"Sounds like Canada," the rebel with a missing tooth said. The others shared a tired laugh.

"Touches it."

The rebels bobbed heads at one another as if Wolf had confirmed their assumptions. "Name's George Perrin." He wiped his hand on his bedroll and stuck it out. Wolf took his hand; the Southerner's grip was strong, not that of a defeated man, but a man waiting for his chance.

"Johannes Wolf."

"Well, Corporal Wolf, your men fought like a bunch of Northern wolves out there the last few days. Running us down in packs. Nipping at Lee's heels. Surprised the hell out of us. Didn't think you bastards had that kind of fight in ya."

Another man, appearing accustomed to hard labor, peered at Wolf, his black-haired head and hairy cheeks made him look like he could be a grizzly bear, or at least a hungry bear. "But we ain't done yet. We'll be free of your Northern oppression."

"And we'll hound you the entire way, until you're beaten." Wolf wasn't one to back down from a scrap, but he was surprised by the steadiness of his words. They flowed like biblical fact from his mouth, just as if Shugart preached or Wilhelm ordered.

The rebels around him grunted their disapproval. "You be ready, Billy Yank. We'll be back. You can count on it."

"Until this war is done, Johnny Reb."

"Until this war is done." The rebels went back to eating and recuperating, the yoke of war unburdened from their shoulders at this moment in time.

Wolf's shoulder ached where the officer's saber had pierced him, but he ignored the wound. It would heal as this nation would heal, with knotty scar tissue that would always be there. A lifelong reminder of the pain and sacrifice.

His body was exhausted and he'd seen enough bloodshed to call it quits.

He knew the glory of war wasn't in a bloody charge, but the bravery it took to bring his brothers home, and he would fight tooth and nail for the men at his side. His unit of outcasts would be there. Ready for the charge. Ready to take the hill. Ready to die for their country. For this country gave them hope for a better life and a better future, and even if the clouds of war shrouded these lands of promise, someday they too would pass and the country would be whole again.

Until peace was found, he would ride with his brothers, run down the enemy, and tear them into submission because he wasn't just Johannes Wolf anymore, but a Northern wolf.

Historical and Personal Note

The Eastern Cavalry Fields are a somewhat forgotten part of the Gettysburg Battlefield experience. This has to do with many reasons, one of which is the magnitude of the battle itself. Over 170,000 men fought in this battle and there were over 53,000 casualties. For the time, these are staggering statistics, making this the largest battle on North American soil. An important note, General Robert E. Lee lost over a third of his soldiers in this battle and, maybe even more importantly, he lost a third of his generals. Both of these dramatic losses would cripple his army in future engagements.

About three miles east and a bit north from the protected battlefield today, you'll find the Eastern Cavalry Fields. Many people don't even make it to see the places where Custer, Stuart, Hampton, and Gregg fought for the rear of the Union line. For a long time, it was considered a side show to the real battle, but in fact, it was a crucial point taking place during the climax of three harrowing days of violence.

Imagine if Stuart had rolled into the Union rear with roughly 5,000 men, successfully pinching the Union line between a force of 12,500 and 5,000 unexpectedly assaulting the rear. Even a fraction of that could have created more than enough chaos among the Union forces to disrupt their attempt to defend the center.

Some historians argue that Stuart's intent was not to threaten the Union rear, but to catch stragglers after Lee crushed the Union center. This is a possible theory, but the manner in which he tried to force his way through Custer and Gregg were the actions of a general who, at the very least, was trying to give the perception of a potential attack to divert Union forces to the rear. However, this is open to debate and, for the sake of the story, I depicted it as a redemptive coordinated assault against the Union rear.

The 13th Michigan is a fictional unit. I used the fictional 13th Michigan Cavalry to be more flexible with the battles the unit fought in and to take more liberties. I loosely followed the 7th Michigan Cavalry experience as a roadmap for the 13th Michigan. The 7th Michigan was mustered in Grand Rapids in October 1862, and they came from all over Michigan, not just the Grand Rapids area.

I attempted to paint Grand Rapids in its true form at the time, a growing midwestern, or western town. Kusterer was a real brewer in Grand Rapids, which today is a town known for its high number of quality breweries. Grand Rapids didn't get a police force until after 1870 and only had a few constables to maintain law and order and, yes, their jail was a beautiful Italianate-style building where the head constable lived with his wife who cooked all the meals for the prisoners.

Wolf's company of immigrants, misfits, and outcasts within the 13th was used to show the experience and bravery of many during such a tumultuous time. We tend to view the American Civil War as a uniquely American experience, but in fact it was much more global. There were over 200,000 native German and 150,000 Irish-born immigrants that fought for the North, and thousands that fought for the South. Approximately 543,000 immigrants fought for the North during the war. They made up 25% of the Union armies. This fact was what prompted me to write about Wolf, the Berleses, O'Reilly, and the Poltorak brothers.

Immigrants also fought for the South, but in much smaller numbers. Many immigrants were fleeing one type of persecution or another and took strongly to the cause of the Union and, generally speaking, were anti-slavery. Some were in it for the financial stability or bounties and others joined because their friends and family had. The reasons matter, but they all were overshadowed by the fact that they fought for a land they were not native to.

Custer's "Wolverines" or the "Michigan Brigade" consisted of the 1st, 5th, 6th, and 7th Michigan Regiments during the Battle of Gettysburg. The only true veteran unit was the 1st Michigan Cavalry led by the sickly Colonel Charles H. Town. He had tuberculosis, and barely could stay in his saddle to charge with Custer at what was to be called the Eastern Cavalry Fields.

I let my characters fall into line and charge with Custer and rescue him. These stories are fact. Other real men spurred their horses to war, fought, held ground, gave ground, lived, and died with Custer. I, of course, let my characters take credit for many of these conflicts and turning points of the battle, weaving history and fiction together as one.

The Boy General did lead a series of charges over the course of the Gettysburg campaign soon after becoming a newly appointed general. This was relatively uncommon among generals, but quickly gained him credibility with his men, as he was willing to lead a daring charge into the enemy at a moment's notice.

This contrasted sharply against his division commander Judson Kilpatrick or "Kill-Cavalry" as he was aptly called by his men, who was aggressive, but ordered men into danger from the rear and often without apparent tactical concern. Of course this is open to modern analysis, his men were generally split in opinion, some loving him to death while others held him in contempt. We know that he did do this on several occasions, including on the South Cavalry Fields of Gettysburg. Elon Farnsworth was ordered to charge a position well after the battle was in hand. Unwilling to lead from behind, Farnsworth led the 1st Vermont and many of his men were slain during the assault that added very little to the Union position.

This very well could have been Custer's fate. Just like Custer, Farnsworth was one of the three fresh and young, newly appointed generals, along with Wesley Merritt, who all received promotion at the same time. They were a part of Pleasonton's replacement of political generals with ones that had proven they wanted to fight. Like his peers, Farnsworth had a chip on his shoulder and was willing to prove himself, even if it meant placing himself in mortal danger. If Custer had followed Kilpatrick's orders instead of Gregg's, who knows, perhaps his career would have ended early instead of at Little Bighorn.

General Wade Hampton is a very real character. He was labeled as one of the richest men from the south, as close to an aristocrat as one could be, rich enough to outfit his entire command on the onset of the war. He also survived the war and became a U.S. Senator and Governor of South Carolina. He had a controversial political career in the Reconstruction South.

His subordinate Captain Marshall Payne is fictional. I used him to exemplify a darker part of the South and its connection to the slavery economic power structure.

Be ready to see more from these complex characters in future books!

Personally, I had multiple ancestors that fought for the North in the Civil War. This is something that brings great pride to our family, and I know that many people feel the same way about their ancestor's service regardless of which side they fought on. People fought for many different things in this war and there is nothing worse for a nation than civil war. This war threatened to tear the very fabric of our country apart, but, like fabric, even when stitched back together there is still a mark. Time heals a nation's wounds, but it does not come without pain, struggle, and scars.

I do believe that, as Americans today, we are thankful that our country survived this war and we are saddened that it cost so many lives to unify us, but conflict also solidified us as a nation. This conflict is a part of our cultural fabric and should be remembered, explored, and hopefully understood because, good and bad, this is a part of us.

My goal was to produce an entertaining coming-of-age tale set in the Civil War time period. A story that brought to life the lives of immigrants fighting to hold a country together that they hadn't lived in for very long. A fact that I am grateful for today. My goal wasn't to vilify anyone who fought for the South, but, as some of them are the primary antagonists for this novel, some have been enhanced for the sake of fiction.

Much of the history was derived from *The Cavalry at Gettysburg, 1862 U.S. Cavalry Tactics, Custer: The Making of a Young General, Union Cavalryman 1861-1865, Custer and His Wolverines,* and *Glorious War: The Civil War Adventures of George Armstrong Custer*. I did take liberty throughout the novel for the sake of story, but tried to adhere to what has been recorded by historians, scholars, and the men/women themselves. While this is a work of historical fiction, it is fiction, and is purely for entertainment value.

Thank you for taking the time to read this novel! I can't wait to share more adventures of Johannes Wolf with you soon.

Best,

Daniel Greene
September 10th, 2019

Thanks for reading! I hope you enjoyed the first novel of the Northern Wolf series. As you may have gathered, there are more books in the series coming your way. Pick up **Northern Hunt Book 2 in the Northern Wolf Series here!**

The Greene Army Newsletter: Want exclusive updates on new work, contests, patches, artwork, and events where you can meet up with Daniel? An elite few will get a chance to join **Greene's Recon Team**: a crack unit of talented readers ready and able to review advance copies of his books anytime, anywhere with killer precision. Sign up for spam-free Greene Army Newsletter today! *Visit http://www.danielgreenebooks.com/?page_id=7741*

Reviews: If you have the time, please consider writing a review. Reviews are important tools that I use to hone my craft. If you do take the time to write a review, I would like to thank you personally for your feedback and support. Don't be afraid to reach out. I love meeting new readers!

You can find me anywhere below.

Facebook Fan Club: *http://www.facebook.com/groups/473698509874575/*
Facebook: *https://www.facebook.com/DanielGreenebooks/*
Instagram: *http://www.instagram.com/danielgreenebooks/*
Website: *DanielGreeneBooks.com*
Email: *DanielGreeneBooks@gmail.com*

A special thanks to all those who've contributed to the creation of this novel. A novel is a huge feat and would remain as a file on my desktop without the contributions of so many wonderfully supportive people. This includes my dedicated Alpha Readers, Greene's Recon Team, Greene Army, my editor, my cover artist and formatters and especially my readers. Without readers, this is an unheard/unread tale. I can't wait to share more stories with you in the future.

About the Author

Daniel Greene is the award-winning author of the growing apocalyptic thriller series The End Time Saga and the historical fiction Northern Wolf series. He is an avid traveler and physical fitness enthusiast with a deep passion for history. He is inspired by the works of George R.R. Martin, Steven Pressfield, Bernard Cornwell, and George Romero. Although he is a Midwesterner for life, he now lives on the East Coast.

Books by Daniel Greene

The End Time Saga
End Time
The Breaking
The Rising
The Departing
The Holding
The Standing (Coming Soon)

The Gun (Origin Short Story)

Northern Wolf Series

Northern Wolf
Northern Hunt
Northern Blood

Made in the USA
Coppell, TX
25 October 2020

40227299R00142